a hope springs novel

Redemption

LAURA LEE

Cover Design: Y'All That Graphic
Editing: Ellie McLove of My Brother's Editor
Proofreading: Christine Estevez of Haven Author Services
Cover Photographer: © Regina Wamba

This book is dedicated to anyone who's known the burden of suffering in silence.

Content Warning

This book contains material that some readers may find disturbing. If you'd like more information, please scan the QR code below:

Prologue
Presley

Worthless. Stupid. Pathetic.

If ugly words are thrown at you often enough, they eventually become your truth. It's a complicated, gradual process carved by years of cruelty. The shift is so diminutive in your everyday life; you don't see the gulch forming until the damage has already been done. At the first fissure, you're second-guessing your own thoughts. Then, as the gap widens, you start questioning your values, no matter how deeply rooted they may be. Over time, little pieces of your soul are chipped away day by day until your self-worth is so diminished, it's living on the opposite end of the canyon. You hardly recognize the person staring back at you in the mirror. The only thing you know for sure is how ashamed you are of what you've become.

I know this because I speak from experience.

For almost twelve years, I'd been meticulously conditioned. Molded by a master manipulator. Barely a woman when Sebastian and I met, I was drawn to him. Curious because he was so sophisticated and drastically different from everything I had ever known. I was flattered by his obvious interest. Surely, a man that successful and attractive could've had any woman he desired. Yet, he chose me—a simple girl from a small southern town, eleven years his junior and hopelessly in over her head. This worldly man wore expensive suits with an impeccable smile as he made pretty promises to mend my broken heart. Alone in a new city and so very desperate to ease my sorrow, I was the perfect little lamb to a vicious wolf.

A freshman in college at the time, I was young and naïve enough to believe the fairy tale. To take his name as my own less than nine months after we met. If only I had the strength to admit the truth on our wedding day. That the man I was about to marry would never have my heart because someone else already owned it. Maybe things would be different. Maybe I would've walked away and never known what a monster Sebastian would become. Maybe, just maybe, I wouldn't be so battered and bruised.

Sebastian had broken me down throughout our marriage, time and time again until all I knew was what he wanted me to know. All I was, was a pretty face on the arm of a powerful man. Here in Manhattan, I'm surrounded by millions of people, but I wouldn't consider any of them a friend. I've alienated every person that ever mattered to me because my husband convinced me I needed no one but him. And as the controlling, abusive side of him came to the surface, I maintained that distance because I didn't want my loved ones to witness my humiliation.

In hindsight, I know that it was all part of his carefully orchestrated plan. Because of him, I have no confidant. Because of him, I have no Plan B. Because of him, I have no escape.

I am his prisoner in a Park Avenue penthouse.

The doctors say I'm lucky—this could've been much worse, but luck is the last word I'd use in this situation. As I glance at my reflection in the little mirror above the sink, I survey the evidence of Sebastian's brutality. I'm a living Picasso, all lopsided features and controlled chaos. Half my face is badly disfigured, while the other half barely has a scratch. Reddish-purple marks mottle my skin, significantly darker around my jawline and the bump on my temple. My lips are split and puffy, with dried blood crusted at the corner. My left arm is resting in a sling, cradling my recently dislocated shoulder, and my right eye is nearly swollen shut from the forceful blow of my husband's angry, drunken fists. I wince as I swallow, carefully prodding the ring of bruises around my neck.

I'm not such a great trophy wife at the moment, am I?

I would laugh at the irony of my condition if I didn't think the movement would hurt so much. Sebastian's typically more controlled, worried I couldn't do my best impression of a Stepford wife during one of his many business functions. Usually, he prefers to work through his rage by slamming his dick inside of me instead of using his fists. I honestly can't decide which is worse. I can't remember the last time I desired sex, let alone enjoyed it during the act. It became a tool I used to pacify the monster because, according to him, a wife's *sworn duty* is to please her husband *whenever and whichever* way he sees fit. Lord knows I've heard him say it enough times over the years.

I gingerly return to the bed, careful not to tug at the IV in my hand as I lower myself to the lumpy mattress. As I lie here listening to the buzz of the emergency room, I can't help but think about who I was before moving to New York. A cheerleader with a perennially sunny disposition. The prom queen who stood proudly beside her adoring king. A young woman with her whole life ahead of her, a smile so bright, it could light up the darkest of nights. Someone who dreamed big, laughed freely, loved wholeheartedly, and believed in happily ever afters.

That was who Sebastian Winters married. That was who he destroyed. That girl, Presley James, died many years ago.

Chapter One
Presley – Age 5

"Presley Anne, come on over here. I want you to meet someone."

I drop my dolly and run at the sound of my daddy's voice. When I make it across the dirt to our big red barn, I find him inside with a man and a boy 'bout as old as me.

"Hi, Daddy!"

He motions me over and tucks me under his arm. "Presley, this is Mr. Armstrong. He's going to be our new foreman. He and his son are moving into Papa's old house. Say hello, honey."

Mr. Armstrong is big like my daddy, 'cept his hair is darker. My daddy has lots of white on his head. Mama says it's from years of trying to run the horse ranch with just him and a couple'a other grown-ups. She says Daddy is stubborn as an old mule when it comes to askin' for help. Mama made him hire a whole buncha new people after he hurt his back real bad.

"Hi, Mr. Armstrong."

Mr. Armstrong goes low to the ground like Mama does sometimes when she's talkin' to me. "Well, hello there, Presley. Aren't you a pretty little thing?"

"Thank you, sir."

He laughs and scoots the boy closer. "Presley, this here is my son, Beckett. According to your daddy, you're both starting kindergarten in the fall."

I give the boy a big smile. Mama says my smile is infected, but that don't make no sense to me. I had an owie get infected once, and it was really gross. Grown-ups are weird sometimes.

"Hi, Beckett. You wanna go see our fishin' pond?"

Beckett looks up to his daddy. "Can I, Daddy?"

His daddy pats him on the shoulder. "Sure, son. You two go ahead. I'll find you when I'm done with Mr. James here."

I pull on Beckett's hand and lead him out of the barn. "The fishin' pond is my second favoritest place on the whole ranch! You can go fishin' and swimmin', but Mama says I'm not allowed to go in the water by myself 'til I'm older."

"What's your first most favoritest place on the ranch?" Beckett asks.

"Oh, that's easy. The horses are my most favoritest things in the whole wide world. One of 'em just had a baby. Daddy let me name her after my favorite flower! He says when she's a little bit older, she can be all mine, and I can ride her anytime I want! Do you like horses, Beckett?"

"I dunno." Beckett's shoulders lift. "My dad was a cattle rancher 'til we moved here. They had some horses on the last ranch we lived on, but only the grown-ups were allowed to ride 'em."

"Where'd ya live before? I've been in Georgia my whole life."

"Brownsville," he says. "That's in Texas."

When we reach the pond, I run down the fishin' dock and pull my shoes off. I like stickin' my toes in the water. It's funny when the fish tickle my feet. "How come you moved to Hope?"

Beckett takes off his socks and boots and hangs his legs over the edge like me. "Mr. Wakefield sold the ranch we were livin' on. He moved away and took my mommy with him. Dad says it's time to make new memories, just us boys, so we came here. He said livin' in a town called Hope Springs was a sign from God that everything was gonna be okay."

"How come she left if she's your mama?"

He runs his finger along the wooden edge of the dock. "My dad says sometimes people aren't fit for bein' mommies and daddies, so he's just gonna have to love me enough for both of 'em."

I kick my feet and giggle when water gets on my face. "Are you sad you don't have a mama no more?"

"Sometimes."

"Well, my mama's real nice. I'm sure she can be your mama, too. She makes the best peach cobbler in all of Georgia. Plus, if I get a boo-boo, she fixes me all up and gives me ice cream after. She's a real good mama."

Beckett kicks the water just like me. "I like peach cobbler."

"It's the yummiest."

"Hey, Presley?"

"Huh?"

"Do you wanna be my friend? My friends call me Beck, so you can, too, if you wanna."

"Okay, Beck." I nod. "I'm gonna be your bestest friend in the whole wide world!"

Chapter Two
Presley

"Mrs. Winters? Is it okay if I come in?"

My eyes follow the sound of the deep voice, and I find a middle-aged man standing in the doorway to my room. I don't know who this guy is, but he looks like some sort of official, which has me instantly on edge. He must sense my discomfort because he digs into his suit jacket's breast pocket and withdraws a wallet.

He flips it open to reveal a badge, but he's too far away for me to see any details. "My name is Derek Simmons. I'd like to ask you a few questions about your attack."

I narrow my good eye in suspicion. "I already gave a statement to the police."

Mr. Simmons nods to the plastic chair that sits against the wall. "May I? I promise I won't take too much of your time."

I give him a slight nod.

"Mrs. Winters—"

"Presley," I insist.

The thought of being Mrs. Winters for a minute longer makes me sick. I can't pretend anymore.

"Presley." He clears his throat. "The statement you gave to the police doesn't match the witnesses' statements or the evidence we have. I'd like to know if you'd care to revise your account of the events that transpired early this morning."

There are witnesses? I guess there'd have to be, but the last thing I remember before waking up in an ambulance is riding the elevator down to my building's lobby.

"Am I being charged with something?"

I wouldn't put it past Sebastian to use his connections to shift the blame to me somehow.

He shakes his head. "Not at all. But I would like to ensure the right person pays for their crimes, and I can't do that without your help."

I release a sigh. "Look, Mr. Simmons—"

"Derek," he says with a smile that's undoubtedly charmed many women out of their panties. "It's only fair."

"Derek." I blow out a breath. "Like I told the first officer who came here, a man broke into my apartment and attacked me. No, I can't give you more details about his appearance because all the lights were off since I was asleep at the time. Somehow, I managed to fight him off and get away. The last thing I remember is riding in the elevator toward the lobby floor. I have nothing else to say."

"What do you typically wear to bed at night, Presley?"

I startle at the sudden change in topic.

"Pajamas, like most people. What does that have to do with anything?"

He gives me a knowing look. "According to the security footage, you were wearing slacks and a blouse when you were found, which, as you've stated, is not your normal bedtime attire. Are you telling me you took the time to change your clothing before leaving your apartment and fleeing the perpetrator?"

Crap. This guy is too observant for my liking. I glare at him again, but I don't think it's as effective as I'd like with only one eye.

"I fell asleep on the couch while I was waiting for my husband to return. I hadn't changed into my pajamas yet."

Derek frowns. "You live in a highly secure building. No one can access the penthouse without a keycard to your private elevator. The doorman confirmed your husband came home around midnight but left again approximately one hour later. Security footage shows you stumbling out of the elevator shortly after that, right before you collapsed onto the lobby floor. Look. I appreciate how delicate this situation is, considering your husband's... influence. I truly don't want to pressure you after everything you've been through, but I can't prevent this from happening again if you don't tell me the truth."

Yeah, right. Like I'm going to trust anything this guy has to say. For all I know, Sebastian put him up to this.

I clench my jaw but forcibly relax when a shooting pain reminds me how many hits it took earlier. "I *am* telling the truth. I have *nothing* else to say."

"Where was your husband going at one in the morning?"

"I have no idea. Not that it's any of your business, but we had a fight, and Sebastian stormed out. Now, if you have any more questions for me, I think I should have my lawyer present as this *conversation* seems to have taken a turn into an *interrogation*."

He releases a harsh exhale as he reaches into the breast pocket of his jacket again. He produces a business card and extends it in my direction. As I eye it warily, making no attempt to grab it, he says, "You have options, Presley. I have *zero* loyalty to your husband, and I can help. Don't let him get away with this. Call me when you're ready to talk."

With that, he stands up, places the card on my bedside table, and leaves the room. When he's out of sight, I pick up the rectangular cardstock.

Derek Simmons

Special Agent

917-555-0156

At the bottom, there's an address to the Federal Bureau of Investigation's Civic Center office. What the heck? Why would the FBI be interested in a case like this? I set the card down and allow my eyes to drift closed, willing the throbbing in my head to go away. The doctor offered me some prescription painkillers, but I declined. Those things make my head fuzzy, and that's the last thing I need right now because my head is already spinning. It probably doesn't help that I haven't slept in over twenty-four hours.

"Knock, knock." I blink rapidly as the nurse who's been taking care of me enters my room. Huh. I must've dozed off for a bit. "I have good news! As soon as I get that IV out, you're all set to go home. Your husband just arrived, and—"

"Could I have a moment alone with my wife, please?"

My entire body stiffens at the sound of his voice. Damn it. I knew it wouldn't be difficult for him to find out which hospital I was in considering the police involvement, but I had hoped I'd have more time. I take a sip of water from the cup the nurse gave me earlier and set it back on the bedside table, this time, directly over Agent Simmons' business card. I'm pretty sure Sebastian would actually kill me if he thought I ratted him out. Hell, he might do it anyway if recent events are any indication.

"Oh... of course," the nurse stutters. "I'll give you two a few minutes. You must've been so worried."

He rushes toward me and grabs my hand. "I've never been more terrified. When the officers showed up at my office, telling me you were attacked during a home invasion, all I could think about was getting to you. Seeing that you were okay with my own eyes."

I fight a whimper when Sebastian's grip tightens in an unmistakable warning not to call him out on his bull.

"Sweetheart, I'm so sorry I wasn't there to protect you."

Our gazes are locked as we wait for the nurse to leave. As always, he's perfectly coifed, not a strand out of place on his thick head of hair or a wrinkle to be found on his five-thousand-dollar suit. The only imperfections marring his beautiful features are the slight scratches on his cheek and neck. The second he's confident we're alone, the air shifts as the real Sebastian Winters leaks through the shiny surface. The concerned, loving husband has disappeared entirely. Instead, a menacing man now looms over me with the devil in his eyes, promising retribution. No longer able to stand the pressure, I avert my eyes. There was a time when this man's baby blues would suck me into his orbit, but now, I go out of my way to avoid eye contact with him, afraid of what I might find.

Sebastian leans over, pressing his mouth against my ear. His thumb idly brushes over the racing pulse on my neck while his fingers span the width of my throat. "Trying to run was incredibly stupid, Presley. You should know by now I'll never let you go, and I don't tolerate disobedience. You're going to have to work *very hard* to make it up to me."

"Sebastian, if you don't let me go, I swear I'll scream." I've been bowing down to this man for too long. After what I learned last night... after what happened when I confronted him about it... I refuse to keep my mouth shut any longer.

"I'd like to see you try." His minty breath teases my nostrils as a dark chuckle falls from his lips. "Matter of fact, please do. I'll enjoy punishing you for it later. And trust me when I say, I *will* punish you, dear wife. I need to make sure you never attempt to do something so stupid again."

I claw at his fingers with my good arm when he puts pressure on my throat. I greedily gulp in air as he jumps back upon hearing someone enter the room.

"Excuse me, but I need to review these discharge instructions with my patient now." The nurse—Mia, I think her name is—turns her icy gaze on my husband.

Said husband straightens his tie as he takes a step back, acting as if he wasn't just trying to strangle me. "Yes, of course."

Mia glances at me out of her peripheral. "I'm sorry, sir, but I'm going to have to ask you to wait in the lobby to protect my patient's privacy."

Sebastian narrows his eyes. "I'm her *husband*. You can say whatever you need to in front of me."

"I mean no disrespect, Mr. Mayor. It's hospital policy." She juts her chin out. "Please don't make me call security. I'm assuming you'd like to avoid making a scene. I'll be happy to escort you to the waiting room myself, so you don't lose your way."

I could kiss this woman for playing the reputation card. The only thing Sebastian cares more about than appearances is control. I wait on bated breath as he decides which course of action he'll take.

His gaze flicks to mine. "I'll be in the waiting room, darling. *Right outside* the emergency room doors, so I can return at a moment's notice."

I don't miss the implied threat.

My nurse straightens her shoulders as she steps aside to let Sebastian walk out first. Right before she leaves the room to follow him, she looks over her shoulder. "I'll be right back."

I nod, too busy trying to swallow the lump in my throat to form any words.

As promised, no more than two minutes later, Mia returns, sliding the glass door closed behind her, sighing as she takes a seat beside me.

"Presley, I hope I'm not stepping over a line, but I have to ask this again. Are you safe at home? Was it really an intruder who did this to you?" She waves a hand toward me. "Or was it someone you know? Perhaps someone close to you?"

I take a moment to formulate my reply. I have no idea what I'm going to do about Sebastian, but I know I can't leave here with him. I'm not about to trust that FBI agent without knowing the motive behind his actions, but something about Mia tells me I can depend on her. This woman heals people for a living. If anyone is a safe bet, it'd be her.

I take a deep breath. "Hypothetically... if I said I wasn't safe at home—which that's not what I'm saying—but if I *did*, what good would that do? I have no money, no friends, nowhere I can stay in this city."

"What about family? Is there anyone you can stay with? Or, if you need me to, I'd be happy to make some calls to check shelter availability."

"No, a shelter would never work." I shake my head. "I could be recognized. And I don't really talk to my family anymore. Even if I could go home, it's almost a thousand miles away. I have no way of getting there."

She gives me a sad smile. "I'd wager a pawn shop would give you good money for those rings. At the very least, you can get a ticket home. They should be open soon."

I gasp, looking at my wedding set. I've been wearing these rings for so long, sometimes I forget they're even there. Sebastian made it clear early on, I was not permitted to remove my rings for any reason. It's not like people don't already know I'm married, seeing as we're in the public eye, but I think he likes having tangible evidence that I belong to him. The overhead lights reflect off the flawless five-carat diamond as I examine it closely, casting tiny rainbows on the wall. It really is stunning, with its Asscher-cut center stone in a pavé setting, but it's been more of a shackle to me than a piece of jewelry, so I lost sight of its beauty. Plus, if

Sebastian ever truly tried to know me—*the real me*—he would've learned I'd never be comfortable with something this flashy and impractical. That should've been my first clue, but sadly, I was too busy nursing a heartbreak to notice.

"I don't..." I toy with the bands on my finger. "I don't even have cab fare to get to one."

"My cousin Joey drives an Uber. I can call him and have him take you somewhere. It's on me. There's a service entrance... you wouldn't even have to cross through the ER waiting area. And they might be a little big, but I have a change of clothes in my locker that I'd be happy to give you to help disguise you as much as possible. You need to decide quickly, though, because I have a feeling the good mayor isn't the most patient man."

You can say that again.

"Can I ask you something?"

Mia nods.

"Why are you helping me?"

"Because I've been there, honey. I was with a horrible man for too long. When I saw the way your husband was standin' over you just now, *I knew* somethin' wasn't right. It felt like I went back in time for a second there." Mia's gesticulating wildly, and her New York accent is becoming more pronounced the longer she talks.

"How'd you get away?" My voice is so quiet, I'm not sure if she hears me.

She shrugs. "I stuffed my damn pride aside and asked for help."

I wonder if that's even an option for me. After all this time, would my family welcome me back home? I know I broke my parents' hearts when I told them I didn't want them to visit. I cringe when I recall the conversation where I implied they would embarrass me in front of my high-society friends. Little did they know, those friends were imaginary. Every time they asked me to come to Georgia, I had one excuse after another, acting as if my new life kept me so busy, I couldn't possibly leave the city. Finally, when Sebastian was elected the mayor of New York City, they stopped asking. Since my wedding day, I haven't seen my parents or my brother, which hurts me so much because we used to be so close. We still talk on the phone, but our conversations are brief, mostly on holidays, and always awkward. I blink back tears when it hits me how badly I miss them.

I sniffle. "Okay."

Her brown eyes widen. "Really?"

I nod. "Yeah."

"Okay." Mia stands up. "I'll be back in two minutes tops with those clothes."

Ten minutes later, I'm dressed in an oversized Giants hoodie and jeans with a ball cap, and I'm sliding into the back seat of cousin Joey's Prius. Mia was kind enough to give me her sunglasses to hide my swollen eye better.

"Good luck, Presley."

"Thank you. For everything." I pull the door closed, giving her a little wave through the window.

As the car pulls away from the curb, I take a deep breath to steady myself. Any minute now, Sebastian will know I'm gone, and once that happens, there'll be no turning back.

Chapter Three
Presley – Age 8

"The fish aren't bitin', Beck. We should go visit the new foals."

"Try casting out a little farther," he suggests.

I do as he says and flick my fishin' rod off to the side, casting the fly halfway across the width of the pond.

I smile. "Like that?"

Beck nods. "Yeah. My dad says the fish bite better in the middle."

I like fishin' with Beck. Sometimes, we come here to sit on the dock and dip our toes in the water. Other times, like today, we try catchin' some fish.

"Hey, Beck?"

"Yeah?"

"Whatcha wanna be when you grow up?"

Beck recasts his line, too. His fly doesn't get as far as mine did, but I don't rub it in because my mommy says that's not nice. "That's easy. I'm gonna be a rancher like my dad."

"On a horse ranch like ours?"

"Maybe." He takes a moment to think about it. "Or cattle. I really like the horses, though. I think it'd be cool to work with 'em. My dad says he'll let me help with the birthin' next summer."

I scrunch my nose up. "Birthin' is messy."

Beck shrugs. "I don't mind."

"Well, I'm gonna be a famous actress."

"That's cool. You sure are pretty enough to be in the movies."

Beck always says nice things to me. "Mama says I can't stay in Hope Springs if I want to be in movies or on the TV. She said I'd have to move to a big city like Hollywood or New York. I told her I don't mind 'cuz I think livin' in a big city would be fun. You could come with me, too. I bet we'd have lots of fun in the city."

Beck's eyebrows pull together. "I like living here."

"Me too, but I wanna see the whole world."

"I bet you'll be super famous, Pres."

I smile. "I can't wait to be a grown-up. You just wait and see, Beckett Armstrong. I'll be a big movie star and make lots of money so I can buy a big ol' piece of land like this and tons of horses. You can be the rancher and take care of 'em. Then, you and me can get married."

Beck holds my hand, 'cuz we do that sometimes. "Okay."

Chapter Four
Presley

"Here we are." My driver shifts the car into park. He took me to a pawnbroker in the Bronx. I've never been to a place like this before—I'm not really sure how this is supposed to work.

Joey seems to sense my hesitancy, so he adds, "Just go in there and ask for Sal. Tell him Joey P sent you."

I grab the handle to open my door, but before I exit the car, I ask, "Hey, I don't suppose you'd mind waiting for me, would you? I'd be happy to compensate you after... well, if he gives me any money."

"Sure thing."

"Thank you."

When I step inside the store, I'm surrounded by a mish-mash of items: guitars, bikes, various electronics and sports memorabilia, power tools, etcetera. Taking up the most real estate is a long glass counter filled with assorted jewelry. Geez, I've never seen so much stuff in such a small space before. It almost feels like I'm on an episode of *Hoarders*.

"You lookin' for something in particular?"

Behind the counter stands a fifty-something man with a big, bushy mustache. Since he seems to be the only person around, I'm guessing he's the one who spoke.

"Uh... I'm looking for Sal. Joey P sent me."

The man gives me a warm smile, the gap between his front teeth somehow making it more enchanting. I'm so used to being surrounded by people obsessed with perfection; it's nice to see someone real for once.

"Well, you've got him. Any friend of Joey's is a friend of mine. What can I do for you?" When I lift my head, Sal's brown eyes widen as he gets a good look at my face beneath the brim of my borrowed hat. "Whoa. You look like you've had better days. *Shit.* That was insensitive. How can I help you?"

I twist the bands on my finger, trying to focus on anything other than the pity in his eyes. "I have these rings, and... I... uh... I'd like to sell them."

"C'mon over, let me have a look." Sal motions me over as he grabs a diamond loupe from a drawer behind him and places it on the counter. He whistles when I drop the rings in his hand. "These real diamonds?" He places my engagement ring—the one with the largest stone—under the lens, not waiting for an answer. "Yep, they sure are. Damn, this is a quality piece. Flawless, if I'm not mistaken. A diamond this size has to retail for at least a hundred-K."

I fidget while Sal takes his time inspecting each ring thoroughly. When he's done, he places them on a little velvet-lined tray and looks up. "I gotta be honest with you; there's no way I can give you even a fraction of what these babies are worth. I just don't have that kind of cash flow. Have you considered trying to sell them privately?"

Tears prick at my eyes. "I can't. I don't have time for that. I need money *now*." I lift my gaze and look him directly in the eye. "Please. Whatever you can give me. I need money to get home."

I tell myself to hold still as his eyes travel over my face.

"The best I can do is ten-K."

I blow out a breath. Ten thousand dollars will be plenty. I don't even care that Sal's offer is significantly below value. I'd donate those rings to a homeless shelter if I didn't desperately need the cash.

"Okay, I'll take it."

Sal lifts an eyebrow. "You sure?"

I nod. "Yes. I'm sure. I need the money, and ten thousand will be more than enough."

"Okay, then." He jerks his head to the left. "Step into my office. We just need to fill out some paperwork, and you'll be on your way with ten-grand in your pocket."

Sal's *office* is really just a drop-down desk at the end of the glass case. He slides a piece of paper across the surface and points to a mug filled with pens on my right.

"These are standard forms, stating where you got

the ring, how long it's been in your possession, an oath that you didn't obtain it by illegal means, stuff like that. I'll need your ID because I have to notarize the affidavit at the end."

Thankfully, I had the sense to grab my cell before leaving the apartment. I don't like carrying a purse on the streets of New York, so I opted for a phone case that doubles as a wallet. I start to pull my license out but pause when I think of a potential problem.

"You're not going to share this information, right? Nobody will know I was here?"

He scratches the scruff on his jaw. "I'm required by law to report any incoming items, but it's not like I'll be broadcasting it on the streets or anything. As long as the rings aren't reported stolen, I don't have to release your name."

I take a moment to weigh the consequences. I suppose it doesn't matter if Sebastian ever did know I was here. It's not like these forms mention where I'm going. Mia suggested I disable the locator feature from my cell so Sebastian couldn't track me. I'm thankful she thought of it because I wouldn't have. If I'm honest with myself, he'll figure out where I'm going sooner rather than later, but if I can get out of New York first, I feel like I'll have a better shot at making it to my destination. Once I'm there, I'll no longer be alone, which makes me less vulnerable in Sebastian's eyes.

Hopefully.

With that decided, I hand Sal my license and start

completing the forms. Fifteen minutes and ten thousand dollars later, I'm back in Joey's car.

"You figure out where you wanna go next?"

I pull the money from my pocket and count ten bills from the stack. Handing them to him, I ask, "How do you feel about taking me to the Newark airport?"

JFK and LaGuardia are too obvious. I hope flying out of Jersey will throw Sebastian off my scent a little.

Joey smiles. "For a thousand bucks, sure. E-W-R, here we come."

A while later, Joey drops me off at the airport, and I make my way over to a nearby check-in area. I feel like bugs are crawling over my skin the entire time I wait in line. I keep the brim of my hat low, but I know people can see how beat up I am, regarding me with sympathy or whispering something to their companions. When it's finally my turn, I walk up to the counter and have to remind myself not to react when the attendant gasps as she gets a close-up look at my face.

"Ho—How can I help you, ma'am? Are you checking in today?"

"I'd like to buy the first available one-way ticket to Atlanta."

I can tell the lady's trying not to gawk while her fingernails tap on the keyboard, but she's not all that successful. "The first flight with any open seats departs at 6:05 p.m., which would arrive in Atlanta at 8:32 p.m."

Crap. I can't wait that long.

"Do you have any earlier flights? Maybe to Montgomery?" I lean forward and lower my voice. "Please. I really do mean *anything*. I don't care how many planes I need to take; I just need to get out of here *as soon as humanly possible*."

Her fingers fly across the keyboard again. "I have a few seats left on a nonstop to Charlotte, leaving in just under an hour." More typing. "From there, I can get you to Atlanta. The layover in Charlotte is about three-and-a-half hours, so you'd be arriving in Atlanta at 6:55."

I sigh in relief. "I'll take it. How much?"

"With taxes and fees, three-hundred eighty-seven dollars and twelve cents. If you're checking a bag, that'll be an extra thirty dollars for the first piece and forty dollars for the second."

I discreetly count out enough cash and hand it to her. Easier said than done when you're not supposed to move one shoulder. "I don't have any bags. It's just me."

She takes the money from me. "I'll just need to see a piece of government identification, please."

I pretend I don't notice her bewilderment as she attempts to match the picture on my license to the woman before her now. I'm sure this whole thing is suspicious as hell in her eyes. It takes the ticket counter lady a few minutes to type everything into the computer before she hands me a boarding pass.

"They're boarding in twenty minutes at gate C-4. You'll need to hurry."

"Thank you." I pocket my ID and pull the brim of

my hat down before heading toward the security screening area.

I barely make it to my gate in time because, of course, I'm flagged by TSA for additional inspection. I'm the last person to board, and my seat is in the back of the plane, so I have to fight through the sick feeling in my stomach as hundreds of curious eyes look me over as I walk down the aisle. Once I'm finally seated with my seat belt securely fastened, I close my eyes and take a few deep breaths. I know once I arrive at the ranch, there'll be a whole new set of shock, pity, and questions I'll have to endure, but the weight that's been crushing my chest all these years finally feels a bit lighter.

Chapter Five
Presley – Age 13

"Great job today, girl."

I close Magnolia's stall door and hang her halter on the hook. Beck finishes stalling his mare, Cinnamon, and meets me at the end of the stable. Cinnamon isn't technically Beck's, but she's taken a liking to him. He assisted his dad with her delivery a few years back, and they bonded right away.

Beck removes his snapback and runs a hand over his head. "Do you know what your mom's cookin' for dinner tonight?"

Beck's dad works late this time of year, so my mom insists he eats dinner with us every night. Then, she sends him home with leftovers for his dad. She's the ultimate mother hen—you're going to get a hot, home-cooked meal every evening whether you like it or not. Beck never seems to mind, though. I swear that boy does nothing *but* eat these days.

"Meatloaf and mashed potatoes, I think."

He gives me a crooked smile. Dang, he's cute when he does that.

"My favorite."

I roll my eyes. "*Everything's* your favorite nowadays, as long as it's in your belly."

Beck's gotten really tall over the summer—way taller than most boys our age. He says it's from my mom's cooking.

He rubs his stomach. "I'm a man, Pres. A man needs to eat a lot to have enough fuel to work on the ranch."

I laugh. "You're getting ahead of yourself, a little bit, don't ya think? You're *thirteen*, Beckett. Not thirty."

"Close enough." He smirks.

"Have you ever kissed a girl? With tongue?"

He sputters a little from my abrupt change in topic. "Why do you ask?"

I shrug. "I dunno. Most of my friends are kissin' boys already. I guess I wanted to see what all the fuss is about."

He props a boot against the wall and leans back. "Well, I couldn't tell ya because I haven't done it. You're the only girl I ever spend time with."

My toes curl inside my boots. I didn't think Beck had kissed another girl, because like he said, he's always with me, but it could've happened at school or something. I see how some of the girls look at him. Okay, *most* of the girls.

"Well, then we should kiss and see what's so special about it."

"W-What?" He pulls the hat over his head again. "Uh… I don't think that's such a good idea, Pres."

I tap my toe in irritation. "Well, why not?"

"You're my best friend, Presley. Friends don't go around kissing each other."

"What the heck is wrong with you, Beckett?" I throw my hands up. "Why have you been actin' so strange lately?"

He hooks his thumbs into the pockets of his jeans and rocks back on his heels. "What do you mean?"

"We've been friends for eight years, and you've never been this way before. Every time I want to hold your hand, or hug you, or go swimmin'—things we've *always* done—you act weird like I gross you out or something."

"You definitely don't gross me out," he mumbles.

"Well, then what's the problem? Is this because I got my period? Because I'm gettin' boobs?"

His head snaps up. "What? *No.*"

Great, now he's staring at my boobs. They're probably not big enough for him—I'm only in an A-cup. I know they'll probably get bigger, but my friend, Nicky, is our age, and she's already wearing a C-cup. I bet he likes *her* boobs.

"Do you think I'm ugly?" I press. "Do I smell bad? Why don't you want to kiss me, Beckett?"

"It's none of those things!" he shouts. "I like you, okay? Are you happy now?"

"Well, of course, you like me. I'm your best friend."

"No, Pres," he groans. "I mean, I *like you*, like you."

Oh.

"Really?"

"Yeah, really." He gulps.

I smile. "Well, then we should definitely kiss."

His jaw drops. "Are you serious?"

"Yes, I'm bein' serious." I step into him and pull off his hat, tossing it to the side. Beckett's eyes widen as I tug on his flannel shirt, so he has to bend over a bit. "Now kiss me, you idiot."

I wet my lips when he stares at them.

"Pres, I don't k—"

Beck doesn't get to finish what he was saying because I press my mouth against his. He's frozen for just a moment, but then his lips soften, and he starts kissing me back. I'm a little startled when his tongue goes inside my mouth—it feels kind of weird—but not gross, I don't think. I mirror his movements, and before I know it, we're full-on French kissing.

Holy crap! Beck Armstrong's tongue is in my mouth!

I can't help it; I start to giggle, which causes him to pull away.

"Am I doin' it wrong?"

I shake my head. "Nuh-uh. Did it seem weird to you?"

He thinks about it for a second. "Not even a little. You?"

"Nope. So, do you wanna be my boyfriend then? Because I want to do that *a lot* more, and we should probably be boyfriend, girlfriend if we're gonna be kissin' all the time."

Beck's eyes bulge. *"Do you wanna be my girlfriend?"*

"Of course I do." I give him a *duh* look. Sheesh, boys are really stupid sometimes.

He nervously rubs the back of his neck. "We have an hour before dinner's ready. Do you wanna make out some more?"

I give him the biggest smile I can manage. "Okay!

Chapter Six
Presley

"This the right place?"

I glance up at the old farmhouse I spent the first half of my life in. "Yes, it is. Thank you again for taking me all this way."

I take out enough money for the meter, plus a generous tip. This poor guy is going to have a three-hour drive back, and it's already after ten.

He smiles as I hand him the cash. "Have a good night."

"Thank you. Drive safe." I take a deep breath and get out of the cab.

As the taxi pulls around to head back down the long drive, its headlights flash right at my parents' bedroom window. It's just after ten, which in New York, the night's just getting started, but on a ranch, it might as well be last call. For as long as I can remember, my parents were up before sunrise, getting a head start on the day. I suppose it doesn't matter if the car's bright lights woke them because I don't have a key to get inside, so I'd have to wake them anyway.

Right before my foot hits the first step, the porch light flicks on. I freeze, mentally preparing myself for what's about to happen. Too bad no amount of preparation could control the flood of emotions that hit me the second I see my father's face through the screen door. God, he looks so much older.

"Can I help you, miss? If you're lookin' for Clayton, I'm sorry to say, you've got the wrong driveway. It's the next one over."

For a split second, I feel like I'm sixteen again, repulsed by the fact that my father assumes I'm one of my brother's many girlfriends. I swear, that boy will never settle down.

Here we go.

"No, Daddy, it's me." I make my way up the stairs to the front porch.

"Presley?" He quickly pushes the screen door open and steps outside. "What are you doing here? Why didn't you tell us you were comin'?" He looks over his shoulder. "Annie, get out here! Presley's here."

My mother arrives just as I'm removing my hat. She slams a hand over her mouth to stifle her gasp as I turn my face into the light. My eyes move over to my dad, where equal parts rage and confusion twist his features.

"Presley Anne, what on God's green earth happened to you? Did you get in some sort of accident?" My father steps forward and reaches for my hand. Out of habit, I instantly recoil, taking a step back. I don't miss the hurt and disbelief in his eyes when I do.

I hang my head in shame. I *hate* that I'm so jumpy around men—I've been this way for years—but ever since Sebastian first... well, let's just say I've learned to shy away from the opposite sex. Especially men who are as imposing as my father is.

"I'm sorry... I... uh... I didn't mean to—"

"Honey, come inside," my mom insists. "I'll make some herbal tea, and you can tell us all about it."

I nod once, following behind them into the house.

My dad pulls out a chair at the same kitchen table where I ate thousands of breakfasts. "Sit."

Nostalgia slams into me as I look around and realize nothing has changed. Not one. Damn. Thing. The black and white checkered valance still hangs above the big window over the sink. My mother's bright red KitchenAid mixer sits on a little rolling cart in the corner. The wooden plaque I made for Mother's Day in the fifth grade is proudly displayed on the wall, declaring Anna James "The Best Mom Ever." A giant Thermos sits on the butcher block countertop next to the coffeemaker, ready to be filled to the brim with French Roast right before my dad gets to work on the ranch. I don't even realize I'm crying until the first drop hits my hand.

I dab at my eyes, hissing when I touch a sore spot. Thankfully, I can open the lid fully now, but the discoloration is so severe, it's not much of an improvement.

My dad runs a hand through his salt and pepper hair. "Presley, honey, I'm trying to be patient here, but I need you to start speaking before I lose my damn mind."

My mom sits in the chair next to mine and gently reaches her hand out. She's eyeing me like a cornered animal, going nice and slow, telegraphing her intentions. When her delicate fingers finally wrap around mine, I hiccup a sob which, unfortunately, seems to release the floodgates. I start crying uncontrollably, weeping for I don't even know what at this point, but I can't seem to stop. I'm not sure how long I sit there bawling. At the same time, my mom whispers words of assurance in my ear before my tears are all dried out. My eyes are even more swollen, making it increasingly difficult to keep them open.

"Please," I sniff. "I'm just so tired. God, so, *so* tired. I promise I'll tell you everything, but I really need some sleep."

It's been a long, long time since I've had a restful night, and it feels like it's all catching up with me at once.

"Of course, honey." My mom stands. "I'll just go put some fresh sheets on your bed real quick, and you can get some rest. We kept your room for you, Pres. Just in case you ever decided to visit."

I shake my head, guilt nagging at my conscience. "Don't worry about changing the sheets, Mom. I'll be fine."

She nods. "Okay, sweetheart. Whatever you want.

There should be some of your old clothes in the dresser if you'd like to make yourself more comfortable."

"Thank you."

I duck my head and slowly make my way up the long staircase. I can hear my parents talking, but they're so quiet, I can't make out what they're saying to each other. I probably don't want to know right now anyway. My entire body aches, so every step is daunting. When I finally reach my old bedroom, I turn the knob and step inside. I don't bother turning on the lamp. There's enough moonlight filtering through the sheer curtains to see the bed, and even if there wasn't, I have every inch of this room memorized. From the little bit I can see, nothing's changed in here either. I step out of my jeans and crawl under the covers, sighing in relief as I hit the soft mattress. It takes me a minute to find a comfortable position with my shoulder, but once I do, I fall asleep so fast, I don't even remember closing my eyes.

———

After only a few hours of restless slumber, I woke up. My physical discomfort caused me to wake, but my brain's inability to shut down is what's keeping me that way. Damn, I really should've filled that prescription before leaving the hospital, but it's too late now. I couldn't stand tossing and turning in bed any longer, so I made my way down to the old swing on the front porch, wrapped in a big blanket to ward off the early morning chill. I had hoped the repetitious motion would make me sleepy, but so far, it hasn't helped. My parents should be up soon anyway, looking for answers, so it's probably a lost cause.

I stare at my phone for what feels like the thousandth time this morning. I know I shouldn't have been surprised, but I was. Shocked is more like it. Sebastian has put me through so much over the years—more than I would ever wish on my worst enemy—but I never, and I do mean *never*, thought he'd cheat. There's too much at stake if he were caught. He's up for reelection soon, and if this got out, it would create a massive scandal. One that could significantly tarnish his precious image.

Mayor Winters can do no wrong in the eyes of his constituents. He's their golden boy, the living Adonis, with the mind of a genius and a golden smile. The youngest person to ever hold his office in state history. The man who led his city, remaining calm yet steadfast during a major health crisis. His efforts during that time were monumental. Tireless. He campaigned for all citizens, young and old, rich or poor; it didn't matter. They were all deserving because they were his people and, therefore, his responsibility. He refused to give up until the city had the resources needed to safely and effectively manage the crisis. Because of Sebastian's leadership, New York City citizens made it through to the other side. Not unscathed by any means, but it could've been so much worse.

I won't ever deny all the good he's done during his time in office, but I also cannot forget the man he is in public is most certainly not the man he is in private. Honesty and family values—the two principles he based his entire platform on—don't mean shit to him. Sewer rats probably rank higher. But he puts on a good show, I'll give him that. More than one media outlet has dubbed my husband a modern-day knight. Others have called him a champion for the people. Then, there's my personal favorite: The Saint of New York.

God, if they only knew.

It looks like the good people of New York might learn the truth about their so-called hero soon enough. The evidence sitting in front of me is pretty hard to dismiss. There's no denying the fact that Mariana Pérez, the First Deputy Mayor of New York City, is the woman on her knees giving my husband an enthusiastic blowjob. She, too, is married, which would only intensify the scandal if this got out. I have no idea who sent this video to me, but someone has the power to expose them, and if that happened, it wouldn't be pretty for anyone. Especially me, considering I'm Sebastian's favorite target.

After what happened the other night, I'm convinced there's no line he won't cross, which is what finally prompted me to run. I was foolish to think otherwise, and I hate myself for not seeing it sooner. I will *never* allow myself to be that vulnerable again. I'm not stupid enough to think Sebastian will give up without a fight —hell, he said as much—but being a thousand miles away, surrounded by family, gives me some room to breathe. To strategize. And a small part of me can't help thinking that maybe this is my opportunity to push the reset button. Move beyond all the pain from my past, both physical and mental, and do things right going forward. Maybe this is my chance for redemption.

The sound of gravel crunching draws my attention toward the left. Damn it. Someone is coming up the driveway at—I check my phone—four-thirty in the morning. Who would show up at this hour? It's a little too early for the ranch hands. My brother, Clayton's place, is nearby, but he has his own driveway about a quarter mile down the road. Shit. Has Sebastian come for me already? How on earth did he get a flight at this hour? He must've chartered a private jet. Oh, God, I need to get inside. I lock my phone, not wanting to draw attention to myself with its light. Thankfully, the sun's not up yet, and I switched the porch light off before I came out here, so I'm cloaked in darkness as I creep toward the front door.

Right as my fingers curl around the screen door handle, it hits me. That's not a car. It's a truck. And not just any truck, but one I'd recognize blind by the throaty purr of its engine. I stand stock-still as the noise gets louder and louder right before the vehicle's headlights come into view. It's dark as hell, and it's been a long time since I've seen it, but there's no doubt in my mind it's the same 1972 two-tone Ford F100 short box I spent a good chunk of my teenage years riding in.

Among other things.

I hold my breath as the driver passes the main house, veering off at the fork heading toward the machine shed. I don't breathe again until its taillights are entirely out of view. Seconds later, the engine shuts down, bathing the ranch in silence once again. This property is massive—over two-thousand acres. There are a dozen outbuildings spread throughout for various purposes, in addition to a few residences independent from the main house. One of them belongs to my brother. Another is reserved for the occasional out-of-town guest.

But there's only one residence that shares the main drive, and that's the original James house my dad grew up in. Now, it belongs to the foreman. More specifically, David Armstrong. That's where that old Ford is currently parked, its driver likely already tucked inside the warm house instead of standing outside in the cold like me. The funny thing is, I overlook the bite of chilly temperature on my skin, even though my blanket is now pooled at my feet, because my mind is too busy trying to fit all the missing puzzle pieces together. Nausea and anxiety roll through me for a whole new reason now. Countless questions are running through my head, but the one thing niggling the most?

Why is the sole reason I left this town, now living on my parents' land? I'm positive it was him—not his father—driving that truck. I could *feel* it. But last I heard, he left town about a year after I did to join the Navy. I had assumed he was off somewhere in the world doing whatever it is that the Navy does. But that's obviously not the case. So, maybe the more appropriate question is, when did he move back? And how in the world am I supposed to face him again after everything that's happened?

Chapter Seven
Presley – Age 16

"Okay, start at the North Star," Beck says.

I locate the brightest star on the tail of the Little Dipper. "Got it. Now what?"

He grabs my index finger and points it slightly lower in the sky, tracing the shape of a weird looking W. "Right there; those five stars. That's Cassiopeia—do you see it?"

"Yeah, I think so."

He pulls me into a side hug. "This is one of the things that I love most about living out in the country. You can't get a view like this in a city."

"It's pretty great," I agree. "But cities have things that you can't get in the country."

He pulls the sleeping bag a little higher. "True… but I wouldn't have been able to pull off this romantic setup in the middle of a bunch of concrete."

I smile and snuggle into him farther. Beck laid out a bunch of blankets and a double sleeping bag in the bed of his truck. The moonlight is reflecting off the pond, and the frogs are really vocal tonight. It might seem like nothing special to some people, but to me, it's perfect.

"It *is* pretty romantic."

Beck's spent the last two years fixing up an old truck with his dad. He just got his driver's license today, so we're celebrating with a campout in the bed of it. Well, not an overnight campout, because our parents put an end to our sleepovers around age ten, but we can stay out until one in the morning during the summer, as long as we stay on the ranch. Thankfully, there's plenty of places to go if we want privacy. This particular spot is our favorite, though. It's where we first became friends, so Beck and I like to call it *our* pond.

Tonight's the night Beckett and I are supposed to finally have sex. We've been officially a couple for almost three years, but I didn't feel ready until now. We've fooled around a lot, but we've never actually gone all the way. I know some of his friends think he's an idiot for waiting for me, but what Beck and I have is real. He's my best friend, and we're in love. There's no other person on Earth I'd want to lose my virginity to. It's even more special because it will be his first time, too.

Beck shifts us so my head is back on a pillow, and he's leaning over me. "Are you nervous? It's okay if you've changed your mind."

God, he really is the most perfect boyfriend. "I'm

not nervous; I want this. I'm ready."

"You're so beautiful, Pres. I don't tell you that enough."

"Beck, I just told you I'm a sure thing; you don't need to keep sweet-talkin' me."

He laughs. "That's good to know, but I'm serious. You're gorgeous, inside and out. I love you so much, Presley. You're my world. I don't ever want to be without you."

I clasp my hands behind his neck. "I love you, too. And don't worry; I'm not going anywhere. I don't ever want to be without you either."

"You know, I haven't forgotten what you said all those years ago."

My eyebrows scrunch together. "Said what exactly? We've exchanged lots of words over the years, you know."

Beck cups my jaw with his hands. "That we're gonna get married one day."

"I did say that, didn't I?" I smile at the memory.

"You did." He nods. "And I want that, Pres. I want to marry you one day. Have kids with you. I know people say this is just puppy love and that we'll grow out of it, but I know that's not true. I want you to be my forever, and that will *never* change."

"Beckett, you have me. For always."

"Yeah?"

"Yeah," I confirm. "Now quit talkin' and make love to me."

He smiles warmly. "Now *that* I can do."

Chapter Eight
Beckett

What the hell was that?

I've seen some messed up shit in my life, and because of that, I've had some pretty fucking disturbing thoughts at times, but I've never questioned my sanity before now. I swear I just saw the girl who wrecked me, standing on her front porch waiting for me like she used to when we were kids. But that would be impossible because the woman hasn't stepped foot on this ranch since the day she left almost twelve years ago. Why would she bother when she has the fancy city life she always dreamed of?

But... there's no one else it could be. I would know that silhouette anywhere.

Or... the more plausible scenario is I've finally lost the plot, and I'm hallucinating. What's one more thing on my list of problems, right? Sanity is overrated.

"Fuck," I mutter, scrubbing a hand down my face.

I glance at the clock above the stove and see that I

have less than an hour to get my ass out to the stables. I don't have time to waste on ghosts from my past. I'm sure this shit is stirring because Nicole and I had another fight. I've been upfront with her from the beginning—I'm just looking to have some fun. Monogamous fun, but casual, nonetheless. It's all I'm capable of, and I make no secret about that. But Nic has decided she wants more. Hell, last night, she pretty much demanded it, issuing an ultimatum that I either put a ring on her finger or she's walking away. When I chose the latter, she begged and pleaded with me to forget she ever said a word. She then proceeded to remind me of all the *fun* we've had over the last two years; hence, why I'm just gettin' home, dead tired.

It's going to be a long day.

After getting changed and eating some breakfast, I figure I might as well head out and get an early start. Right as I'm scooping up my cell from its spot on the kitchen counter, it buzzes with an incoming call. When I look down and see Mrs. James' name on the caller ID, I immediately pick up, worried something may have happened to her husband.

"Is everything okay?"

There's a pause on the other end before she says anything. "Hi, honey. I'm glad I caught you. I heard your truck passing just a little bit ago, so I figured I'd call before you came over this morning. I know this will sound strange—and completely out of left field— but I need you to stay away from the house for a while. There's been... well, we have an unexpected visitor, and

I think it's best if you get your morning coffee from your own kitchen. At least for now. I'm sure she'll... I mean, I think—"

"Anna, what's going on?"

She blows out a frustrated breath. Probably because I rarely address this woman by her first name. It's usually ma'am or Mrs. J. She tried convincing me to drop the formalities when I was a kid, but the woman had a hand in raising me almost as much as my father did, so I feel like I owe her that respect. If I'm dropping the formalities, she knows I mean business.

"She's back, Beckett." Mrs. James' voice is so quiet, it barely qualifies as a whisper, but I heard every word loud and clear.

"*Who's* back, Mrs. J?"

We both know who *she* is, but I need to hear her say it. At least I know she wasn't a figment of my imagination. That's a mark in the plus column, I suppose.

"Presley." Why is her voice so shaky? "And things aren't right, Beck. She'd be so upset if she knew I was calling you, but she doesn't know you took over for your father yet, and I know she wouldn't want anyone seeing her like this, so—"

"See her like *what*, Mrs. J? *What's wrong with Presley?*"

I shouldn't care. Not after Pres walked away from everything we had and married another man less than a year later. A goddamned politician douchebag at that. Logically, I know this, but logic is the last thing on my mind when I hear the anguish in her mother's tone.

"She's in an awful place, honey. I have my suspicions about why, but I need to have a long talk with my daughter to confirm whether or not it's true. I'm not going to assume anything and give the gossipmongers any fodder based purely on a mother's intuition."

"I would *never* feed the rumor mill about anyone, Mrs. J, and quite frankly, I'm insulted you'd think so. And let's not forget, you're the one who called me."

Another sigh. "I know you wouldn't, and I'm sorry if I implied that, Beckett. I just meant it's not my story to tell. The only reason I'm even calling you is to protect her. She's not in the right mind to face you right now, or anyone for that matter. Just please, stay away from the house until I give you the okay to return."

I pinch the bridge of my nose. "There's one problem with this little plan of yours."

"What's that?"

"Well, seeing as I'm the foreman of this ranch, I'll be all over the property doing my job. How exactly am I supposed to avoid her then?"

Mrs. J takes so long to answer, I have to check my phone to make sure the call didn't cut off.

"I don't think that'll be a problem."

"Why not?"

"Because I don't think Presley will be leaving this house anytime soon. I have a feeling it's going to be hard enough coaxing her out of her room."

My eyebrows draw together. "What the hell does that mean?"

"I've already said too much. I think she's up, so I

need to go. Can I depend on you to honor my wishes, Beckett?"

"Yes, ma'am. Of course."

"Thank you."

"You—"

Mrs. J ends the call before I can finish my sentence.

I take deep breaths, trying to get a grip. I don't even know why I'm so pissed. The fact that Presley's here? The fact that she left in the first place? The fact that she's spent over a decade in another man's bed? The fact that had she not run away to New York, I wouldn't have felt the need to flee either? And if I didn't do that, maybe I wouldn't be so fucked in the head? How in the hell am I supposed to do my job, knowing she's so close, but still completely out of my reach?

"Damn it!" I slam my open palm against the wall in frustration.

I fill my lungs a few more times before telling myself to man the fuck up and get out there because I have a job to do. There's no room for mistakes when you're working with powerful animals all day. And there's *definitely* no room in my life for a woman who tossed me aside like yesterday's trash.

Fuck Presley and whatever problems she came rolling back into town with. She's not my concern anymore. She hasn't been for a long time.

Chapter Nine
Presley – Age 17

"Touchdown!" the announcer calls over the PA. "Number thirteen, Beckett Armstrong, just threw his third touchdown pass of the night, with two seconds to spare in the fourth. That's another win for the Knights, ladies and gentlemen!"

I jump up and down, my gold and navy pom-poms waving high in the air, as Beck and his teammates celebrate their fourth consecutive win. Beck is the starting quarterback this year, which is unusual for a junior, but he's been rocking it. There's something to be said about small-town football. Everyone bands together each Friday to put the games on and support the home team as much as possible.

"Presley, that man of yours is on fire," my fellow cheerleader, Nicky says. "If you ever get sick of him, I'll take him off your hands."

I playfully whack her with my pom-pom. "Sorry, Nic, he's all mine forever and ever."

She fans herself mockingly. "Oh well, a girl can dream. Oh, look, Mr. Hotness is making his way over here now."

I can barely contain my joy as Beck runs across the football field in my direction. He's sweaty, and he has helmet hair, but he's still drop-dead gorgeous. I squeal when he pulls me into him and nuzzles my neck.

"Beckett, stop! Don't be startin' something you can't finish."

He kisses me hard. "Don't worry, baby. There will be plenty of *finishing* later."

I giggle. "Well, as long as you make sure I *finish* first, I'm good with that."

"Honey, I *always* make sure you *finish* first." Beck pulls me into a kiss that's not so appropriate for a school event, but I can't seem to help myself whenever he's around.

"Gah! You guys are so adorable, it's nauseating," Nicky complains.

"I can't help it if my girlfriend is the prettiest, smartest girl in the great state of Georgia." Beck winks. "No offense, Nicky."

She laughs. "Yeah, yeah, none taken. I'll leave you two lovebirds alone so I don't barf up those nachos I ate earlier. Presley, I'll see you at the bonfire later?"

After every game, our running back, Miles, hosts a bonfire on his property. It's our chance to celebrate together if the team won, or commiserate with each other if they lost.

"Yep, we'll be there," I say.

Beck waits until Nicky is out of earshot. "And I'll meet you by my truck after I get cleaned up?"

"Sure. Maybe we can take the long way to Miles'?"

Translation: Let's park somewhere and do it in the truck.

He grins knowingly. "I wouldn't have it any other way, Pres."

Chapter Ten
Presley

"**P**resley Anne, what are you doing out here in the dark?"

I blink as my mother flips on the porch light. "Just thinkin'."

She gives me a sad smile. "Come inside. I'm just about to get breakfast started."

I nod, wrapping the blanket more securely around my shoulders. "If you don't mind, I'm going to take a shower first. I can meet you in the kitchen after."

"Sure, honey."

She avoids looking at my face, and I can't say I blame her. When I got a glimpse in the mirror above my dresser, it didn't look any better than it did last night. In fact, I think it may look worse. If I'm not mistaken, the purple bruising is a shade or two deeper now.

Like the coward that I am, I take my sweet time in the shower. It's already taking me longer than usual, trying to do everything with only one arm, but when I grab the apple-scented shampoo off the shelf—the same shampoo I favored in my teenage years—I lose it. I sink to the bottom of the tub in the fetal position and cry like a baby. I make no effort to move, even as the icy water pelts my skin and causes my teeth to chatter. My chest squeezes as I think about the events that led me here.

I startle when I hear the familiar hum of the private elevator that leads directly into our penthouse. As the steel doors open, Sebastian's eyes widen when he sees me sitting on the couch. I can't say I blame him; I'm not usually up this late. It's not uncommon for my husband to work well into the evening. However, ever since I got this anonymous text, I wonder how many of those nights he legitimately spent working. Most days, I go to bed early, hoping that when he does return home, he's too tired for sex. It doesn't always work, but on the nights it does, I breathe a sigh of relief.

"Darling, what are you doing up this late?"

I rise from the couch, my arm falling to the side. "I was waiting for you."

"Is that so?" He gives me a wolfish grin as he removes his suit jacket and drapes it over one of the foyer chairs. "Is there something you want from me? I've had a long day, but I wouldn't be opposed to having those pretty lips of yours wrapped around my cock. You'd like that, wouldn't you, baby? I know how much you enjoy pleasuring me with your mouth."

Sebastian saunters toward me, loosening his tie and unfastening the top button of his shirt. I have to fight a shudder as his eyes travel the length of my body; I can see him hardening beneath his slacks.

I hold my hand up in a stop gesture as he unfastens his belt. "I wanted to talk to you about something I learned today."

He frowns. "We can talk tomorrow. Right now, you're going to get on your knees and suck me off like a good girl."

I take a step back when Sebastian reaches out, presumably to push on my shoulders until I'm kneeling before him. That's his preferred method of receiving. No doubt, because he can lord over me while I'm forced to perform the act.

"No, Sebastian. I'm not. We're going to talk."

He releases a sardonic laugh. He's not used to me fighting back. I've learned Sebastian's not nearly as rough if I just keep my mouth shut and pray for it to be over quickly. On occasion, he'll even pretend like he's a generous lover and performs oral sex on me. Despite his irrefutable talent in that area, I haven't orgasmed once in over ten years, not that he would care to notice.

I used to love making love. The physical gratification, being emboldened by watching the man I love coming apart from the pleasure I give him. The intimacy of being as close as two people can be... I adored everything about it. At one point, I was worried there was something wrong with me, that my libido might be a little too high, but that thought is absurd now. While my husband has never technically forced himself on me, I wouldn't exactly consider myself a willing participant either. I suppose you could say I've become indifferent.

Or, more likely, dead inside.

When sex is never on your terms, desire fades more and more each day, until one day, it disappears entirely. That's how it's been for me, at least. I can say without a doubt, I'd be perfectly content never having sex again. Of course, that doesn't work for Sebastian's delicate ego—God forbid a woman reject him, especially his wife—so I've spent many years pretending otherwise. Sebastian's fuse is short, and one thing that'll blow that fuse faster than anything is telling him no, for any reason, on any matter.

On the rare occasion I couldn't convince myself to submit to his advances, I'd regretted it almost immediately while I was serving as his punching bag. My husband needs an outlet for the beast raging inside of him, especially if he's been drinking, and he's decided I'm that outlet, one way or the other. Allowing him into my body is the best way I've figured out how to manage the situation because when he gets off, he's much more pleasant to be around. And more often than not, he'll fall asleep within minutes after he orgasms, which affords me some much-needed peace, no matter how temporary.

"Fine. We can talk after I come all over your tits." He gives me a smarmy smile. "C'mon, baby. I know how much you love my pearl necklaces."

I've been such a fool, haven't I? All these years, I've been playing along to keep the monster at bay, but I thought for sure he knew—whether he was willing to admit it or not— that my compliance wasn't out of love or loyalty, and defi-nitely not out of lust. For some reason, it made it easier for me to stomach. Sure, I was a puppet to his whims, but if he knew deep down I didn't really want him, it made his abuse more palatable in my head. It was a small victory I clung to, to help me get through the worst of it. Sebastian's arrogance knows no bounds, but he's a brilliant man. After our first two years together, fear and self-preservation—and okay, shame, too—have been my only motivators. But now, seeing that look in his eye, I've no doubt, he actually thinks I want him, that I crave his touch. And if that's true, the man's genuinely unhinged.

Either that or my acting is so phenomenal, I should have won ten Oscars by now.

"Oh, this should be good. What could possibly be so important that it comes before your wifely duties?"

I unlock my phone, hit play on the video, and extend my arm, turning the screen toward him. "This. This is what's so important."

His blue eyes harden as they narrow in on the screen. His hand lashes out like a viper, grabbing my wrist, yanking my arm to bring the phone closer. "What the fuck is this?"

I lift my chin, refusing to acknowledge the pain from his grip. "I think it's fairly obvious what it is, Sebastian. My question is, how long has this been happening? Is she the only woman you're screwing behind my back, or are there more?"

"Don't play games with me, you bitch! Where the fuck did you get this?!" Spittle flies on my face as he screams. I cry out when he twists my wrist as he pulls the phone out of my hand. "Where. The. Fuck. Did. This. Come. From. Presley? What are you up to?"

"What am I up to?" I'm screaming now, too. "I'm not the one who's cheating, Sebastian! How could you do this to me? It's not like you're not getting enough sex at home. After

everything... how could you? I've put up with a lot from you, but I won't put up with this. I refuse to be humiliated any longer! I w—"

"You ungrateful cunt! I'm going to fucking kill you!"

I stumble as his fist slams into my mouth, cutting off my words. I'm stunned for a moment as I press my fingertips to my lips, and they come back coated in red. This isn't the first time he's hit me. Hell, it's probably not even the hundredth. But out of all the other times, I've never seen him so manic. Sebastian's threatened to kill me before, but I never felt the weight of those words like I do now. There's no doubt in my mind that if I don't get out of here, he might just live up to that threat. I do the only thing I can think of.

I run.

"Where the fuck do you think you're going?" Sebastian booms, grabbing my long hair and pulling backward. "We're not finished here."

My stomach drops as he slams me to the floor, jabbing a knee into my lower spine. I whimper as he starts yanking at my pants, pulling roughly on my panties to get them down as well. "Sebastian, don't. Please."

A dark chuckle falls from his lips. I can smell the whiskey on his breath as he nudges the bridge of his nose against my earlobe. "You don't get to make demands, darling. What you do get to do is accept your punishment for being so disrespectful. I mean, really, is that any way to treat the man who's been caring for you all these years?" He brushes my hair aside and clamps his teeth down on my neck, licking the same spot when I cry out in pain. "The man who loves you, who vowed to take you as his wife until death do us part."

I tremble as he spears me with two fingers, pumping them in and out. I'm bone dry and in no way prepared, but he doesn't seem to notice, or maybe he simply doesn't care. His fingernails scratch my insides as he works the digits in and out, whispering words of encouragement, telling me what a good girl I'm being, how good I'm going to feel around his cock. I hate myself for allowing this, but I'm paralyzed with fear. I squeeze my eyes shut, trying to find the strength to fight back. If he does this, if he takes my body without consent, I don't know if I'd ever recover from that. After everything he's done over the years, that's the one line I never thought he'd cross. It seems ridiculous now—if he felt no remorse beating the shit out of me, why would he have any now?

I scramble when Sebastian flips me over but freeze when his hand wraps around the front of my neck. "I wouldn't do that if I were you." He squeezes tightly in warning. "I can end your life in a second, Presley. Do you really want that?"

I actually consider it for a moment.

Sebastian grins when he sees the tears pouring down my face. I shudder when he licks a path over my cheek, collecting the salty liquid with his tongue. "Mmm, I love the taste of your tears. So. Fucking. Sexy."

"Sebastian... please... don't do this. It doesn't have to be like this."

His face twists in anger. "When are you going to learn? You don't make the rules, Presley!" With one hand manacled around my neck, he uses the other to yank my shirt open. Buttons go flying right before he pops open the front clasp of my bra, exposing my bare breasts to his greedy eyes. He circles my areola with his finger, pinching the tip until I cry out in pain. "Ah, there's my gorgeous tits. Every time I see them, I want to thank Dr. Malcolm for doing such a fantastic job."

I was perfectly happy with my smaller breasts until one too many less-than-subtle hints from my husband about surgery ate at my self-esteem. I thought the augmentation was my idea at the time, but if I had to do it over again, I wouldn't.

My eyes slam shut as he seals his mouth around one nipple, then the other. I press my lips together to stifle my scream as he moans, and I feel his dick jerk against my thigh. My fear seems to excite him more, and the last thing I want to do is encourage him. I want nothing more than to buck him off, but I know trying would be futile. Sebastian has almost a hundred pounds on me, and he's using every bit of that to his advantage right now, pinning me to the hardwood floor. A calmness settles over me as I accept what I have to do. Getting out of this alive needs to be my top priority. If I make him any angrier, my chances of escaping this apartment are slim to none. That doesn't mean I won't try to appeal to any shred of humanity he might have left, though.

"Sebastian... please. Don't do this. If you really love me, you won't do this."

He removes his mouth from my breast to work his pants down over his backside, just enough to free his erection. "Shut up and pay your penance, bitch."

I whimper, accepting my fate.

When he notices I'm no longer struggling, he cants his head to the side, assessing me carefully. I look him directly in the eye with as much hatred as I can possibly manage. If Sebastian insists on doing this, I'm going to make damn sure he knows it's not freely offered. I'm going to leave no doubt as to how much he disgusts me. And when it's over, one way or another, I'm going to do everything in my power to ensure it's the last time he ever gets his hands on me.

A cruel smirk forms on his lips as he enters me. Despite his earlier attempts, there's no lubrication, but he somehow forces himself inside anyway. One of his hands remains on my throat, daring me to give him a reason to squeeze, while the other digs into my hip with bruising force as he pistons in and out of my body. Sebastian is well-endowed, so the pain steals my breath. I bite my tongue and cheek, dig my fingernails into my palms. I do anything I can think of to distract myself from the horror of it, so I don't give him the satisfaction of crying out. This man has had enough of my tears, and I refuse to give him any more.

Sebastian takes my silence as a challenge, one I readily accept. No matter how roughly he drills into me, no matter how hard he pinches my nipples or digs his thumb into my inner thigh, I refuse to make a peep. It's the most remarkable performance I've ever given because while I may appear stoic on the surface, I'm dying on the inside. Any inkling of hope I may have been holding on to has been shredded beyond repair. The longer it goes on, the more enraged he becomes when I don't give him the response he's looking for. When his body stiffens, and he spills his seed into me, I breathe a sigh of relief, knowing it's almost over.

But my relief is short-lived as I see the look on his face when he pulls out and tucks himself back into his pants. He's *deceptively calm, so much so, I ask myself if this is the moment I die? My husband's fists come flying at me so fast, I don't even have a chance to blink before they meet my flesh. Sebastian doesn't say a word as he rains blow after blow down on my body. My face, my ribs, my stomach, nothing is off the table. He's no longer concerned about limiting his punches to non-visible places. I finally break and scream so hard my throat is raw when he twists my arm at an unnatural angle, causing excruciating pain in my shoulder. When he releases me, my arm falls limply to my side, completely useless. I'm almost certain he pulled it right out of its socket. I double over, vomiting all over the expensive rug. The last thing I see before blacking out is Sebastian's designer loafer coming at the side of my head.*

Chapter Eleven
Presley – Age 17

I drum my fingers over the kitchen table, overwhelmed by all the possibilities before me. I drove to Atlanta this past weekend with Nicky to go to a college fair. There were representatives from over two hundred different universities. Community colleges, private or state universities—the choices were endless. I have packets from at least half of those spread out before me.

I finger the corner of an NYU pamphlet. Beck and I have talked at great length about which school we'd choose. We'd both like to major in business, so we have flexibility. The University of West Georgia seemed to be our best option—it's only about two hours from Hope Springs, and we'd get in-state tuition. I love this town, and I especially love this ranch, but I've been itching for something more for years now. I want to experience life outside of small-town America. I want to know what it's like to live in a city surrounded by millions, eating all the takeout you can imagine, exploring the arts, and experiencing various cultures. What better time to do that than your college years?

New York City was never on my radar. Still, after meeting with their admissions representative, I can't lie to myself and say the idea doesn't intrigue me. Honestly, it *excites* me. I can't stop thinking about how much I'd be able to see and do daily. I'm torn because I thought we had this all figured out, and now I'm being pulled in a different direction.

The only thing I know for sure is that I want to be close to Beck. Not because I don't think our relationship wouldn't survive distance—I know it would. I just don't *want* to be without him, and he feels the same way about me. We've been together almost every day for the past thirteen years. He's not only my boyfriend—he's part of my soul. Nobody knows me like Beck. He's my best friend. My confidant. He makes me feel loved and safe. When I'm away from him for any length of time, it feels like a part of me is missing. I don't want to dive into college with that kind of emptiness.

I look up when I hear the screen door squeak. Beck walks into the kitchen, looking gorgeous as ever in his flannel, jeans, and boots. The main house is just as much his home as mine, so knocking isn't something he's ever needed to do.

"Hey," he says with a big smile.

"Hey." I discreetly flip over the NYU brochure as I stand up to greet him with a kiss.

He looks at the pile on the table. "What's all this?"

I know I have to approach this delicately. Beck loves everything about living here. He's never been drawn to city living—he'd be happy staying in Hope Springs forever. The only reason he even wants to go to college is that he wants his own horse ranch one day. He's already had all the hands-on experience he needs with the animals, but he wants to learn more about running a successful business. I don't know what I want to do after school, but a business degree is transferable, so I figured it's not a bad way to go.

I follow his eyes to the table. "I brought home a bunch of stuff from the college fair I went to with Nicky."

"Why? We already know where we're going. I thought you only went so she didn't have to make the drive by herself."

"Well, that's how it started. But there were hundreds of schools there, and some of them seem *amazing*, Beck. It wouldn't hurt to have options, right?"

He frowns. "What's going on, Pres? Are you changing your mind?"

"No! Not exactly, anyway. But what if we went out of state? Don't you think it could be fun?"

"I don't know," he says. "I thought we decided to stay close to family. And staying in-state is a lot cheaper."

I shrug. "It's not like we'd be leaving forever."

He scrubs a hand over his face. "Where are you thinking? Did any of them stand out more than the others?"

I take a deep breath and pick up the NYU pamphlet. "This one."

"*New York City?* Are you shittin' me, Presley? Why would you ever want to go there?"

"Why not? It could be fun."

"Yeah, if you like concrete," he mutters. "Or getting mugged."

"Beckett, I'm serious. Think of all the things we could experience. Would you at least consider it?"

He eyes the brochure like it's coated in anthrax and releases a big sigh. "Yeah, Pres. I'll think about it."

I hand it to him and lift on my toes to place a kiss on his lips. "I love you."

He pulls me into his strong arms and rests his chin on the top of my head. "I love you too, darlin'. More than anything."

Chapter Twelve
Presley

"Come sit down, honey. I made your favorites: banana chocolate chip pancakes, bacon, and hash browns."

I slowly make my way into the kitchen and take a seat at the table. My stomach rumbles when my mom sets a heaping plate before me. I inhale the delicious aroma for just a moment before pushing it away.

"Do you by chance have any scrambled egg whites or turkey bacon?"

My mother frowns. "I could manage the egg whites, but the only bacon we have is the kind sitting right in front of you. What's the matter? Do you not like pancakes anymore?"

I don't know. I haven't had pancakes in over a decade because my personal trainer had me on a strict low-calorie, low-carb diet. If my size zero pants got a little snug, he dropped my calorie allowance even further, tacking on an extra forty-five minutes of cardio to my workout.

"Um... no, it's not that. It's just, I..."

"It's just *what*, honey? Eat up. You're wasting away. I haven't seen you this small in... well, probably not since you had your first period." She gestures to my clothing. "You were tiny in high school, and yet, you're practically swimming in that outfit."

I sigh. When I dug through the dresser for some old clothes, I was shocked when I saw all the size fours. People used to tell me I was too skinny back then. I can't imagine what they'd say if they saw me now. I don't know why I'm making such a big deal out of it, anyway. It's just one meal. I slide the plate closer to me, pick up a fork, and take a tentative bite.

"Oh, my God," I mumble around a mouthful of heaven.

My mama preens. "See? They can't be all that bad if they put that smile on your face."

Was I smiling? I reach up to touch my cheek but think better of it when I feel how swollen it is.

My mom takes the seat across from me with a sigh. "Talk to me, Presley. Please. This is killing your daddy and me."

I finish chewing before speaking again. "Where is Dad anyway?"

"He had business up in Macon. He didn't want to leave without saying goodbye, but you were taking so long in the shower, and I thought maybe it would be easier for you to open up if it were just the two of us.

Now, tell me what happened, sweetheart. Who did this to you?"

I take another bite, stalling as long as I can. Unfortunately, after only five bites, my stomach can't handle any more food.

I can't bear to see the look in her eyes when I say it, so I carefully study the tabletop. "Sebastian. Sebastian did this."

She doesn't say a word, so I finally look up and meet her tear-filled eyes. "Has he... done this before?"

"Never this bad, but... yeah. Quite a few times."

"How long, Presley?" she croaks. "How long has he been puttin' his hands on you?"

I hang my head in shame. "Almost the whole time."

My mom gasps. "Oh, baby, why didn't you say anything?"

I lift my good shoulder. "I was scared. And ashamed."

"I'm going to kill that son of a bitch if your daddy or brother don't get to him first."

I shake my head. "No, Mama. You have to promise not to do anything. Not to say anything. I know you have to tell Dad, but I just want this to go away. I just want to move on with my life."

"How can you say that? You can't let him get away with this, Presley! I find it hard to believe you'd even consider it. I raised you to stand up for yourself."

"Mom, please. He's too much in the public eye. I don't... I can't..." I sniff as a new wave of tears makes my nose run. "I can't stand the thought of anyone knowing what I went through. They'll either judge me or pity me, and I don't want either. Besides, with his connections, who do you think they're gonna believe if I start pointing fingers? It's my word against Sebastian's, and in their eyes, he's their messiah. I got away. I don't know what I'm going to do, but I do know I'm never going back. That's what matters."

"Presley..."

I hold my hand up. "I know it's hard to understand. Unless you're in the middle of a situation like that, there's no way to truly understand why some people do what they feel they have to do. But... I just want to put it behind me. I have to believe karma will get to him one of these days."

She gets out of her chair to envelop me in a hug, careful not to jostle my shoulder. "I don't like it, baby, but you're a grown woman. Just know you're welcome to stay here as long as you need."

"Thank you. I—"

"Damn, Ma, I hope you have extras because that smel—"

Both mine and my mother's head lifted at the sound of my brother's voice.

His jaw drops. "Presley?! What are you doing here? *And what the hell happened to your face?*"

I just sit here like an idiot, blinking as he looks me over in confusion.

My mom places her hand on his chest and starts gently pushing him out of the room. "Clayton, shush. We'll talk later."

"What the hell, Ma? Somebody needs to explain what's going on. Why does she look like that? Who do I need to kill?"

I can hear them whispering as she's ushering him out of the house. After about a minute, she comes back in and starts washing dishes like the whole thing never happened.

"Mama?"

"Don't worry about your brother, baby. His lips are sealed. He's working this evening, but you two can catch up at dinner tomorrow night." She turns around and throws a dishtowel over her shoulder. "Speaking of catching up... there's something you should know, Presley."

The look on her face tells me exactly who she's talking about. "Why didn't you tell me he was back?"

Her eyes widen. "You knew?"

"I saw his truck this morning. I couldn't actually see *him*, but I knew he was the one driving it. Is he visiting his dad or something?"

Sadness washes over her face. "Oh, no, honey. Dave passed away about five years ago. Died in his sleep of a heart attack."

"Oh." I rub at the sudden tightness in my chest.

Mr. Armstrong was like a second father to me. The fact that he died *years* ago and I had no idea doesn't sit well with me. Poor Beck. He was really close with his father.

"Why didn't you tell me?"

My mom frowns as she retakes a seat. "Presley, you

told us *on more than one occasion* you didn't want to hear about what was going on here, *especially* not any news related to Beckett. The last time I tried, you practically bit my head off through the phone, and I didn't hear from you again for almost a year. What was I supposed to do?"

I remember that phone call. It was the morning after an awful beating. Sebastian had just left for work—he was the deputy mayor back then. I felt sorry for myself and really needed to hear my mama's voice, so I called her. Within the first minute, she brought up Beckett, telling me she had some important news, and I completely freaked out on her. I never did find out what she was trying to say, but I assumed at the time that maybe he was getting married, and she was trying to break it to me gently. She sounded so sad, I couldn't think of anything else she could possibly have to tell me.

"I still wish I knew."

"He's buried at the old cemetery. When you're... feeling better, maybe you can go for a visit and make your peace."

"Yeah, maybe," I half-heartedly agree. "I still don't understand why Beckett's here. I thought he was going to make a career out of the military."

Despite my refusal to talk about Beck, my brother felt compelled to sneak some bits and pieces in. We'd be chatting about something totally unrelated, then bam! He'd slip in some information about Beck and go right back to the previous topic as if it never happened.

I'm surprised he didn't find a way to tell me about Mr. Armstrong's passing.

"Well, as you know, sometimes, plans change." My mom shrugs. "Once Beck was... uh, once he had some time to grieve his father's passing, he asked about the foreman's position. Your daddy and I couldn't think of anyone more deserving or qualified for it."

Beck always did want to be a rancher.

"Well, I guess that worked out well then, huh? Good for him."

My mom's hazel eyes narrow. "What's with the bitter tone? I've gotta say, Presley, I know you've been through a lot, but that boy has, too. You have no right to be upset that he's found his way, especially since you're..." She looks away. "Never mind. Now's not the time."

I stand up. "No, let's do this. Especially since I'm *what*, Mom? Especially since I'm the one who left?"

She releases a harsh exhale. "You know I would never fault you for leaving, Presley. I know you were hurtin' and you felt getting away was the best option at the time. But I don't understand why you had to cut us out of your life, too. That part never made sense."

I gesture to my beat-up face. "I didn't want you to see this. I was afraid you'd know. If we talked too often, or if you came for a visit, I was afraid you'd see right through me. I was so ashamed. I *am* so ashamed."

Great, now I'm crying again.

"Oh, honey." My mom pulls me into her arms and

lets me cry on her shoulder until my tears are all dried out.

"Sorry." I wipe the tears off my face. "Lord, I'm so sick of crying."

My mother gently frames my face with her hands. "I have a feeling you've been saving up a lot of tears. You cry as much as you need to."

And now I'm blubbering.

"Look, Presley. Why don't you go upstairs and rest for a while? You look like it's been an awful long time since you've had a good sleep."

It has.

"Okay. That's probably a good idea. If... if I sleep through dinner, will you please wake me?"

She nods. "Of course. Get some rest, dear."

I give her a quick one-armed hug. "Thanks, Mom."

My mom pats the back of my head. "Anytime, baby."

Chapter Thirteen
Presley – Age 17

"Good lord, Beck, where did you learn how to do that?"

He flashes me his sexy smirk. "You liked that, did you?"

I roll onto my side and pull him into a kiss. "I *love* anything you do. You always know what my body wants before I do."

It's Saturday night, so Beck and I have spent the last few hours under the stars in the back of his pickup. It's been cooler than average lately, but we never have any problems keeping warm when it's just the two of us beside our pond. Beck rolls me onto my back and hovers over me. I can feel him hardening against my thigh, even though we just finished making love a few minutes ago.

"That's because you're part of me, Pres. I'll always know how to take care of you. In *every* way."

I laugh when he wags his eyebrows at the innuendo. "So confident, aren't you?"

He lowers himself down for a kiss. God, this man can get me going with the slightest effort.

"It's part of my charm," he says when he pulls away. "You know you love it."

I wrap my arms around his neck. "I can't wait to become your wife one day."

He flashes his blinding smile. "Me neither."

We're not officially engaged, but that's been our plan since we were about fifteen. We'll get married right after college and have our first baby by twenty-five. I can't imagine anything I want more. We have it all mapped out, except where we'll be living. It's been almost a month since I gave Beck that brochure on NYU, and we haven't talked about it since. I'm trying to give him time—I know I'm asking him to go way out of his comfort zone—but the application deadline for the fall semester is approaching. He needs to make a decision soon.

"Hey, have you thought about New York?"

His muscles tense. "Yeah, I've looked at the brochure some, but I can't say that I understand why it appeals to you so much."

"Because… this is our chance to see what life's like outside of the country."

"Pres, you're acting like we've never been to a city before."

"Not any like New York, Beckett. And a short trip isn't enough time to get the full experience, anyway.

We'd actually be *living* in another city during college. It's our chance to see what's out there in the world."

"What's wrong with *this* world? It's been perfect for us."

"I know it has, but don't you want more, Beck? Aren't you curious?"

He shakes his head. "Not really."

I sigh. "Can't we just apply and decide what to do from there? If we don't get in, we have nothing to even talk about."

He searches my eyes. "This is something you really want?"

"It really is."

He lowers his forehead to my shoulder. "Okay, Pres. Let's fill out some more application packets."

I pull his head away so I can look him in the eyes. "Really?"

Beck smiles. "Haven't you figured out by now that there isn't anything I wouldn't do for you? *You're my everything, Pres.* If New York is going to make you happy, then we're going to New York."

"You're too good to me, Beck."

"No such thing." He grinds his stiff length into my thigh. "Are we done talkin' now?"

I gasp when he begins circling his thumb against my hot flesh. "Yeah, we're done talking."

"I was hopin' you'd say that," he says, right before pulling me into a drugging kiss.

After that, we're incapable of words for quite some time.

Chapter Fourteen
Beckett

"Hey, man." Clay pops the top off a bottle of Coors and sets it in front of me on the bar. "You look like you could use this."

I scoff. "I could use *a lot* more than this."

"Yeah, I thought so. That's why I have this." Clayton lines four shot glasses on the bar and fills each one to the brim.

I raise my eyebrows. "You trying to get me drunk and take advantage of me, sweetheart?"

"You should be so lucky." He laughs, picking up a shot and downing it in one go. "Half of these are for me. The women in my life are driving me nuts."

I pick up a glass and clink it against his. "I'll drink to that."

We each swallow our second shot and chase it with a beer. I'm not sure he's supposed to be drinking on the job, but the man does own the place, so who am I to judge?

Clayton observes me as I take a long pull from my bottle. "I take it you heard?"

"Yeah, I heard." I tip my head back as I drain the last drop of beer. "You see her yet?"

He nods. "This morning. I stopped by my folks' place."

I told myself I wasn't going to dig. I thought I had actually managed to convince myself by the end of the workday, yet here I am.

I quirk my head to the side. "What's that look for?"

"What look?"

I gesture to him. "You look like you're ready to lay someone out."

He points to me. "You always were a smart one, Cowboy."

I roll my eyes at Clay's use of my call sign. When one of the guys from my unit found out I grew up on a ranch in the middle of nowhere, he dubbed me Cowboy, and from that point on, I was stuck with it. I made the mistake of telling Clay about it once after a few too many drinks, and now he's decided he likes that name better than the one I was born with.

"So, what gives?"

Clay swallows hard. "I don't know yet. But I have my suspicions."

"What's that supposed to mean?"

Clay pops another bottle open and hands it to me. "I take it you haven't seen her."

"Nope." I take a swig. "I've been banned from the house until further notice, per your mother's request."

"That's probably for the best."

Why is this damn family so secretive all of a sudden? I've known Clay practically my whole life. He's like a brother to me. It's not like him to be anything other than a straight-shooter.

"What's going on, man?"

He looks around to make sure nobody's listening. "Between you and me, I think that Presley's dickbag hus—"

"Hey, baby. You didn't say you were comin' here tonight." Small hands wrap around me from behind while a set of firm tits press against my back.

I grab Nicole's hand and guide her to the stool on my left so I can hear her better. "That's because I wasn't planning on it. Just came to talk to Clayton."

Nicole glances at the bartender-slash-owner of this joint with more than a little disdain. "Clayton."

His mouth forms into a cocky grin. "Nicky."

She glares. There's definitely no love lost between these two. "It's *Nicole* now, remember? I haven't gone by Nicky in a long time."

"Nah, I think I'll stick with Nicky." He winks for added measure before walking away to take someone's order at the end of the bar.

My lips twitch as I fight a smile. For some reason, Nicole got it in her head that Nicky made her sound childish, so she's pretty much demanded nobody call her that ever again. Considering we all grew up in this town, I think it's a little ridiculous, but whatever. It's not my name. Clayton never seems to miss an opportunity to fuck with her, though. I should probably care more about that, considering I am sleeping with her, but I can't really find the will when I think it's funny as hell.

"Ugh, he's so annoying." Nicole turns toward me, giving me a quick flash of her underwear beneath the short denim skirt she's wearing. Or should I say, her lack of underwear? "Did you know I used to have the biggest crush on him in high school? What was I thinking?"

She obviously doesn't remember the night Pres and I caught her fooling around with Clay. If I'm not mistaken, he's the one who popped her cherry. I should probably have some kind of feelings about that, too, but I don't really care one way or the other.

"I'm sure we all did questionable things as teenagers."

She chuckles. "Oh my God, you can say that again. You and Presley being a perfect example."

"What does that mean?" Everyone around here knows talking about Presley is a no-go zone with me. The only people who are the exception to that rule are the ones related to her. I wonder why Nicole's bringing her up all of a sudden. In the two years we've been seeing each other, she hasn't done so once.

Nicole rolls her eyes. "Oh, don't get all defensive, Beckett. I'm not baggin' on your precious Presley. I'm just sayin—"

"Hey, kids, did I hear my sister's name?" Clay pops his head in between us like a goddamn whack-a-mole.

"Jesus, Clayton!" Nicole places her open palm over her heart. "You scared the shit out of me."

He laughs. "Gotta pay better attention, Nicky. You never know who's gonna sneak up on you. Now, what's this I hear about my dear old sis? You heard the buzz she's back, I take it?"

Ah, fuck. He just had to go there, didn't he?

"What?!" Nicole shrieks, drawing the attention of everyone in this damn place. "Since when? Why? More importantly, when's she going back to New York?"

All questions I'd like answers to, and if Nicole hadn't interrupted my conversation with Clay, I'd probably have them by now.

"Retract your claws there, kitten." Clay holds his palms out, laughing. "I thought Beck would've told you, that's all."

She whips her head over to me with an accusing glare. "*You knew?*"

I blow out a breath, pinching the bridge of my nose. Why this jackass is stirring up trouble right now, I don't know, but it's starting to piss me off. "I don't know any more than you do, Nic. I just found out this morning."

"And you didn't think to tell me at any point today?"

I clench my jaw, giving Clay a look that says, *thanks a lot, dick.* "No, I didn't, seeing as I've been working all day. I don't see why it matters anyway."

She laughs, but there's no humor behind it. "Of course, you don't."

"Jesus fucking Christ," I mutter, rubbing my

temples. "What is the right thing to say here, Nicole? Because I feel like you're mad at me, but for the life of me, I can't figure out why."

Nicole stands and hauls her giant purse over her shoulder. "No surprise there, Beckett. I'll see you later."

I groan and thunk my head on the bar after she walks away.

"Yeah, I hear ya."

I sit up and point a finger at Clayton. "Don't start with me. You're on my shit list, asshole."

Twin dimples pop on his cheeks as he laughs. "You know what I can't figure out?"

"What's that?"

"Why you're still with Nicky. I mean, she's fuckhot, obviously, and that thing she can do with her tongue..."

I make a hurry-up motion. "Move the fuck along with that train of thought."

"All I'm sayin' is I don't get it. She's not your type. *At all.* We both know you have a thing for blondes and that she-devil's hair is black as night. Plus, she's so fucking uptight, man. *Also,* not your type. I mean, who the hell cares if someone calls her Nicky?"

"She does, evidently."

"No, kidding." A shit-eating grin lights up his face. "Hence, why I use it every chance I get. I just meant, what's the big deal? There's nothing wrong with the name."

"I gave up trying to figure her out a long time ago, bud. Now, are you going to tell me what I want to know, or what?"

Clay's expression instantly sobers as he pours another shot. "Whatever's going on, it ain't good, Beckett. That's all I'm saying for now."

I give him a wry look before I tip it back. "Wow... that's really helpful. Thanks for absolutely nothing."

"Look, man. I love you. You know that."

"I told you, Clay, I don't care how drunk I get or how much you sweet-talk me. I'm not sucking your cock. I will *never* be that hard up."

He flips me off. "Very funny, dickhead. The point I was trying to make is you're like my brother, but she's always going to be my baby sister. And as much as I want to run this by someone and speculate 'til I can't see straight, I need to respect her right to privacy. When she's ready to talk, she'll talk."

I nod, digging some bills out of my wallet. Clay tries waving them off, but I pin the cash under one of the shot glasses. "You cool if I pick my truck up after I get done workin' tomorrow?"

"It's all good. You need me to find you a ride?"

"Nah." I take my phone out of my pocket and send a text. "I'm texting Colby. I'm just going to wait for him out front."

Clay nods. "You doin' okay with all this, Beckett?"

I appreciate his concern, but the last thing I want to do is have a heart-to-heart about this shit right now. I need to figure out what the hell's going on inside my head first.

"I guess we'll find out soon enough." I shrug,

honestly not sure how else to answer that. "I'll see you later, man."

He lifts his chin. "Later."

A few minutes after I step out into the starry night, Colby Mitchell, also known as Sheriff Mitchell, also known as my best friend since high school, is pulling up in front of *Dive Bar*, Hope Springs' one and only drinking establishment.

He rolls the window down on his Explorer. "You know the sheriff's office is not your personal Uber service, right?"

I belt out a laugh. "If we had a damn Uber service in this town, I wouldn't need you. It does come in handy the station is right down the road, though."

"Yeah, yeah. Hop in, asswipe."

He waits until I'm buckled up before pulling out of the lot. "What's going on, man? It's not like you to throw 'em back when you have to work the next day."

I groan, looking out the window. "Presley's back in town."

He whistles. "Shit. That's rough, buddy."

"Tell me about it. Even better, I think something's wrong, Colby. Clayton and Mrs. J. are being extremely vague, but I have a feeling whatever brought Pres back after all these years isn't good."

"And you're concerned about that? After what she did to you?"

"I sure as hell don't want to be. My life's fucking complicated enough. Nic's pissed I didn't tell her the second I found out."

Colby laughs. "I bet. But to be fair, it doesn't take much to piss that woman off."

I laugh with him. "True."

"So, what are you going to do?"

"I don't know." I shake my head. "I don't fucking know."

Chapter Fifteen
Presley – Age 18

"Please be negative," I beg. "Please be negative."

This shouldn't be happening. I'm on the pill, yet my period is eight days late. When Mama figured out that Beck and I were having sex, she drove me to the doctor's office the very next day to get me on birth control. She said, "There's no way you're making me a grandma right now. It's bad enough I have to worry about your brother and his philandering ways." I don't know how she knew, but I'm a terrible liar, so I didn't even try denying it. She told me we were too young, and she didn't like it, but she also remembered what it was like to be young and in love. If I had to be sexually active, at least it was with a boy she loved as much as her own children. I was sixteen at the time and haven't missed a single pill since then.

I stare at the little white stick from across the bathroom. I drove two towns over immediately after school to buy a pregnancy test. I wasn't going to risk bringing it home, so here I am, standing in the restroom at the drugstore, waiting for my results.

I take a deep breath when the timer goes off on my phone. As I approach the counter, I say one more little prayer that my whole future isn't about to blow up in smoke. I pick up the test and immediately hone in on the pink plus sign staring back at me.

"No-no-no-no-no! This can't be happening!"

I drop the stick when there's a knock on the door. "Miss, are you okay in there?"

Crap, I must've said that too loud.

"Uh… yep. I'll be right out."

I wrap the white stick in toilet paper, toss it in the garbage, and wash my hands before exiting the restroom.

The gray-haired pharmacist is looking at me with concern. "Are you sure you're okay, dear?"

I fight back tears. "Yes, thank you. I'll be fine."

I get to my car as fast as possible and start the ignition. Once I'm a safe distance away, I pull over on the side of the road and proceed to break down. Fat tears roll down my face uncontrollably as I calculate that I must be only four or five weeks along. What am I going to do? I'm too young. I just turned eighteen a few weeks ago! How am I going to tell Beck? My parents? Everything I thought I knew about my future is gone now. Beck and I were both accepted into NYU. We just received our letters last week. Now, instead of moving up north in the fall, I'm going to be a giant pregnant lady going into my third trimester. I can't have a baby right now. How would we even support one?

There's a women's clinic about an hour away. I can ditch school and drive there tomorrow morning to discuss my options. Oh, what am I saying? I fully support a woman's right to choose, but I can't imagine myself doing that. Especially not with a baby that Beck and I made.

I gasp and place my hand on my stomach. "Oh my God, there's a baby in there. I have a baby inside of me."

As soon as I can hold back the tears to see clearly, I pull back onto the road and head straight for the ranch. I need to talk to Beck, and then we can worry about what to do together.

I spot him coming out of the machine shed as I make my way up the long drive. Instead of parking in front of the main house, I pull up beside him and push the passenger door open.

"Get in, Beck. We need to talk."

He places his hands on the roof of my car and leans in the open door. "What's going on, darlin'?"

I take off my sunglasses so he can see my bloodshot, tear-filled eyes. "Please just get in. We need to talk, and we can't have this conversation here."

He purses his lips when he gets a good look at me. "Give me a second to tell my dad I'm taking a break."

"'Kay," I say, sniffling.

A few moments later, Beck slides into the passenger seat and slams the door shut. "What's going on, Pres?"

"Just hold on a sec. Not here." I shift my car into

drive and head toward the pond. My car isn't made for off-road, so it's a little bumpy getting there, but I manage. I park the car and immediately step out toward the dock. I can hear Beck's footsteps behind me, but he hasn't said a word. He's waiting me out.

The water's too cold to put my feet in this time of year, so I take a seat, curling my legs under me. Beck sits down next to me and wipes a stray tear from my cheek.

"Presley, what's wrong? You're freaking me out here."

"I'm freaking out too, Beck! How could this have happened?"

"How could *what* have happened?" His eyebrows pinch together.

I look him straight in the eye. "I'm pregnant."

His eyes widen. "Seriously?"

"Do you think I'd joke about something like this?"

He rubs the back of his neck. "Holy shit, Pres. How far along?"

"About a month, I think. I just took a home pregnancy test; I haven't seen a doctor yet."

"But you're on the pill."

"Obviously, it didn't work," I sniff. "What are we going to do, Beck? This ruins everything."

"Hey, look at me, Pres." He grabs my hand. "Why does this have to be a bad thing? We have a baby on the way—that should be celebrated."

"Are you crazy?" I jerk my hand away. "What about New York? How are we supposed to be parents, Beck?

We still live with our parents. And we sure as hell can't raise a baby in a dorm room."

Beck grabs my hand back. "Presley, take a deep breath and just listen, okay?"

I take a few calming breaths. "Go ahead, Beckett. Tell me why you think this will all work out."

"Well, I don't have all the details ironed out since I've known about this for two whole minutes, but we can make this work. My dad was going to take me on full-time at the ranch after graduation. It's a good-paying job; we can find a little place to rent until we can afford to buy."

"You were only supposed to work full-time through the summer to get some extra cash for school."

"That's true, but he needs help. He was going to hire someone else come fall. Now, he doesn't have to. I'll be able to take care of us, Pres. *All three of us.* Besides that, you know damn well our parents are going to want as much time with their little grandbaby as possible, so it's not like we'll never have time to ourselves again."

"What about college?"

He rubs the back of his neck with his free hand. "Well, obviously that's gonna have to wait. And when we're ready, we'll have to take online courses for a while until we figure something out. New York's not an option anymore, but it doesn't mean we can't go to a local school eventually." He squeezes my hand. "This is going to be a good thing, Pres."

I look up to find him smiling. "How can you say that, Beck? How are we going to tell our parents?"

"C'mere." He pulls me into his lap, so I'm on my knees, straddling him. "We're legal adults. This baby was conceived in love. How can that ever be a bad thing?" He places a soft kiss on my lips. "We were planning to do this one day anyway. This just bumps the timeline up."

"Beckett, it's not that simple. This isn't what we planned. We're still in high school, and I'm pregnant out of wedlock."

He smooths some hair out of my face. "We're graduating in two-and-a-half months, and we can get married whenever you want. We'll make this work, Pres."

I don't know what else to say, so I just fall into him and let him hold me. I'm not nearly as optimistic as Beckett is about this, but if nothing else, I can find a few moments of solace in his arms.

Chapter Sixteen
Presley

"What can I help with?"

My mom shoos me away. "Nothing. I've got it all taken care of. Why don't you go join your dad and brother in the living room? You used to love watching football with them."

That was before when I used to enjoy a lot of things.

I shrug and drop down into the seat at the kitchen table. "I don't think either one of them wants to look at me right now."

She falters for just a moment before wiping her hands on her apron and turning toward me. "Why would you say a silly thing like that?"

"Mom, I appreciate what you're trying to do, but we can't pretend I don't look like I went a few rounds with Connor McGregor." I motion to my face. "And when they look at me, they look like they're ready to launch into battle to defend my honor, but they're frustrated because I made them promise to leave it be. They may think they're sly, but I see the questions in their eyes. They're wondering why I didn't leave long before now. How I could stay with a man who abused me for years and years. I should probably just eat my dinner up in my room, so I don't make anyone uncomfortable."

I jump when my mom slams her clenched fist on the countertop. "Pardon my language, but that's the biggest crock of shit I've ever heard, Presley Anne! Your daddy and Clayton love you. *I love you.* You could never make any of us uncomfortable by just being in the same room. If you see *any* kind of expression on our faces, it's because when you hurt, *we* hurt. That's what love is. There was a time when you knew that."

I hang my head in disgrace, feeling the weight of her words. There *was* a time when I knew love inside and out. I knew how to give it and receive it. But it's been so long since I've done either, I don't think I'd even recognize it anymore. Apparently not, if I can't read my father or brother like I used to.

"I don't know, Mama. It just feels strange. Being back here is... confusing."

"Confusing how?"

"Because physically, everything's the same. It's like a time warp or something. And all the players are the same—you, Daddy, Clayton." There's a pregnant pause as we both silently acknowledge the one person I intentionally left out. "But when I walk around this house, sit at this table, I feel like a stranger. I feel like my memories don't belong to the person I am now."

"Oh, honey, no one can take your memories from you. That's the beauty of 'em; they're inside your head. And as painful as some of them might be, you never want to lose sight of them. They can warm your heart or tear it to pieces, but those experiences are what shape you. I think you just need some practice remembering the good to balance out some of the bad."

"Wow..." I sniff. "That's pretty deep, Mama. When did you become a philosopher?"

"It's called being a mom, honey. You'll learn one day." Her face falls when I start crying. "Oh, honey, I didn't mean to upset you."

I take a second to collect myself. "It's okay. It doesn't take much these days."

"Presley, your life isn't over. You're barely thirty. There's still plenty of time to have kids if that's something you want."

I shake my head. "I don't think kids are in the cards for me."

"Why not?"

"Because... I just can't see it anymore. It's not like I have this biological need to procreate. I'd only want children because I'd want a family with a man I couldn't live without. I know what great love feels like, and I don't see that ever happening for me again. Thirty may not be old in a physical sense, but some days, Mama, I feel ninety on the inside. I feel like there's nothing left for me in this world."

My mom slams a hand over her mouth to cover her sob. "Oh, baby."

I wave her off like it's no big deal that I have nothing to live for. "It's the hand I was dealt. My poor choices have led me to this point, so it's my fate to accept."

She wraps her arms around me from behind. "Presley, kids, or no kids, you have *a lot* of life ahead of you. And you're allowed to make mistakes. The important thing is that you learn from them, change course accordingly, and move on. I think maybe you've been surviving for so long, you forgot what *living* feels like. Some days are going to be tough; you'll feel like you're nothing more than a pile of ashes. But on the days you actually get to live life to its fullest, when that fire inside of you burns bright, those are the days you have to hold on to, knowing that each new day is an opportunity for another just like it."

"There you go, being all profound again."

She chuckles. "My wisdom is finally catching up with these gray hairs of mine."

I wipe the remainder of my tears away. "Thanks, Mom."

"Anytime, sweetheart." She punctuates her statement with a gentle squeeze.

I stand up and smooth out my shirt. "I think I'm going to go freshen up in the bathroom and join the boys after."

A wide grin stretches across my mother's face. "I think that's a great idea, Pres."

"Thanks for dinner, Ma. It was amazing, as always." Clayton bends down to pull my mom into a hug.

"You know you're welcome anytime." She pats his cheek condescendingly. "Lord knows you'd never eat a solid home-cooked meal again if left to your own devices."

"Hey, I cook!"

She gives him a wry look. "Frozen dinners or left-over pizza doesn't count."

Clayton smirks. "I'm a single guy, Ma. I'm pretty sure leftover pizza and frozen dinners cover all the major food groups of bachelorhood."

Mama whacks the back of her hand against his chest. "You're thirty-two, Clayton Daniel. Not twelve."

"Shit, she middle-named me. I must be in trouble, now." Clay looks to me for sympathy.

I think I surprise all three of us when I belt out a laugh.

"Ah, there she is!" Clay points to me. "I was wondering when I'd get to see the old Presley."

My laughter dies. "I think I'm going to call it a night. It was good seeing you, Clay."

"Pres, hold up," he calls my name as my foot hits the bottom stair. "Walk me out?"

I look over my shoulder and meet his pleading eyes. "Yeah... okay."

All the ranch hands have gone home by now, but

that doesn't stop me from grabbing an old snapback and pulling it low over my face. If my brother notices what I'm doing, he's kind enough not to call me out on it.

I lean up against the side of Clay's shiny black F-350, waiting for the questions I know are coming.

He kicks some gravel around. "So... you give any thought to what you're going to do?"

"What do you mean?"

"Well, I'm assuming you're sticking around for a while, right?"

I haven't really thought about it, but that option certainly makes the most sense.

"Most likely. Why do you ask?"

Clay gestures to the house. "Well, I'm assuming you'd eventually want to get your own place, right? I love Mom and Dad, but I can't imagine still having to live with them." He shudders in mock disgust.

"Oh, please." I roll my eyes. "You live on the same property, and the way I hear it, you're over here mooching food several times a week."

He laughs. "Yeah... but it's nice having my own place to entertain my lady friends. My many, many, lady friends."

"Well... *entertaining* anyone is low on my list of priorities right now." I shake my head. "Very, *very* low."

Clay rubs the back of his neck. "Regardless, if you're thinking about getting your own place eventually, you'd need a job, right?"

"I suppose," I agree. "But Clayton, I've only been

back a few days. I have a lot of stuff to figure out right now."

"Let me take one thing off your plate then. When you're ready—and I don't care how long that takes—I could use a little help around the bar. I know it's not the most glamourous job, but—"

I reach up on my toes to pull him into a hug, mindful of my sore shoulder. "Thank you, Clay."

After he gets over the surprise, he hugs me back. "You're welcome, kid."

I scoff. "I'm hardly a kid."

He pulls back and musses my hair. "You'll always be my kid sister, no matter how old you get." His blue eyes watch me carefully. "What are you going to do about your husband, Pres?"

"I don't know," I admit. "I'm honestly shocked he hasn't tried contacting me yet. It's not like him to just accept defeat. He's not dumb; he has to know where I am."

Clay scowls. "Well, he doesn't really have a fuckin' choice but to accept defeat in this case. If he comes sniffing around here, Pres, I can't promise you I won't do something about it. I'd say the same applies to Dad."

I draw circles in the gravel with my toe. "I kno—"

The roar of a truck engine cuts off my words. A few seconds later, that old Ford comes rolling down the drive. I use my brother as a shield as I watch it drive away toward the road. I release a deep breath the moment it's out of sight.

"Yeah, so..." I jerk my head toward the house, feeling

like a complete fool for hiding behind Clay. "I guess I'll see you later then."

I start walking back toward the porch when Clayton's words stop me right in my tracks. "He never gave up on you, Pres."

"What?" I blink rapidly, positive I heard him wrong.

Clay inclines his head in the direction the truck just went. "Beck. He'd kill me for saying this, but he never gave up on you. Whether he wants to admit it or not, he never stopped loving you."

"I don't..." I shake my head. "I mean... that's impossible. Isn't he married?"

My brother's laughter is so loud, it echoes through the wind. "He'd never let anyone get close enough for that to happen. I think he's been holding out hope you'd come back someday."

I slump down on the top step. "I don't know what to say to that, Clayton. It doesn't matter if he still has feelings for me—which I highly doubt, by the way. I'm not the same girl he fell in love with. I've been through so much... it's changed me."

"You're the same where it counts." He shakes his head. "But just so you know, he's not exactly the same guy either. He's been through some really messed up stuff. Things that stick with you for a lifetime."

I tilt my head to the side. "His dad dying?"

"That was just the icing on the shitastic cake. He was gone for over six years, Pres. A lot happened during that time."

"In the military?"

Clayton nods.

"But... I thought the Navy was one of the safest branches of the military."

He scoffs. "Not when you're a SEAL."

My eyes widen. "He was a SEAL?!"

"You didn't know?" My brother tilts his head to the side.

"I had no idea." I sigh. "You two are still close, I take it?"

"Yeah, we are."

I look my brother right in the eye. "You can't tell him what I went through, Clayton. I don't want him to know."

My family got the *extremely* watered-down version of events, but I'm sure they're smart enough to fill in the gaps. Allowing anyone to witness my shame was hard enough to stomach... but for some reason, the thought of Beck knowing what happened—what I put up with for too many years—makes it so much worse.

Clay opens the door to his truck and hops on the running board. "It's not my story to tell, Pres. The same goes for the demons he's living with."

As I watch my brother drive away, I can't help but replay our conversation in my head. The idea that Beckett Armstrong is still in love with me after all these years is ludicrous. It's been *twelve years*. I'm probably nothing more to him than a girl he used to know. Yet... part of me can't help but wonder if it *is* possible.

Because the thing is... that same part of me knows I never stopped loving him. That when I walked away from this ranch all those years ago, he was holding a piece of my heart that I never got back.

Chapter Seventeen
Presley – Age 18

"Oh, honey, you look beautiful!"

"Thanks, Mom," I say.

My senior prom is tonight. I won't be engaging in the post-prom bonfire/drink fest that all of our friends will be at, though. I convinced Beck to keep the pregnancy a secret until after graduation. Neither one of us are big partiers, but we've definitely had some alcohol during get-togethers and such. Since I don't want to explain *why* I'm not drinking, we've avoided those types of gatherings. I'm fortunate that I've had minimal morning sickness, so I haven't raised suspicion in that respect either. I know it will be a shock, especially to my parents, because I waited so long to tell them. Call me crazy, but I just wanted to get through graduation feeling like a high school student, not a mom-to-be.

"That dress looks absolutely perfect on you. I'm glad you went with it."

She doesn't know that I chose this dress because the

eggplant color and layered chiffon hide imperfections well. Or, in my case, a small baby bump.

I touch up my pink lip gloss. "Thanks, Mom. Beck should be here any minute, so get your camera ready."

Her eyes light up as she grabs her Nikon off the table. "I can't believe this is the last time I get to do this! How are you about to graduate high school already?"

Or become a mom.

"Hello?" Beckett calls from the other room.

"In here!" I say.

I turn as my mother gasps, and I do the same. Beck never fails to take my breath away, but holy hell, Beck in a tux is a magnificent sight. I can feel my skin heating as my eyes travel over his purposely messy hair to his broad shoulders down to his toes. Then I do it all over again in reverse. These damn pregnancy hormones aren't helping either. I thought I was bad before, but all I want to do lately is have sex. Of course, Beck doesn't seem to mind, and it's not like I need to worry about getting pregnant, right?

"Hey." He smirks, obviously picking up on my ill-timed arousal.

"Hey." I smile. "You look incredible."

He steps into me and grabs my hand. "You're *stunning,* Pres." He turns to my mom. "Hello, Mrs. J."

She smiles. "Hello, Beckett. You two are so gorgeous! Go on over by the fireplace so I can get some pictures."

We deal with my mother's exuberance for a good twenty minutes before she finally lets us out the door.

When we get to school, we walk straight to the gymnasium. Navy and gold balloons float through the air, and fairy lights are twinkling from every available surface. It's impressive what dimmed lighting and a few decorations can do to completely transform a space.

"Wow, the prom committee did an excellent job."

Beck jerks his head toward the dance floor. "Care to dance?"

"I'd love to." I smile. "But I thought you didn't dance."

He smiles. "For you, I dance. Just don't be mad if I occasionally step on your toes."

I laugh. "Deal."

We say hello to several friends as we make our way to the makeshift dance floor. When Beck pulls me into his loving arms, everything else disappears. I don't know how he does it, but this man has a way of making me feel like there's nothing we can't handle, as long as we have each other. Initially, I was upset when I learned I was pregnant. I'd be lying if I said I wasn't scared, but that doesn't mean I'm not happy about it. Beck was right; we're legal adults, and this baby was conceived in love. He or she is a *product* of our love. Plenty of children have been brought into the world under lesser circumstances.

Beck's hand moves from my hip over to my baby bump. I'm not sure if it's a conscious move, but he's been doing that a lot lately. I don't know how many songs we've danced to at this point, but we haven't moved out of our close embrace, regardless of the music's tempo.

He rests his cheek against mine and whispers, "You and this baby are everything to me, Pres. I can't wait to officially make you mine."

I tighten my hold on him. "I've been yours since we were five years old, Beck."

He pulls back and smiles. "You wanna get out of here?"

"Sure." I take his hand as he leads me out of the building. I had assumed we were heading to the parking lot, so I'm confused when he takes me to the football field. "What're we doing here?"

Beck walks backward, still holding my hand until our toes touch the sideline. "I can't wait any longer to do this, but I didn't want an audience. This should be ours."

My eyebrows pinch together. "*What* should be ours?"

I figure it out quickly enough when he gets down on one knee and produces a small velvet box from his jacket pocket. "Presley Anne James, I've been in love with you practically my whole life. You're the reason I look forward to each new day. You're the reason I strive to be a better man." He briefly glances at my stomach. "You've given me the ultimate gift, and I can't wait to show you how grateful I am by being the best daddy that I can be. Pres, you're my best friend, and I would be honored if you'd also be my wife. Will you marry me?"

I nod furiously as tears drip down my face. Marrying Beck was always a *when*, not an *if*, but having an actual proposal makes it official.

"Yes, Beckett. I'd marry you ten times over if you asked me to."

He jumps to his feet and slides a beautiful diamond ring onto my trembling hand. "It's not much—it's all I can afford right now, but I promise to get you a bigger diamond one day."

I shake my head as I stare at the thin platinum band with a small round diamond in the middle. "I don't want another one, Beck. This is perfect."

He grins. "Yeah?"

I sniffle. "Yeah. I love it, Beckett. So much."

He cups my face in his hands. "I love you, Pres. *So much.*"

"I love *you* so much."

He pulls me into a sweet kiss. When we break away, he says, "I want you to be my wife before the baby is born. What do you think about making it official this summer? We can have a small ceremony on the ranch —just a few friends and family."

"That sounds perfect, Beck. Absolutely perfect."

Chapter Eighteen
Presley

"You were so good to me over the years, old girl. I'm sorry it took me this long to come back to you."

Magnolia eagerly takes the sugar cube from my flattened palm while I stroke her forelock. Now that my bruises have faded enough to hide with strategically applied makeup, I can roam freely around the ranch. Unsurprisingly, the stables were the first place I gravitated toward. Being here, smelling the horses and the hay brings me a sense of peace I haven't known in far too long. I spent my entire childhood on this land, interacting with the animals daily. I never realized how much I missed this until now. How much I *needed* it.

I close my eyes and suppress a shiver as electricity suddenly shoots through my veins. My heart is beating wildly. My lungs are momentarily robbed of breath. I'm no longer the only person standing in this stable—

of that, I've no doubt. I can *feel* every atom in my body lighting up like a summer storm. I knew this moment was inevitable—I've been expecting it—but the thought of facing Beckett Armstrong after all these years terrifies me. Yet... I'd be lying if I said there wasn't also some underlying excitement. I can't remember the last time I looked forward to *anything*, but having him this close, is almost... exhilarating. I have few memories of my childhood that don't include this man. He was the love of my life. I gave him all of my firsts. He breathed life into me by merely existing. When I left this town, I not only left pieces of my heart behind; I left part of my soul, too. I just didn't realize how much of it until this very moment.

I take a fortifying breath as I step away from Mag's stall.

"So the rumors are true."

The timbre of his voice is much deeper than I remember. That southern twang rolls over me like Tupelo honey—thick and sweet and oh, so seductive. I worked really hard on ditching my accent when I first moved to New York, but Beck's time away seemed to do nothing to diminish his.

"What rumors?" I slowly turn around and do my best to quell the shock from seeing him in the flesh.

Neither one of us dares to look away. It's like the space between us is shrinking, even though we're both frozen in place. The wasted time, the buckets of tears, the ache of longing. It's all passing between us right now, zinging back and forth, hitting its mark, driving the pain of our shared loss deeper and deeper. Countless *what-ifs* and *never-beens* thicken the air, making it nearly impossible to breathe.

God, he's so devastatingly handsome, my chest constricts. Any traces of boyhood are long gone. His jaw is stronger now and lined with heavy stubble. His shoulders are broader, and his arms have significantly more bulk. As Beck clenches his fists tightly, I can't help remembering how those hands easily spanned my torso. How his calloused fingertips felt gliding along my bare skin. Lighter streaks weave through his dark blond hair, producing memories of all the times I'd run my fingers through those thick strands, as Beck hummed in appreciation. My hands itch to do just that, to see if it's just as silky as I remember, then I remind myself this man is no longer mine to touch.

Although, if I simply looked into his eyes, I'd have all the reminders I needed. The dark chocolate colored orbs I spent so many hours staring into belong to a stranger now. They're harder. Wiser. Shadows lurk beneath the surface, hinting at the many secrets living within. The one thing that hasn't changed is how expressive they are. Growing up, Beck's eyes usually glittered with humor, or love, or heat. None of those emotions are present as he looks at me now. He's rough around the edges like I suspected he would be, but I wasn't in any way prepared for this. I would've never imagined the boy I loved half my life was capable of feeling such contempt toward me. I swallow a lump in my throat as I absorb the impact of his glare.

"That you finally came back."

My skin tingles with awareness as his eyes leisurely roam my body. Okay, so the lust might still be there, but it's clearly laced with revulsion.

"What happened to your arm?"

I startle from the question. My shoulder still has a ways to go before it's healed, but I'm no longer wearing my sling, so I'm not sure how he can tell something's wrong.

"What do you mean?"

He nods toward my left side. "You're favoring your right arm. Looks like you're avoiding using the left entirely."

"I got mugged," I lie. "Dislocated my shoulder when I fell down."

"Ah, the joys of living in the big city," he mocks. I glare back at him, but it doesn't seem to faze him. "Where's your husband?"

"New York," I snap. "His work keeps him very busy."

I'm so afraid he'll see right through me, I mentally erect my protective barrier. It's something I've excelled at over the years. It was the only way I could survive my marriage. I'd force myself to withdraw... to become remote as if I wasn't really inhabiting my body when Sebastian was working through his rage.

"How long are you in town, Presley?"

"Why does it matter?"

"It doesn't. Not to me, anyway. I'm simply

wondering how much longer I'll have to tiptoe around you. It's making my job a lot harder than it needs to be, and that's getting tiresome real fast. You've been here, what? Almost two weeks now? I'd imagine your husband misses you back home."

I shift slightly as my shoulder muscles tense. I'm sure the only thing my husband misses is the control he had over me. I highly doubt he's missing sex, considering the deputy mayor is gladly providing that service.

"I never said you had to tiptoe around me."

His full lips turn up in the corners. Like his eyes, Beck's smiles are capable of saying many things without speaking a single word. This is his *I know something you don't* smile.

"Maybe not. But somebody did."

What? "Who?"

"C'mon, Presley. I thought you went to New York to get an education. Use your brain." He snaps his fingers. "Oh, but wait, the way I hear it, you dropped out after a year to become a socialite, so maybe your brain isn't accustomed to such strenuous activities. My bad."

God, who is this guy? The Beck I knew would never fling an insult at a woman. *Any* woman. He was the true definition of a southern gentleman. I know I can't maintain this fake bravado for much longer. The last thing I need is for Beckett to see the truth about why I'm here, so I decide to step the bitchiness up a notch.

"What do you want, Beckett? You obviously sought

me out for a reason. Just get it out so I can move on with my day. I don't have time for your bullshit."

His jaw sharpens as the vitriol flows from my mouth. He pulls a ball cap from his back pocket and takes a moment to fix the brim before placing it on his head. Looking me straight in the eye, Beckett delivers a verbal sucker punch that hurts worse than Sebastian's fists ever did.

"Naw, darlin'," he sneers. "I don't want *anything* from you. Do us all a favor and head back to New York sooner rather than later."

Beck turns around and slowly walks away, rapping his knuckles against the doorframe as he leaves the stable. There's a toughness to his gait that wasn't there before. His movements used to be so fluid, he practically had a full-time swagger. His personality drew you in without any effort whatsoever. There was a lightness to him that attracted complete strangers, hoping for a chance to bask in his warmth. His kindness and affection were given freely.

Nothing about this Beck is approachable. He's made up of bunched muscles and hard edges. Anger radiates off him in waves. This guy slings words meant to cut deep, but the harshness of those words pales in comparison to that look in his eyes. The one that says I'm inconsequential. That none of the good we shared matters. That I'm nothing more than a vapid gold digger, undeserving of his time. I've never felt so small in my life, and that's saying a lot considering how often Sebastian belittled me.

The last time Beck and I saw each other, I was the one walking away, breaking his heart in two. If he felt even half as bad as I do now, I hate myself even more for putting *anyone* through that, especially him.

125

Chapter Nineteen
Presley – Age 18

Graduation day is finally here. A few hours after we walk across the stage to accept our diplomas, Beck and I will break the news to our family that we're engaged and having a baby this November. I went to the doctor for an official diagnosis and due date a few weeks back. Thankfully, since I'm eighteen, he couldn't say a word to my parents. As of today, I've hit the sixteen-week mark. In another month, we get to see our little one on ultrasound and find out the sex. Beck and I are really excited about that part.

Everything seems to be falling into place. Beck begins working full-time on the ranch tomorrow, and we've already found this cute little two-bedroom cottage to rent. We'd like to get married on July fifteenth, which will be here before we know it. Knowing my mom, she'll insist on flittering about to make our ceremony as perfect as can be. Neither Beck nor I care what the ceremony is like, but we figured we'd let her have this to focus on since we're dumping such a huge bomb on them tonight.

I rub the firm bump on my belly as another cramp hits me. Man, these growing pains have been really getting to me today. They never tell you ahead of time that while you may not have a period while pregnant, you'll still get to enjoy the pain of one on occasion.

"Hey, beautiful." I turn around to find Beck leaning against the doorframe to my bedroom, smiling.

I give him a hug. "Hi. Are you ready for tonight?"

He smirks. "Honey, if I had my way, they would've known on the day we found out."

"Yeah, yeah." I roll my eyes. "Are you guys about to leave?"

Beck's dad insisted on driving him to the ceremony today. Something about having a man-to-man talk on the way over, whatever that entails. There's no sense in wasting gas, so I'm going to ride over with my parents and meet him there.

He nods. "Yeah, he's out front waiting for me. I just wanted to say goodbye before we head out."

And by goodbye, he means kiss me until I'm breathless.

"Beck, your dad's gettin' anxious to leave," my dad calls from the bottom of the stairs. "He said, hurry the hell up."

"I'll be right down," Beck promises with a smirk. "I'll see you there, okay?"

"'Kay."

Right before he descends the stairs, he calls out to me. "Hey, Pres?"

I peek my head out of the doorway. "Yeah?"

"You look gorgeous—I didn't tell you that before. And I love you."

I smile. "I love you too, Beck. Now get on out there. I'll see you in a bit."

I finish curling my hair into soft ringlets and step into my kitten-heeled shoes. After one final glance in the mirror to make sure everything's in place, I head down the staircase to find my mom smiling back at me.

"Oh, Presley, you look beautiful. I can't believe my baby is graduating today."

And your baby is having a baby.

"Thanks, Mom."

"Your father's just finishing washing the truck. He insisted on sprucing it up since today is a special day."

"Annie!" he calls from outside. "Are you ladies ready to go?"

She props the screen door open. "We'll be right there, Dan. Just hold your horses."

My mom turns back to me and winks. "See what I did there?"

I can't help but laugh. She has the corniest sense of humor, but I love it. Damn it, I have to pee again before we hit the road. This baby makes me feel like my bladder is as big as a grain of rice.

"Mom, go ahead. I'm just going to use the bathroom real quick, and I'll be right out."

"Okay, honey. I'll be in the truck with your father."

As I head down the hall, something strange happens. My panties are suddenly sopping wet. Crap, did I really just pee myself? I jog the rest of the way until I'm safely enclosed in the bathroom. I pull my underwear down as I'm takin' a seat on the toilet, and I'm instantly frozen in shock. My panties are soaked, but it's not urine. Bright red blood is pooling in the middle, threatening to spill over the sides. *Oh my God, what is happening right now?* I'm not a doctor, but I know bleeding while pregnant is not a good thing.

I'm trying to remain calm, but I find myself sobbing and shaking as my butt is perched on the seat. My cell phone is in my purse by the front door, so I do the only thing I can think of: scream for my mother as loud as I can until she comes inside. It's probably less than a minute, but it feels like hours before she hears my cry for help and comes running.

She knocks on the powder room door. "Presley Anne, what on God's green earth is going on?"

"Mom, open the door," I cry, thankful that I didn't lock it. "I need help."

She cracks it open and looks at me in confusion. I'm sure I'm a hot mess, sitting here with my panties around my ankles and mascara running down my face. She spots the blood and thinks she's figured out the problem.

"Oh, honey, did you just start your period? I thought your cycle was at the end of the month. No need to get so upset. I'll just run upstairs and grab a tampon with some new briefs."

Before she can leave, I shout, "I'm not on my period, Mom. *I'm pregnant!*"

She whips around so fast it would be comical under different circumstances. "What did you say?"

"I'm four months pregnant," I sob. "We were going to tell you tonight. Something's wrong with the baby, isn't there?"

My mother gives me a sympathetic look and says in a surprisingly calm voice, "Okay, honey. This is what we're going to do. I'm going to head upstairs to get you a maxi pad and some clean briefs. Then, you and I are going to take a quick trip to the hospital, just to be sure everything's okay."

I nod, making a futile attempt to wipe my tears away. "Okay."

She must've run because she's back with the items she promised to deliver in no more than thirty seconds. "I'll meet you out in the kitchen once you've cleaned up."

"Mom, I need to call Beck. My phone's in my purse."

"You can call him on the way, sweetie. I'm sure the baby's fine, but you can never be too careful in these situations."

"Okay," I repeat.

The baby's fine, I tell myself. The baby *has* to be okay. I clean myself up and meet her by the front door. She already has her car keys in hand and my purse slung around her shoulder. She's unbelievably stoic right now. I look at her in question when I see that my dad's truck is no longer in the driveway.

"I sent him to the school," she explains. "To drive Beck to the hospital to meet us."

I get into the car and buckle my seat belt on autopilot. "What did Daddy say? Is he mad at me?"

She waves her hand dismissively. "Oh, don't worry about your father right now. Just close your eyes and take some deep breaths. We'll be there in no time."

I dig through my purse to grab my phone. "I need to call Beck first."

"Of course, honey."

My call goes straight to his voicemail, so I try again but get the same result. I dial his dad's number, thinking maybe his battery died, but there's no answer there either.

"He's not answering."

My mom glances at me. "Presley, just breathe and do your best to relax. Your father will get him there."

I lay my head back and do my best to follow her instructions. She's right; my dad will come through. Beck will probably get to the hospital right after we do. After about twenty minutes, we're pulling into the Tri-County Medical Center lot. My mom parks close to the emergency entrance and guides me inside.

"May I help you?" the woman at the counter asks.

I try speaking, but the words won't come out, so my mother does it for me in a hushed tone.

"My daughter is four months pregnant. She started bleeding about thirty minutes ago, so we think we should see a doctor."

"Of course," the woman says, flashing me a sympathetic look. God, I'm getting really sick of those already.

I hear the lady asking my mom questions so she can check me in, but I'm not really paying attention to what they're saying. Everything is hazy as I'm ushered into a room and asked to change into a gown and hop on an exam bed. I guess that's one good thing about this—small-town hospitals don't make you wait very long. While we're waiting for the doctor to arrive, I snap out of my daze.

"Have you heard from Daddy?"

My mother looks down at her phone. "He just texted me. He's at the school now, trying to find Beck. He said it's a bit chaotic over there."

"Maybe I should try calling him again."

She shakes her head. "Your dad's been trying, but he's not having any luck either. Don't worry, honey. He'll find him any minute now."

A middle-aged woman walks into the room, rolling a cart with a monitor and keyboard on it.

"Hi, I'm Dr. Morris. I hear you're having some bleeding. I'm just going to do a quick ultrasound to take a look at the baby and see what's going on." She gestures to my mom. "Is it okay for her to be in the room? I need to lift your gown over your belly."

"It's fine," I say. "She's my mom."

The woman nods and turns the monitor on. My mother gasps when the doctor lifts my gown and tucks it under my breasts. I know she's looking at the evidence of my pregnancy, wondering how she missed such a telltale sign. My bump is small, but it's pretty apparent there's a baby inside of me. She's probably connecting the dots in her head, just now realizing how many of Beck's T-shirts I've been wearing lately.

Dr. Morris squirts some cold blue jelly over my stomach and spreads it around with a wand. The screen is black at first before it slowly transitions to something comprehensible. In the middle of a black oval is a distorted image of the baby. I know he or she is still really tiny, but all of the parts are formed into this tiny little human. My mom squeezes my hand as tears silently crawl down my face. The doctor's face pinches with concern as she moves the wand around.

"Is something wrong?" I ask her.

"You said you were sixteen weeks?"

"Yes, exactly sixteen today," I confirm. "My due date is November first."

"The baby measures a little small." She punches a few buttons on the keyboard, and the screen switches to another view. "Let's check the heartbeat."

The doctor frowns as two thick white lines shoot across the screen. She punches a few more buttons and turns a dial before removing the wand from my abdomen and wiping the gel off my skin. I already know what she's going to say when I see the look in her eyes.

"I'm sorry, sweetie. There's no heartbeat."

A high-pitched keening sound echoes throughout

the small room. It takes me a moment to realize it's coming from me.

My mom hovers over the exam bed and wraps me in her arms. "Shh, Presley, I've got you, baby. Shh…"

"I'll give you two a few moments, and I'll be back to answer any questions you might have."

"Why, Mom?" I ask, as the doctor leaves the room. "Why did this happen?"

"I don't know, honey. I don't know. Sometimes, it just happens."

I grab on to her like she's my lifeline. She strokes my hair and whispers soothing words, just holding me as I mourn the loss of my child. Of the beautiful future Beck and I have planned out. God, how can this happen? I'm in my second trimester. Everything's supposed to be okay after you make it to the second trimester.

"It's not fair," I sob.

"I know, sweetheart." My mom's sentence is choked off by her own sob.

After a while, the doctor comes back in telling me that I'll need to have a minor procedure because I'm so far along. The whole time I listen to her talk about why miscarriages happen and what to expect in the next few days, I ask myself where Beck is. Why isn't he here by now? I need him more than I ever have, and he's nowhere to be found.

"The room is yours for as long as you'd like," Dr. Morris says. "Take all the time you need. We'll call you when we've scheduled the D&C, but you call us if you have any questions beforehand. Okay, Presley?"

I sniff. "Okay."

My mom hasn't let go once—she's rocking me from side to side like she used to do when I was a little girl.

"Has Daddy responded yet?"

She pulls away from me to dig her phone out of her purse. "Your dad found Beck, and they're on their way. They should be here any minute, actually."

She's typing a message to my father as I lie curled on my side, staring at the wall. A few moments later, there's a light knock on the door, so my mom jumps out of her chair to open it. I can make out my father's voice in their hushed conversation, but I don't bother moving from my position. After the door clicks shut, soft footsteps approach, and I breathe a sigh of relief that Beck has finally made it.

He crouches down beside me and pushes some hair away from my face. "Pres, darlin', are you okay?"

I meet his glassy eyes. "What took you so long to get here?"

"My dad and I left our phones in the truck. I didn't know anything was wrong until your dad pulled me out of the ceremony during the principal's speech." He clears his throat. "He told me what happened. I'm so sorry, baby. I'm sorry like hell that this happened and that I wasn't here for you."

I sob when he rests his cheek against mine, and I feel our tears mixing together. "I am too, Beck. I am too."

"I love you so much, Pres." He places a soft kiss against my temple. "We'll get through this. Everything will be okay."

I wish I had his confidence. Right now, it feels like *nothing* will ever be okay again.

Chapter Twenty
Beckett

Christ.

Could I have been any more of a jerk? I don't know what came over me, but seeing Presley in person for the first time in over a decade, stirred up feelings I've refused to acknowledge for a long time. Everything was converging on me at once, the most prevalent of which was the gut-wrenching sense of betrayal I feel whenever I think about her marrying another man. After Clayton broke the news of her engagement, I was in denial. It had been less than a year since Presley had been gone. Maybe that's long enough for most people to move on, but I sure as hell wasn't ready for that. And I refused to believe she was either after everything we shared throughout the years. Hence, why I convinced Clay to give me her address right before I hopped on the first plane to New York.

I'll never forget the way she looked that day. I waited outside her swanky building for hours, contemplating what I was going to say to her. How I was going to talk her into coming back home with me. But then I saw her getting out of a black limo with *him,* and I knew it was hopeless. The girl I fell in love with was nowhere to be found. In her place was this plastic imitation. Gone were the T-shirts, denim, and boots that were staples of her wardrobe. This Presley wore a crisp, white linen dress with skyscraper heels. The long, wild blonde locks I used to love running my hands through were chopped into a sensible pin-straight shoulder-length bob. The girl who only wore makeup or jewelry on special occasions had her face painted in color, and her left hand was weighed down by the gaudiest diamond ring I had ever seen. We were nineteen, for fuck's sake, but she looked more like thirty.

As if all of that wasn't bad enough, when she tilted her chin up at that bastard, gifting him with the same bright smile she used to aim at me, it felt like someone had stabbed me in the heart. Physically, Presley looked like a completely different woman, but she also looked *happy.* When she left Hope Springs, she was deeply depressed. No matter what I did or said, she wouldn't shake out of it. I had never seen someone so over-wrought with sadness, and I had no idea how to make it better. I knew at that moment that no matter how badly it was going to hurt, I had to walk away. I had to step aside so she could live her life with another man who somehow managed to give her what I couldn't.

Joy.

When I got back home, self-destruction became my way of life. I started sloughing off of work, drinking myself into stupors more times than I could count, and getting into fights with anyone who dared to look at me the wrong way. I was a mean, miserable bastard trying to do whatever he could to drown out the memories I was haunted by at every turn. When Colby's dad, the current sheriff at the time, forced me to sober up in a cell after finding my belligerent under-age-drinking ass stumbling down Main Street, I knew something had to change. I was turning into someone I didn't want to be. Sheriff Mitchell sat me down the next morning and asked if I ever considered enlisting in the military. He shared some stories about his troubled teenage years and how joining the army whipped him into shape. When I really took some time to think about it, I knew that would be the best course of action. I couldn't stay in Hope Springs any longer.

After quite a bit of research, the Navy caught my attention. More specifically, the SEALs. Although I hadn't been in any hurry to leave Georgia, the possibilities began to fascinate me. The thought of being at the front of the action, doing some good in the world, gave me an objective to focus on. I knew it would be demanding. I knew my odds of making it past BUDs were slim. But it sure beat the hell out of wallowing in my own misery, so what did I have to lose? I enlisted the next day, and shortly after that, I was on a plane headed to boot camp.

Despite the ugliness I'd seen in humanity during my

time in the Navy—and some of it was *really fucking ugly* —I loved being a SEAL. I quickly learned I'm a bit of an adrenaline junkie. During those six years, I had regular opportunities to feed that compulsion. I got to see parts of the world I would've never imagined and become part of a brotherhood that I'll have for the rest of my life. Our actions helped make this world a better place, and that gave me purpose. I had every intention of sticking with it as long as my body could handle the ride.

Unfortunately, Fate, being the fickle bitch she is, had other plans. One minute, we were riding in the Humvee on a routine patrol, giving each other shit like we always did, and in the next, an IED changed our lives forever. I was one of the fortunate ones, walking away with partial hearing loss, minor nerve damage, and a fucked-up head. Sure, it sucks having permanent injuries, but at least I made it out with all of my limbs intact. One of my brothers lost a leg. Another went home in a box. I consider myself pretty fucking lucky, all things considered.

The Navy offered me a desk job, but I couldn't see myself doing that. I needed to be active. Being idle did nothing but give me time to think. To remember everything I'd rather forget. So...at my dad's request, I came back home to work with him. As difficult as it was coming back here and facing another set of demons, I like to think things turned out the way they were meant to in hindsight. If I hadn't been injured, I would've missed the last few months of my father's life.

Life had already taught me to never take things for granted, that it could all be ripped away in an instant. But that didn't lessen the shock when my fifty-three-year-old father didn't wake up one morning. The man took care of himself. He ate well, and he was physically active. There was no reason to suspect anything was wrong. But that didn't prevent the blood clot from forming in his artery. Nor the massive heart attack that occurred as a result. One day he was here, the next he wasn't.

Fuck.

I pull off my hat and rake a hand through my hair. What the hell am I going to do about Pres? I told myself not to follow her, but when I saw her heading toward the stables, looking like an apparition from the past, I couldn't imagine myself being anywhere else. When I got my first glimpse of her up close, I felt like I was going to burst out of my skin. Desire and longing fought for dominance as the Presley I once knew stood before me. She looks as incredible as she always did. In fact, she might be even more beautiful now. Her hair is long again, falling down her back in loose waves. She was wearing makeup, but it was subtle, just enough to enhance her features, not mask them. She's a bit thinner—probably a little too thin—but her jeans and simple cotton tee hugged her curves in a way that had me itching to explore.

There is one big difference, though. Presley's breasts are significantly fuller, which caught me off guard. I never thought she felt a lick of self-consciousness when it came to her body, but there's no doubt she had surgery. Granted, from what I could tell, they look entirely natural. She didn't go overboard by any means. If I didn't have every inch of her body memorized, I would've never suspected she had implants. I won't lie and say the thought of mapping the new topography of her body with my hands didn't get me going. Despite my anger with her, I had to keep my fists clenched to prevent myself from touching her.

Have I said fuck yet? Because fuuuuuck.

"You look like you've seen a ghost."

I glance to the side where Clay is hopping off the ATV he drove over here. "Feels like it."

Clayton comes up beside me, ensuring he stays on my left. Leaning over the paddock fence and jerking his chin toward the new arena we're having built, he says, "It's coming along nicely. Everything still on track?"

I nod. "Ahead of schedule, actually."

"If I haven't told you already, I think this is a really good thing you're doing, Cowboy."

"Thanks, man."

Mr. J had wanted to build an indoor arena for a while, but construction didn't start until last month because it took quite some time to get funding and all of the permits in order. Having an enclosed riding space will offer a controlled environment for the new equine-assisted therapy program we're launching. When I came back from overseas, I was a fucking mess, as much as I tried to deny it. Losing my dad so soon after my return didn't help. But the more time I spent on the ranch with the horses, the better I felt. It's a daily struggle, and I've come to accept it might always be that way, but for the most part, I've found ways to cope.

I saw a counselor for a while after the blast. We talked a lot about how animals can provide emotional support, especially to those suffering from post-traumatic stress disorder. Horses have been proven to offer a unique advantage over other animals because they have such a strong awareness of emotional temperament and nonverbal cues. You can't just force a horse to do your bidding. You need to learn to collaborate with the animal and build a trusting relationship—skills that would carry over to the people in your life. I certainly saw the benefit in it, and when we started drawing plans for the new arena, I brought my proposal to Mr. and Mrs. J.

Not only were they onboard, but they also wanted to take it a step further than I had imagined. In addition to the new arena, we also have a crew building a small lodge that will serve as guest housing. Licensed therapists will be on staff to provide counseling during a twenty-one or twenty-eight-day retreat where guests will have daily interactions with the animals. Our ultimate goal is to offer trauma survivors a quiet place to develop the necessary skills to better manage their triggers and anxiety.

This program is something I'm incredibly passionate about, and I'm grateful to have the James' support. They've always been like family to me, but they've proven that ten times over in recent years. After Pres left, part of me was worried things wouldn't be the same, but Mr. and Mrs. J, and Clayton, for that matter, made it crystal clear from the start that my father and I would always be part of their clan, regardless of whether or not Presley and I were together.

"So... how'd it go? Did you and Pres have a big happy reunion filled with fluffy bunnies and rainbows?"

I scoff. "I'm pretty sure it was the exact opposite of that. She's probably packing her bags right now to get as far away from me as possible. I probably did her husband a favor."

Clay raises his brows. "That bad, huh?"

"It sure as shit wasn't good." I hop off the fence. "I should probably get back to work."

Clayton kneads the muscles at the back of his neck. "She'd be pissed if she knew I was telling you this, but I don't think she's leaving anytime soon, Beck. If Presley tried going back to that bastard, I'm pretty sure my parents would chain her to the barn to prevent that from happening. Hell, if they didn't, I would."

I frown. "Why?"

He stares at me for a moment. I get the feeling he's trying to tell me something without actually saying the words. "He doesn't deserve her. For many, *many* reasons, he doesn't even come close to deserving her."

"What the hell does that mean? Why is everyone so damn cryptic all of a sudden?"

Clayton hops back on the four-wheeler. "Let's just say you're not the only one who's experienced trauma in your time away from this ranch. If you want more than that, you need to get it out of Pres."

I scrub a hand down my face as Clay drives away. What kind of trauma could Presley have possibly been through in her cushy life? And why should I care? That woman had no trouble casting me aside as if our past meant nothing to her. After all this time, I should be able to do the same.

So, the question is... why can't I stop wondering what secrets she's hiding and what I'm going to do to uncover them?

Chapter Twenty-One
Presley – Age 18

Today should've been one of the happiest days of my life. I should be wearing a pretty white dress and walking down a makeshift aisle to marry the man I've loved my whole life. Instead, I can't stomach the thought of leaving the safety of my bedroom and facing the world. It's been just over six weeks since my miscarriage. Six weeks of cursing God, wondering why this happened to me. A month-and-a-half of dragging my lifeless body around just to meet my basic needs of eating, bathing, and using the bathroom. I still can't manage to use the powder room where all of my dreams went down in flames. I avoid that hallway at all costs.

One of the biggest downsides of living in a small town is that nobody can keep a secret for long. As one could imagine, my father caused quite a stir when he ripped Beckett out of the graduation ceremony. It wasn't hard to figure out that I was the reason. It took only two days before my phone started blowing up. Apparently, somebody's cousin was sitting in that ER the day I was admitted. She told someone who then told someone else, and so on and so forth.

"Presley, honey," my mother calls through my closed door. "Beckett's walking toward the house. I'm going to send him up, okay?"

Beck's been coming over every day, trying to coax me out of my room.

I finger the small diamond on my engagement ring. "Okay, Mama."

The door cracks a few moments later, and he slips through before closing it again. I can't stand the way he looks at me now. The way they *all* look at me—my parents, my brother, all of the ranch hands. I know they mean well, that they care, but I can't handle the pity on their faces. I don't want their pity—I want my baby back. I feel like I'm losing my mind half the time. I still *feel* pregnant sometimes. I wake up and lovingly rub my stomach, but I'm quickly shocked back into reality when I feel how flat it is now. Hell, maybe I *am* going crazy. I certainly don't feel like the same person I was before miscarrying.

The bed dips as Beck sits down and curls his hand over my hip. "Pres, you need to get out of this house. It's not healthy, darlin'. Everyone is worried about you."

"Tell them not to worry. I'm fine."

He scoffs. "The hell you are."

I sit up, breaking away from his hold. "I said I'm fine, Beckett. Leave it alone."

He cups his hand around my jaw. "No, you're not, Pres. And that's okay. But you're not going to get better if you stay holed up in this bedroom all the time. Why don't we go for a ride? Mag's been wondering where you've been."

I feel a pang of guilt when he mentions my beloved horse. Magnolia and I would go for a ride every day, but I haven't been to the stables once since this happened. The only time I've even left the house was when I had a follow-up appointment with my doctor.

I fight back the tears. "I can't."

"C'mon baby, I can get her tacked up for you and bring her to the front of the house. You don't have to do anything but ride."

I know what he's doing—why he's pushing this. Magnolia and I have always had a special bond. Our relationship is symbiotic—we bring each other joy. I need her just as much as she needs me. *And I've been abandoning her.*

"Okay." I nod. "I'm not up for riding, but I do want to visit her."

He gives me a gentle smile. "I'll be right there with you, Pres."

I slide out of bed and throw some clothes on. Thankfully, we don't run into anyone on our way to the stables. I can't help but wonder if Beck had something to do with that. There are always people milling about, especially in the summertime when enrollment is maxed out on riding lessons. Beck holds my hand the entire time but doesn't say a word. I think he's giving me time to adjust. I try ignoring how oppressive the air feels with each step that I take. I can feel the heat of Beck's gaze as my boots kick up the dirt. He's watching… waiting for me to crack like some delicate piece of china. I hate that we've been reduced to this. If I'm not crying, I'm closed off… robotic almost. He's so careful with every action, every word. We've never had to censor ourselves in front of one another or guard our feelings before. It's almost as if we're strangers sometimes.

I inhale as we reach the stables and feel my chest loosen. The stalls must've been mucked within the past hour; the scent of cedar shavings and hay is much stronger than usual. The ventilation system whirls above my head, keeping the air fresh and cool. The animals stir as we walk down the corridor until we reach the final stall, which belongs to my beautiful girl. Magnolia snuffs as her muzzle peeks out over the door.

I reach out my hand and allow her to sniff my upturned palm as I approach her from the side. "Hey, girl, how are you?"

Beck studies me as I stroke her soft chestnut coat. I can see him out of the corner of my eye—I can tell he wants to say something, but he refrains, watching me like I'm a complicated puzzle he's trying to piece together. I can't stand his scrutiny, so I hide my face behind Mag's neck as my eyes water. I've no doubt he knows what I'm doing—why I'm hiding. But he's allowing me the retreat because he knows I need it.

After a few minutes, he says his first words since we

left the house. "Pres, why don't we take her out? I'll saddle Dakota, and we can ride out to the pond."

I shake my head. "I can't."

"Why the hell not?"

"Because I don't want to."

"Again, I'll ask. Why not?"

Magnolia is starting to get agitated, so I take a few steps back.

"Because I can't go on pretending like nothing's wrong!" I shout.

"I didn't ask you to!" He removes his snapback and runs a hand over his head in frustration. "Goddammit, Presley. Stop shutting me out! Talk to me!"

Our shouting has all of the animals stressed now, so we head out of the building.

"You wouldn't understand, Beck." I hang my head in defeat.

He sighs. "I lost a baby, too, Pres. I'm just as sad as you are about it; I just can't show it because I have to be strong for you."

"You don't have to be *anything* for me!"

"What the hell does that mean?"

"You don't understand, Beck. You *can't* understand what it feels like to have a human being growing inside of you one day, and the next, it's not. I still wake up almost every morning, expecting to see a growing belly, and I cry every time I find my flat stomach instead. I might not look pregnant, but I still *feel* pregnant. I still feel our baby growing inside of me. I know that's crazy—*I know it*—but it's how it is. I have to relive the heartbreak of losing my child. Every. Single. Day. Some nights, when I close my eyes, I wish for God to take me in my sleep, so I don't have to go through that feeling again."

His face falls. "Pres, please just let me in. We should be doing this together. It was *our* baby. *Our* loss. Stop shutting me out."

"I can't!"

"Tell. Me. Why?"

"*Because you weren't there!*" I scream. "You weren't there when I lost the baby! You weren't there when I had to listen to the deafening silence of her missing heartbeat! You. Weren't. There!"

His head jerks back as if I slapped him. "I didn't know, Pres. I came *as soon as I knew.*"

Tears are pouring down my face as I start walking back toward the main house. I know we're causing a spectacle, but I don't even care anymore. "I know, Beck. But it doesn't change the fact that you weren't there when I needed you more than I ever have in my life."

"I can't change what happened," he chokes out. "But I can help make it better if you'd let me."

"It's not that simple."

"I'll do anything for you, Presley. You know that. If you still want to get married this summer, let's get married. If you want to try for another baby, we'll try for another baby. Just tell me what you want."

My jaw drops, appalled. "*You think trying for another baby is the answer?!* Are you kidding me, Beckett?"

He scrubs a hand over his face. "I don't know what to think anymore! Just please tell me what I need to do to make you smile again, and I'll do it. I don't know how to make this better, and it's breaking my heart, Pres. Just tell me what to do!"

I turn toward him when we reach the front porch. "I wish I knew, Beck. Right now, all I want is for you to go back to work so I can go back to sleep. If I'm asleep, it doesn't hurt as bad."

I stiffen when he pulls me into his arms. "Call me if you need anything. *Anything.* My phone is never leaving my side again."

I nod in agreement as I pull out of his embrace. As I'm opening the screen door, I say, "I need more time, Beck. Just give me more time."

"I love you, Pres."

If only love were enough to save our baby.

Chapter Twenty-Two
Presley

It's been almost three weeks since I've left New York, and I've yet to hear from Sebastian. I'm so on edge with the uncertainty. I feel like he's going to jump out at me at every corner. But then again, patience is not my husband's virtue. You'd think if he was coming for me, he would've done so by now. I've kept my phone turned off for the most part, but Sebastian hasn't even tried calling my parents. Is it because he's too busy managing a scandal? I've been checking online, and there hasn't been a single mention about his tryst with his second-in-command. I don't get it. If someone took the time to send me that video, there had to have been a reason, right? I don't have any friends in New York. No one would've sent that to me out of loyalty, so the only thing I could think of was whoever it is, wanted Sebastian to know that he's being watched. That he's been caught with his pants down. Literally.

I blow out a breath, fingering the business card in front of me. Okay, I can do this. I have to go with my gut that Agent Simmons is on my side. I look around my father's office to ensure I'm alone before picking up the phone. Shaking my head about the fact my parents still have a landline, I dial his number.

"Agent Simmons." He picks up after the first ring.

I clear my throat. "Hi... uh... I don't know if you remember me, but—"

"Presley? Is that you?"

My jaw drops. "How'd you know?"

He chuckles lightly. "Your maiden name on the caller ID was my first clue, but you have a distinctive voice. I can tell you try masking it, but you still have a slight southern lilt at the end of certain words. I've lived in New York my entire life, so it stands out. Now, since you're calling, I'm assuming you're ready to talk?"

Crap, I forgot about caller ID.

"I..." I swallow, trying to alleviate the sudden dryness in my throat. "Um... I was hoping you could help me with something."

"I'll do my best."

"Well, it's been almost three weeks since I've been gone."

"You mean since you've been staying at your parents' house?"

The man's done his homework. I shouldn't be surprised; he does work for the FBI, after all.

"Right." I nod, even though he can't see me. "And I haven't heard from my husband once. There's no doubt he's figured out where I'm at by now. My phone's been off, but he has my parents' numbers. I think maybe even my brother's, too. He's had plenty of opportunities to reach out to me, yet he hasn't. I was hopin' you might know why. Is there something going on that's keeping him occupied?"

"Something like trying to prevent a scandalous video from getting into the wrong hands?"

"You know about the video?!"

"Yes, I know about the recording of your husband engaging in a sexual act with the deputy mayor."

"How?"

"Presley, I need you to hear me out before you say anything."

I frown, not liking the direction this conversation is heading. "Okay..."

"I know who forwarded that video to you."

"Excuse me?" I couldn't have possibly heard that correctly.

"A private investigator I work with sometimes had it," he explains. "If I had known he was going to send it to you beforehand, I would've stopped him. He had no idea your husband was so... uh..."

I laugh humorlessly. "The word you're looking for is abusive, Agent."

It feels strange admitting that out loud... yet, it's also cathartic.

Derek clears his throat. "Yes... well, like I said, if I had known beforehand, I would have stopped him. I wouldn't have put you in that situation."

"Because you *did* know how Sebastian would have reacted?"

"Yes, I knew. I *know*. I'm well aware he's a spineless piece of shit who has no qualms about hitting a woman."

"How?" I pinch the bridge of my nose.

"You're not his first victim, Presley. There have been at least three that I know of."

I inhale sharply. "How... why... how can that be? He's never been arrested. There haven't been any accusations."

I don't think anyway.

Agent Simmons sighs audibly. "Your husband is a wealthy, well-connected man. Even before his time in office. Unfortunately, none of those women pressed charges."

"Because he paid for their silence?"

"Two of them, yes."

"And the third?" I hold my breath, waiting for his answer.

"His first wife...took her own life."

I slam a hand over my mouth. "Oh, God."

I knew Sebastian had been married for about five years before he met me—a woman named Sabrina. Her official cause of death was a prescription opioid overdose. Supposedly, it was accidental. Sebastian rarely talked about his late wife. I thought it was because thinking about her was too painful, but now, I wonder if it was because he was afraid I'd uncover the truth.

That maybe Sabrina was so desperate to escape him, she took control the only way she knew how.

I can't say I haven't thought about it more than once.

"There's something else you should know, Presley."

"What's that?"

"Bri—his first wife—was my sister."

I choke back a sob. "That's why you said you had no loyalty to the man."

"Among other things, yes."

"I'm sorry for your loss, Derek."

"Thank you."

Neither one of us says anything for a few beats. Finally, I decide to get to the reason behind my call.

"I have a question."

"Go ahead."

I pick up a pen from the desk and begin twirling it between my fingers. "Why is the FBI interested in my husband?"

"The FBI has no official interest in your husband."

"With all due respect, Agent, if you want me to trust you, it has to go both ways. How 'bout this? What do you need from me? I'm assuming that's the reason you came to see me in the hospital. Because you need my help with something regarding your case against my husband?"

Derek takes a moment to reply. "I don't need your help with anything, although I reserve the right to change my mind down the road. I wish I could nail that bastard with something, but my employer has no interest in your husband."

"Then, why bother?"

"Because I'm not a narcissistic sociopath? Because maybe I see a little bit of my sister in you? Or, how about the fact that I couldn't save Bri eats me alive, so I'm doing what I can to ensure you don't suffer the same fate? Take your pick. I just wanted to help, Presley, and I saw an opportunity to introduce myself."

"How'd you know I was in the hospital? How'd you get access to my building's security footage?"

"You know that private investigator I mentioned earlier? I've had him trailing your husband. Look, I apologize for misleading you about my involvement in the police investigation, but I tried getting you to talk so you wouldn't go back to him. I wanted to offer to help you make a clean break."

Oh.

I dab at the tears pooling in the corner of my eyes. It's been so long since I've had anyone standing in my corner. Yes, I know my family will always have my back, but I suffered in silence for over a third of my life. My family had no clue how bad things were with Sebastian because I cut them out of my life, despite their best efforts to remain close. And if I'm honest with myself, a small part of me felt like maybe I deserved it. That maybe Sebastian's abuse was my penance for leaving this ranch. For breaking the hearts of everyone I loved by running from my problems instead of facing them together.

I hang my head in my hands, weeping for all the mistakes I've made. All the time I've lost. For the many things that will never be the same again.

"Presley? Are you still there?"

I sniffle. "Yeah. Sorry. I sort of got lost in my head for a moment there."

"No need to apologize. Is there anything I can do?"

I nod. "I don't suppose you know any good divorce attorneys? I think I'm going to need one."

"As a matter of fact, I do. I'm married to one."

"That must be interesting, being married to someone who spends their days dealing with fighting spouses."

"Eh, it makes her appreciate me more."

I chuckle, despite the gravity of the situation. "You're a lucky man."

"I am," he agrees.

I take a deep breath. "I'll be heading into town tomorrow to get a new phone number. Can I follow up with you then?"

"Sure thing, Presley."

"Thank you, Derek. For everything."

"You can thank me by staying safe. You are okay where you're at, right?"

"Physically? Yes. As for the rest... I think I will be."

Eventually.

"Good. Call me when you get your new number, or if you'd prefer to text, this is my cell, so that's fine, too."

"Okay. We'll talk soon. Bye, Derek."

"Bye, Presley."

Chapter Twenty-Three
Presley – Age 18

"Presley, you need to tell him. You're runnin' out of time."

I sigh. "I know, Mama. I asked him to meet me by the pond about an hour from now."

My mother takes a seat beside me at the end of my bed. "Is there anything I can do to change your mind? I know it hurts, honey, but my gut is telling me this is the wrong move. Just take a little more time, and if you still want to go to New York by the time winter term rolls around, so be it."

I squeeze my eyes shut, warding off the tears. "I can't stay here anymore. *Everything* reminds me of what I lost."

She gives me a pained smile. "And that includes Beckett?"

"*Especially* Beckett," I admit. "I can't... I don't know how to talk to him anymore. There's this giant void between us I don't know how to overcome. He's so sad

—I know he is—but Beck tries hiding it because he thinks he has to be strong for me. Like, if he showed me his sorrow, it'd make mine even worse. We used to be able to tell each other anything. Now... now, it's like every conversation is forced. It's so awkward. We're walking on eggshells around each other, and I hate it."

"So, tell him that."

"I did!" I throw my hands up. "But Beck's a problem solver. He refuses to give up until he can find a way to fix me. Fix *us*. I wish it were that easy, but I don't know if I'm capable of being whole again. You know, I've spent these last two months being angry at God, but when NYU got back to me, sayin' they still had room for the fall semester, I felt like maybe it was a sign. Maybe this is God's way of puttin' me on the path to healing. I need a fresh start, and New York will give me that fresh start."

"Presley, that boy loves you with his whole heart. There isn't anything Beck wouldn't do for you. Love like that doesn't come around very often. Some people go their whole lives and never find it. If you walk away... if you leave him... it's going to break his heart. And if you do that, you may never get another shot. Beck will eventually move on. He might fall in love. Not that once-in-a-lifetime kind of love you two share, but he could find enough happiness with another woman to make a life with her. They could get married and have babies... all things you two were meant to do together. Are you really willing to risk losing that?"

My tears are falling freely now. The thought of

losing Beck forever is terrifying. Picturing him marrying another woman, having babies with her makes me want to curl into a ball and die. But I'm no good to him like this. I need to figure out how to fix myself before I can be the woman he deserves.

"If Beck and I are meant to be together, it'll work itself out. My mind's made up, Mama. I have to do this. I *am* doin' this."

Now, she sighs. "I hope you don't regret this, Presley Anne."

Me too, Mama. Me too.

Chapter Twenty-Four
Presley

I can't get over how much growth this area has seen in the time I've been gone. I've been driving around in my dad's old truck for over an hour, taking it all in. Right on the outskirts of town, there's a relatively new shopping center with various stores, including a Piggly Wiggly, a CVS, and a Walmart. Luckily for me, they also had a Verizon store, so I didn't have to travel forty-five minutes each way to get a new phone. For obvious reasons, I needed to get rid of my joint account with Sebastian. As much as things have changed around here, I'm pleased to see Main Street seems relatively untouched, except for a few new businesses, namely the coffee shop I've got my eye on. It's not even noon yet, and I'm already dragging, so I decide a caffeine boost is in order.

I haven't slept well in quite some time, but it's been even worse over the last few weeks. I've been plagued with these horrible dreams about the night I confronted Sebastian. I keep reliving that moment again and again with startling clarity. When I wake up, my heart is racing out of my chest, and I'm so distraught, falling back asleep is next to impossible. Last night was especially rough because I had only been asleep for two hours before the nightmare woke me.

A bell dings over the door as I walk into Java House. I take a deep breath inhaling the aroma of freshly ground coffee. When I look up and see a familiar face behind the counter, my eyes widen.

"Nicky?" Damn. She was always pretty, but she's become even more beautiful over the years.

Nicky's pale blue eyes narrow, and her lip curls. *What the heck?*

"It's Nicole now."

"Oh. Um... okay. How've you been, Nicole? It's good to see you."

I don't understand why she's giving off such hostile vibes, but I know I do not imagine it. Is she mad at me for not reaching out to her after I moved? We were friends in high school, but we weren't especially close. She wasn't the person I confided in or spent any significant time with except cheerleading. Beck and I were together so often, we didn't see our friends much outside of school or bonfires.

Nicky... uh, Nicole smiles. It's a practiced smile, one I'm familiar with. Whenever Sebastian needed me to attend a business function with him all night long, I'd be on the receiving end of those plastic smiles.

"Why, I've been great, Presley. Aren't you sweet for askin'?"

I don't miss the fact that she doesn't ask how I've been.

"Sure. Of course." I look around the cute little shop. "So, you work here?"

Nicole straightens her spine. "I own it. All by myself."

"Oh, that's great. Congratulations."

There's that smile again. "Aw, bless your heart."

Okay, I've been up north for a long time, but I haven't forgotten the versatility of that statement. In the South, "Bless your heart" can serve as a genuine sign of sympathy or concern. But when it's spoken in *that* tone—the one that's sugary sweet but laced with arsenic—it's typically a precursor to an insult.

I tilt my head to the side. "I'm sorry, Nicole, but I get the feeling you're mad at me for some reason. Is everything okay?"

She places her open palm against her chest. "Of course, it is. Everything is *wonderful*. Business is great. I have a sexy, *oh-so-talented* man to warm my bed *all night long*. What could be bad about that?"

Well, this is awkward. I don't remember Nicole being so brash.

"Uh... good for you. I hate to cut this short, but I really need to get back to the ranch. Could I please get a twelve-ounce vanilla latte for the road?"

"Sure, hun." Nicole gets to work brewing some espresso and steaming the milk. "How long are you in town, Presley? Beckett mentioned you were back, but he wasn't sure how long you were stayin'.'"

My chest tightens as she says his name. "You still talk to Beckett?"

"Of course, I do, silly. Well, when we're not too busy burnin' up the sheets, anyway." Nicole winks.

I blink rapidly, stunned. "You and Beckett are... seeing each other?"

She nods. "For about two years now."

"Oh." I swallow the sudden lump in my throat. "Is it... are you two serious?"

I know I have no right to ask, nor reason to care, but the words just seem to fall out of my mouth.

She chuckles. "Well, we were recently talkin' about marriage, so I think that's pretty serious, don't you?"

Wow. I don't know what to say. I never expected Beck to be a monk, but I'm caught off guard by the fact that he's dating one of my old friends. Like the song says, I guess that's just how it goes when you break up in a small town. Obviously, my brother was wrong about Beck not letting anyone get close to him.

"Speakin' of marriage... if you don't mind me pryin'. I notice you're not wearing a wedding band." Nicole sets the to-go cup on the counter. "You poor thing. Is that why you're back? Because your marriage to that handsome billionaire failed?"

My face flushes with anger. Nicole was always insecure, which I never understood because she's absolutely gorgeous. But I don't ever remember her being downright nasty. Her motive couldn't possibly be any

more apparent. She's not happy I've returned—probably because she considers me a threat due to my
history with Beck—and she's going to do her
damnedest to cut me down, so she can make herself
feel better. Too bad for her, I'm well-versed in this
game, and I have no intention of letting her walk all
over me. I'm *so* over biting my tongue. That was something Presley Winters would do. Well, as this scornful
woman is about to learn, Presley James is making a
comeback.

I dig a ten-dollar bill out of my purse and set it on
the counter before grabbing the cup of coffee. "Nicky, I
know you're threatened by me, but let me assure
you—"

"Threatened by you?!" she sputters. "Hardly."

I hold my hand up. "*As I was saying*, let me assure
you, I am *not* in the market for a man, so you need to
get that through your head now. If you and Beck are
havin' troubles, that has *nothing* to do with me. Your
relationship with him is none of my business, just like
my relationship is none of yours. Don't project your
insecurities onto me. I've got plenty of my own shit to
worry about; I definitely don't need any of yours piled
on top of it."

"You have some nerve!" Nicky folds her arms over
her ample chest. "I don't have *a single thing* to be insecure about, least of all my relationship with Beckett. If
anyone's projectin' somethin', it's *you*. If you think he'll
come running back to you, you're sorely mistaken,
Presley. He wants nothing to do with you after the way

you treated him. In fact, he once told me he'd prefer it if you *never* came back, so maybe you should think about *that* next time you want to throw around accusations. You're *nothing* to me and *nothing* to Beckett."

This is pointless. Nicky obviously has no interest in listening to reason.

I hold up the coffee. "Thanks for the latte. Good luck with everything."

Her shrill scream is cut off as I leave the store. I'm in such a hurry to get out of there, I'm not looking where I'm going until it's too late.

"Shit!" I stumble backward after bouncing off a hard chest, hot coffee spilling all over my hand.

"Damn it!" a deep voice booms, reaching out to steady me. "What the hell, Presley? Where's the fire?"

I gasp as his large hand curls around my elbow. My eyes are trained on his white T-shirt, more specifically, the spot where my coffee has soaked through the cotton, making it cling to his rippled abs. *Jesus.* Beckett had a great body when we were younger, honed by good old-fashioned manual labor, but this is the body of a *man.* My stomach flutters, stirring up feelings I thought were long gone. I don't know which one of us moves first, but we're suddenly so close that only a few inches of space exist between us. I close my eyes, inhaling the same woodsy cologne he wore when we were together. Beck drops his head, our foreheads nearly touching as I breathe him in.

He releases my arm and moves the hand lower until his fingertips are digging into my denim-clad hip. The hunger between us is palpable. There's an urgency to it that scorches my insides, overwhelming my senses. The outside world doesn't matter. It's just me and him, drawn together by this magnetic force neither one of us could ever deny.

My toes curl when Beck groans, then whispers, "Pres."

I lean in a little farther, closing the gap between us. I think I moan when my peaked nipples brush against his upper abs. "Beckett."

My voice is breathy, needy in a way I didn't know I was capable of any longer. Like a rubber band stretched too thin, as soon as the words leave my mouth, Beck snaps back, breaking the spell we seemed to be under. We both look at each other, bewildered, as the cloud of lust dissipates and reality sets in. Now that I'm thinking clearly, I remember why I was in such a hurry in the first place.

My eyes narrow. "Excuse me. Obviously, I didn't mean to ruin your shirt. If it doesn't wash out, I'd be happy to replace it."

"I don't need you to replace my goddamn shirt, Presley," he growls. "I just need you to watch where you're goin'."

"Duly noted. Now, if you'll excuse me..." I try stepping around him, but Beckett's hand lashes out again, grabbing my wrist.

"Hold on a second."

My eyes flicker to my wrist. "Let go of me, Beckett. I didn't give you permission to touch me."

He pulls back again, shaking his head. If I didn't know better, I'd swear he was confused about how his hand got there.

"Where are you off to in such a hurry?"

"Why does it matter?" I let out a tired sigh.

Beck's bourbon eyes fall to my cup before making their way back to my face. Ah, I get it now. He's wondering what just went down inside that store.

I roll my eyes. "Why don't you go ask your girlfriend? You might have better luck."

He briefly glances over my shoulder. We're off to the side of the coffee shop, so I don't think he's able to see Nicky, but it's obvious he's thinking about her.

"What did she say to you?"

I scoff. "Don't you mean what did *I* say to *her*? Don't worry, Beck. I'm sure her precious feelings are just fine."

He looks me dead in the eye. "*What did she say to you, Presley?*"

I startle, thrown off guard by the vehemence in his tone. I take the few steps necessary to get to my vehicle. Beck doesn't try grabbing me again, but his eyes follow my every move.

"Nothing special. She was just needlessly marking her territory."

His forehead creases. "I'll make sure it doesn't happen again."

I hold my hand up. "Don't bother, Beckett. I'm a big girl. A few bitchy comments aren't going to break me. Trust me, I've been exposed to much worse. Catty women are nothing in the grand scheme of things. Now, if you'll excuse me, I need to get back. Send me the bill for your shirt if the stain doesn't come out."

He opens his mouth to say something but snaps it shut when I open the truck door and seal myself inside. I can feel Beck watching me through the windshield as I put the key in the ignition and crank the engine. I can still feel the burn of his stare as I'm backing out and driving away. The buzz crawling beneath my skin doesn't subside until I've turned a corner, completely cutting off his line of sight. I curl my shaking hands around the steering wheel, telling myself to calm down. I shiver when I remember the feel of his warm body pressed against mine and how strongly I reacted to his proximity.

Seriously, what the hell was that? How can Beckett still have that kind of effect on me? After everything we've been through, after everything *I've* been through since, it shouldn't be possible. Yet, as I glance down at the evidence of my arousal poking through my shirt, I know it's true. My mind and my heart may be in tatters right now, but my body remembers his touch.

And unfortunately for me, it desperately wants more.

Chapter Twenty-Five
Presley – Age 18

"Hey. Thanks for meetin' me here." I take a seat next to Beck on the tailgate. He backed his truck up against the edge of the pond, so we're facing the water.

His eyes roam over my face, digging, searching for answers. I don't know how, but he knows I'm leaving. There's no doubt in my mind.

Beck grabs my hand, weaving our fingers together. Neither one of us looks away from our joined hands. "Just say it."

I take a deep breath, trying to ignore the sharp pain in my chest. "I'm leavin', Beckett. I emailed the admissions office at NYU, explainin' my circumstances. I asked if they still had room for me in the fall semester, and... they said yes. My flight leaves in the mornin'."

His grip on me tightens. When I look up, I see his eyes are closed, his head hanging low. When he opens them, they're filled with tears, begging me to change my mind.

"Pres. Please don't do this."

His choked off plea is nearly my undoing. I almost tell him I'll stay. That I'll find a way to not be so sad, I want to die sometimes, just to make it go away. But I can't. Being here isn't healthy for me right now. I need to go someplace where I can keep busy. Where my mind won't have time to focus on all the hurt. I need to make a drastic change, and New York City is pretty much the polar opposite of Southwest Georgia.

"I have to, Beck. *I have to get away from this place.*"

"Then, let's go together." He tilts my chin up with his finger. "I don't care where we are, Pres, as long as we're together."

Tears roll down my face as I shake my head, pulling away. "I can't do that."

A sharp crease forms between his eyebrows. "Why not?"

And here it is—the moment of truth.

"Because..." I know it's cowardly, but I look away. I can't face this beautiful, broken boy as I say the words that have the power to ruin us forever. "I need to get away from you too, Beckett. I can't... I can't be around you right now. I can't stop thinking about what we lost when I look at you. It hurts too much."

I risk looking at him then. There's a shadow casting over us from the giant Spanish moss to the side. But there's a gap in the leaves, where a ray of sunshine hits his eyes, making their glassy surface sparkle even more. In a matter of seconds, I see so many expressions flicker through them—love, longing, sadness, hopelessness, and finally, acceptance. Beck says nothing as he stares at me because words are rarely necessary between us. He knows there's nothing he can say to stop me. He knows we may never be the same again. He gently frames my face with his hands, leaning down before placing soft kisses over each one of my eyelids. The moment he pulls back, I fall apart. Beck gathers me to him, positioning my body until I'm straddling his lap. We hold on for dear life, clutching each other, bodies shaking with grief. I'm not sure how much time passes until our tears run dry, but once they do, a new kind of desperation takes over. We move in sync, lunging for each other until our lips are crashing together.

We kiss each other until we're both panting for breath. I'm suddenly thankful I took the time to put on a dress today, trying to look pretty on the outside since my insides are so dark and gloomy. I fumble with Beckett's belt buckle while he pulls on my panties with such force, they tear in two. Damn it, that stung, but it was also so, *so* hot.

"Holy crap, I thought that only happened in books."

Beck flashes his signature smirk as he tosses them over his shoulder. In the next moment, he kicks off his boots and lowers his boxers and jeans in one go. I help him pull the denim down until one leg is free, but we're both in such a frenzy, we don't bother with the rest. He scoots back until his head is resting against the window, taking me with him. I lift up just enough to position myself over his hardness before sinking down slowly. We both groan as I take him in deeper and deeper until my backside is touching his legs.

This is crazy; we both know it. It's the middle of the day. We're far enough removed from the ranch's main activity, but still, anyone could happen upon us. We've never been this careless, but neither one of us seems able to stop. My beautiful boy and I—the love of my life—make love under the hot summer sun, slowly, tenderly, until I'm crying out in bliss. He follows me only moments later, saying my name like a prayer, over and over again. I can feel him softening inside of me, but neither one of us are in any hurry to move.

When we do finally disconnect, Beck removes his T-shirt to help me clean up. My underwear is ruined, so there's not much else I can do there. He hops off the truck bed to straighten the remainder of his clothes while I take the tie from my wrist and pull my hair into a pony. Once he's fully dressed from the waist down, he extends his hand, helping me to the ground. He folds me into his chest, placing a kiss against my temple. We stand there just like that for a few minutes before I finally get the nerve to speak.

"I'm not leavin' because I don't love you with every-thing inside of me. That's never gonna change, Beck. No matter how far apart we are."

But I'll be getting on that plane anyway, no matter how badly it breaks both of our hearts.

"I know, darlin'." Beck squeezes me tighter. "Doesn't mean I'm going to hate it any less."

Chapter Twenty-Six
Beckett

I'm so fucked.

I told myself I don't care. That it doesn't matter if Presley stays in Hope Springs because she's leaving her douchebag husband. That I don't want to know every detail of her life since she's been gone and what demons she's runnin' from now.

Then, I got to hold her in my arms again.

In a matter of seconds, the impenetrable fortress I've built over the years came crumbling down. Now, as I stare down the road long after Presley's gone, I can't stop thinking. Wondering. Mentally listing all the ways I can coincidentally—okay, purposefully—cross paths with her, hoping for the chance to hold her again. But I know I've got my work cut out for me. There's darkness living beneath her beautiful hazel eyes. I don't know what exactly Presley's experienced in her time away, but I'm confident it's not good. She has that same haunted look about her I see in the mirror every day. I know what it feels like to keep unpleasant thoughts stuffed inside until you feel like you're about to implode, and that's exactly what that woman is doing. She's well-practiced at it, too, which makes me madder than a pack of wild dogs.

I know I need to tread carefully because trying to solve Presley's problems is what got us into this mess in the first place. She's a grown-ass woman, a stubborn one at that, and trying to sniff out the problem so I can fix it isn't going to do either one of us any good. Speaking of problems... there's one that I've needed to take care of for quite a while now, and I can't afford to put it off anymore. The bell rings as I open the door to Nicole's shop. A quick glance around tells me we're alone, so I launch straight into it before that changes.

A smile stretches across her face as she comes from behind the counter. "Well, this is a nice surprise. What the heck happened to your shirt?" Her grin quickly dies when I step aside, dodging the kiss she tried planting on me.

"Are you free tonight? We need to talk."

Nicole's sky-blue eyes widen in panic before she remembers to mask it. She knows nothing ever good happens when I say we need to talk. Unfortunately, every time I've tried having this conversation, she's successfully distracted me. This time, I'm not going to allow my dick to get in the way. And to ensure she doesn't attempt to dissuade me again, we're going to have this discussion in public.

"Can you meet me somewhere later? Clay's bar, maybe?"

"You wanna go out for a drink?" Her brows pinch together.

"And talk," I remind her.

"We don't need to go out for that." She places her open palm on my chest, leaning in. "I have plenty of your favorite whiskey at my place."

I take another step back, shaking my head. "I don't think that's a good idea, Nic. Meet me at Clay's. Say at eight o'clock?"

"Why don't you come to pick me up instead?"

"Can't. I'm going to be working late tonight. I had a quick errand to run on my lunch break, but I need to get back." I push open the door and step over the threshold. "I'll see you at eight."

Nicole's still frowning as I exit the store, but I pretend not to notice. I'm not trying to be an asshole, but I don't want to spend the next thirty minutes listening to her attempted negotiations. I really do need to get back to the ranch.

As I'm rolling up the driveway, I see Mr. J's truck parked in front of the main house, so I know Presley's made it back. It takes every bit of willpower I possess to continue driving until I reach my place. As I exit my pickup, I catch movement out of the corner of my eye. They're a ways away, but there's no mistaking the gorgeous Arabian nor the stunning blonde walking beside her, taking her by the lead. I know I'm witnessing something special as I watch them. Magnolia's not wearing a saddle, which tells me Presley has no intention of riding her. The woman may have grown up around horses, but she couldn't ride bareback to save her life, and I doubt that's changed during her time up north. This moment between them is intimate, almost, and I feel like a bit of a voyeur, but I can't force myself to look away.

I move closer, drawn to the wild beauty of it, but I'm mindful about keeping my distance. It's obvious they're reconnecting, and the last thing I'd want to do is interrupt like I did last time. Presley strokes the horse's mane lovingly, and when Magnolia lowers her muzzle to nudge her companion, Presley's face lights up in laughter. Mag drops her head even farther until their foreheads are touching. Pres runs her hand along the animal's neck as she's speaking softly to her. They remain that way for quite some time, the light breeze blowing Presley's hair around as the two re-establish the bond they once shared as if they had never been apart.

Christ. I don't think I've ever seen anything more beautiful in my life.

When Presley finally lifts her head, her eyes wander, as if she can sense she's being watched. When her gaze locks on mine, she freezes. We stare at each other across the space between us, and something shifts in the air. Like an acknowledgment of sorts, mutual respect for our past. Life may have shaped us into different people in some ways, but what happened on that sidewalk earlier proves that not *everything* has changed. And that small but significant fact has me contemplating something I haven't thought about in a long time: maybe things between Presley and me aren't over after all.

Chapter Twenty-Seven
Presley

"Okay, I know you're still supposed to take it easy on your shoulder, so why don't you stick to beer and shots for now? Once you're operating at one-hundred percent, we can work on some of those girly cocktails chicks love."

I whack my brother with the dishtowel that was slung over my shoulder. "Sexist much?"

Clayton holds his hands up. "What? It's true! I seem to remember you havin' a fondness for Cosmos back in the day. You're a chick, and drinks don't get much girlier than that."

I roll my eyes. "That's because I was a teenager who didn't know any better. I also thought Boone's Strawberry Hill was fine wine."

He belts out a laugh and swings his arm around my neck, pulling me into his side. "I'm sure your tastes are much more refined after living in a big city, huh?"

I shrug out of his hold, suddenly not finding the moment so amusing. "I guess."

The truth is, I rarely drink. When you've been on the receiving end of alcohol-induced rages like I have, you tend to lose your taste for it. I know the irony behind taking this job, but it's not the same here. Here, things feel normal. Like, maybe this is where I'd be going on a Friday night if I hadn't moved away. Even if my brother wasn't standing right next to me, I'd still feel safe. In a town of less than five hundred, nearly everyone who walks through those doors knows everyone else. And Clayton has assured me he's not afraid to cut someone off before things get out of hand.

Throughout the night, I see many familiar faces. I have a lot of conversations that end in some variation of: "Let's get together and catch up sometime." Clayton's stuck close by for the most part, but he seems to have figured out how important it is that I don't use him as a crutch. Tending bar is definitely not something I'd ever enjoy doing long-term, but it's a step in the right direction. I can't stay holed up in that house anymore, wondering if and when Sebastian is ever going to make his move. I texted my new number to Agent Simmons earlier, and he promised to have his wife call me first thing Monday morning. I suppose once I file for divorce, Sebastian will have no choice but to acknowledge me.

Dive Bar also sells pub food, so we had a rush around suppertime, but we're having a bit of a lull right now. Since it's Friday night, Clayton says business will really start picking up around nine. I'm due to clock out at the same time because he didn't want to over-whelm me on my first day, but I might hang out for a while after my shift. It's refreshing having this little slice of normal, being around people who don't have a pretentious bone in their body. The front door opens, and I silently amend my previous statement. I guess I spoke too soon.

Nicky—I refuse to call her Nicole after the way she treated me earlier—saunters in, wearing a skin-tight red dress that pushes her boobs up and a cute pair of brown cowgirl booties.

My brother whistles from the other end of the bar, closest to the door. "Damn, Nicky."

My lips twitch as she pins him with a glare. "Kiss my sweet ass, Clayton."

Clayton rests his elbows on the bar top and leans forward. "Well, I've already been there, done that, honey, but if you're lookin' for a repeat, I will gladly oblige. You just say the word."

I duck my head, shaking with silent laughter. This boy hasn't changed one bit, has he? Clay would *never* move in on another man's girl, especially not one of his friends, but that doesn't stop him from flirting with everyone bearing a pair of tits. Nineteen or ninety, it doesn't matter. He can't seem to help himself. The only exceptions to that rule are the women he's related to.

She huffs. "You wish. Have you seen Beckett? He's supposed to be meetin' me here."

Lovely. I knew this was bound to happen eventually, but I hoped I wouldn't have to deal with it on my first night. Especially after Beck and I had that weird… whatever it was earlier.

Nicky's eyes wander around the room before turning back our way. She must not have noticed me before because as contemptuous as I thought her expression was then, it's nothing compared to now.

"Presley." She looks me up and down, taking in my outfit with a sneer. I'm not sure what her problem is. My wardrobe choices are limited to the things I wore when I was eighteen, but thankfully, I had a pretty timeless fashion sense back then. My shirts are a little tighter than they used to be because my breasts are two cup sizes fuller, but it's not revealing in any way. "What are you doin' behind the bar?"

Before I can answer, Clayton swings his arm over my shoulders and says, "Didn't you hear? Presley's sticking around. She's gonna be helping me out for the foreseeable future. Isn't that great?"

Nicky's face transforms into what could only be described as severely constipated. "Yeah. Just great." Her tone says that it's anything *but* great. "I'm grabbin' a table in the back. When my *boyfriend* gets here, will ya send him on back, hun?"

I give her a saccharine smile. "Sure thing, *hun*."

I shove Clayton's arm off when she walks away. "You just had to antagonize her, didn't you?"

"She makes it too easy." He laughs. "What's the deal with you two? I get the sense this isn't the first time you've run into each other since you've been back."

"It's not."

His eyebrows lift. "You gonna explain that?"

I fold my arms over my chest. "Nope."

He shakes his head. "You're no fun."

"Not everything's fun and games, you idiot. You can't go ar—"

My words are cut off when the door opens again, and the breath whooshes from my lungs. Beck makes a beeline for the bar the second he sees me.

"Presley. Can we talk?"

"No. I'm working."

Beck frowns. "You're workin' here now? Since when?"

"Since today." I wipe down the spotless bar to keep myself occupied. "Now, if you'll ex—"

"Go ahead and take a break, Pres. I don't mind."

My eyes snap to my meddling brother. "No, thank you. I'm good."

Clay looks between Beck and me, his eyes twinkling with mischief. "Really, I don't mind. You've done a great job tonight. In fact, if you wanna cut out early so you two can go somewhere and *talk*, feel free."

I glare when he uses air quotes around the word *talk*. "I said, *no, thank you*." My jaw is clenched so tightly, I'm surprised I can get the words out.

Beck clears his throat. "Pres—"

"Hey, baby, there you are!" Nicky curls her arm around Beck's bicep, pressing her breasts into him. "I've got us a table in the back. C'mon." Beck hesitates, which does not please his girlfriend one bit. "Beckett, did you hear what I said?"

He glances at her briefly before returning his eyes to me. "We'll finish this conversation later."

I shake my head. "I have nothing to say."

Beckett smirks. "Well, too bad, because I do."

I hold my chin high, hoping he can't read me like he used to. If he can, he'd know I'm lying through my teeth. I have so many words to say to this man, if you put them on paper, the first volume alone would make *War and Peace* look like *CliffsNotes*. I'm afraid if I started, the word vomit wouldn't stop until all my deepest, darkest secrets were exposed. I can't bear the thought of him knowing what I went through when it never would've happened if I had listened to him, my mama, or anyone else who told me I shouldn't go to New York.

Nicky tugs on Beck's arm, trying to drag him to the table she had claimed. He finally gives in and goes with her, but not before looking back at me one more time.

Clayton chuckles under his breath. I'm a little annoyed he finds this whole thing so funny. "I need to grab a new keg. You okay up here by yourself for a few?"

I wave him off. "Go do what you need to do."

"Well, I'll be damned. I heard you were back in town. You look great, Presley."

I glance up at the man who just sat down at the bar. It takes me a second to recognize him because the police uniform threw me off, but his pale green eyes are a dead giveaway.

"Well, look at that: Colby Mitchell in the flesh. What can I get you?"

He raises a single brow. "You workin' here now?"

I shrug. "I'm just helping Clayton out for a bit. Now, how 'bout that drink?"

"I'm on duty, so a Coke is fine."

I scoop some ice in a glass and fill it with soda, as they call it up north. I place a cocktail napkin down in front of him and set the glass on top.

"So...sheriff, huh? When did that happen?"

He takes a sip before answering. "About a year ago, when my dad retired. I've been with the force for almost ten years now, though."

"You like it?"

"Most days. Not much happens in this town, and ladies love a man in uniform." He punctuates his statement with a wink.

Geez, I almost forgot Colby is as incorrigible as my brother when it comes to flirting.

"What happens on the days you don't like?"

His mouth kicks up in the corner. "Usually, some punk-ass kids are bored and causin' trouble."

"Oh, you mean like you used to do?"

"Exactly." He laughs. "Little bastards."

"Colby, what did I tell you about hanging around here scaring off my customers?" Clayton grunts as he sets the keg down. "How are folks supposed to engage in some good old-fashioned debauchery when the town sheriff is watching their every move?"

"It's never stopped you," Colby challenges.

Clay points to him. "That's because I have dirt on you."

My head swings to the sheriff. "What kind of dirt?"

"The kind a gentleman like me never talks about." He winks again.

"Oh, lord." I shake my head.

"Gentleman, my ass," Clay teases. "Just last week, you—"

"Are you kidding me?!" All three of our heads swing toward the back of the seating area where the shrill voice came from. "You're unbelievable, you know that?"

"Oh, shit," Colby and my brother say at the same time.

I, however, don't say a word because I'm too busy watching the drama unfold.

"Nic, calm down." Beck reaches for her as she stands, but she shakes him off.

"Calm down? *Calm down?!* This is because of her, isn't it?" Nicky points directly at me. *"Isn't it?!"*

Beckett pinches the bridge of his nose and says something to her that I can't hear.

"Oh, screw you, Beckett Armstrong! You're going to regret this, I can promise you that."

Nicky storms through the bar, leaving a giant spectacle in her wake. Beck is still sitting in the booth, looking like he's fighting off a migraine. He probably is after being screamed at like that. After a moment, he slides out of the seat and goes after her.

Nicky flashes all three of us a nasty glare as she passes us on the way out.

Right before she reaches the door, my brother calls out, "Bye, Nicky. You have a wonderful evening, sweetheart."

She flips him a double bird as she's stepping outside.

Beck throws a dirty look over his shoulder as he's walking out. "Not helpin', Clayton."

Clayton finds this especially amusing if his laughter is any indication.

Colby whistles softly. "Shit, he finally did it."

"Looks like it," Clay agrees. "About damn time."

"Finally did *what?*"

"Cut Nicky loose," Colby explains. "He's tried multiple times, but she always managed to sink her claws in and convince him to give her another shot. I don't know what the hell he was thinkin', doing it in public, though. He had to have known she'd make a scene."

"She wouldn't be Nicky if she didn't," Clay adds.

Beck tried breaking up with her before? What about all the supposed marriage talk? And why do I care?

"I need to hit the ladies' room. Be back in a bit."

I take off like my butt is on fire, heading down the long hallway to the bathrooms. I duck inside the ladies' and take a few deep breaths once I'm safely behind the closed door. My eyes widen when I see my reflection in the mirror above the sinks. My face is flushed, and my eyes are wild. My chest is heaving like those women in the historical romances I used to enjoy reading before Sebastian sucked all the joy out of them.

I turn on the tap and run my wrists under cold water, trying to calm my racing pulse. Why am I having such a strong physical reaction to what just went down with Beck and his girlfriend? *Ex*-girlfriend, I mean. Was she right? Did Beck just break up with her because I'm back in town? Based on my first encounter with him, I'd dismiss the possibility entirely. But after what happened earlier, I don't know. I think it just might be entirely... possible. But why? I'm not single. Not technically. And it's not like either one of us can just forget the last twelve years happened and go back to the way things were. There are so many obstacles in the way, it's almost comical.

The question is, why am I actually considering facing them one by one until nothing is standing in our way?

Chapter Twenty-Eight
Presley

I'm woken by the buzzing under my pillow. I have no clue what time it is, but it's still dark outside. I reach for the phone blindly until my hand finds purchase and hit the accept button.

"Hello," I mumble.

"Hello, Presley. Did I wake you?"

I'm instantly alert as Sebastian's voice registers. Damn it, if I wasn't half-asleep when it rang, I would've thought about the fact that no one that has this number would be calling me before sunrise.

I switch the bedside lamp on and sit up. "How did you get this number?"

"Now, is that any way to speak to your husband? Especially one as forgiving as I am?"

"Forgiving?" I scoff. "You're one of the least forgiving people I know, Sebastian. Now, how did you get my number?"

He releases a dark chuckle. "Did you really think I

wouldn't find you? That I wouldn't have people watching you? I knew where you were heading the moment I realized you had left the hospital. Getting a new phone number was a cute attempt to evade me, I must admit, but I've grown tired of this game, Presley. People are starting to question your absence. Visiting your parents for three weeks is a bit excessive, don't you think?"

My blood runs cold. It's one thing if he knows where I'm at. It's an entirely different ballgame if he genuinely has eyes on me. I've been expecting him to possibly show up, but not once did I consider he'd have me followed. If Sebastian came to Hope Springs, he'd stick out like a sore thumb. My family knows him; half this town knows what he looks like. I'd have a warning, and I could ensure I had a barrier in place. An unknown threat seems almost worse. If I don't know what to look for, how can I protect myself? I think back to the two times I've been in town. Was someone following me? Was there anyone suspicious in the bar last night? I take a deep breath to gather the strength I need.

"First of all, it's not a game, Sebastian. Secondly, I'm not comin' back. In fact, I've hired an attorney to file for divorce." Okay, so I will be hiring an attorney on Monday. Close enough. "You should expect to hear from her soon. If you have anything else to say to me, you can do it through her."

I'm just about to hang up when he says, "I wouldn't

do that if I were you, Presley. You're not going to like the consequences."

"I'm quite familiar with the *consequences* you're capable of deliverin', Sebastian. I have several broken bones that never healed properly to prove it. Nothing you say will make me change my mind. I'm done livin' with your abuse."

"Trust me when I say you have *no idea* what I'm capable of if you push this, Presley. I didn't spend the last twelve years of my life trying to smother your inner country bumpkin to have it all thrown away over nothing. Do you even hear yourself? After only a few weeks back in the Deep South, your hick is showing."

"Nothing?!" I shout, completely ignoring his remark about my accent. Fact is, I've *never* been able to conceal it when I get fired up, but since I so rarely fought back, he wouldn't know that. "Did you forget about the part where you continuously beat me? Or when you cheated on me? How about the part right before I left where you *raped me?*"

"I did no such thing. We both know you wanted it. That you get off when I'm rough with you because you're my dirty whore. Now, I won't repeat myself, watch how you're speaking to me, or you're going to force me to punish you twice as hard."

I throw the covers off my body and leap out of bed, enraged. "Fuck you, Sebastian! I am your *nothing!* You don't get to tell me what to do ever again! I should've left years ago! There's not a snowball's chance in hell I will *ever* come back, so you'd better prepare yourself now. I *will* be filin' for divorce, and I will no longer be your wife. If you want to push me, trust me when I say *you* won't like the consequences. Don't forget about that little video I have on my phone."

Holy shit. I can't believe I just threatened him! Don't get me wrong; it's long overdue, and I won't take it back, but my lord, I didn't think I had it in me. As much as I'd like to pretend I'm not afraid of Sebastian, you can't just reverse over a decade of psychological warfare by creating a little distance. There's complete silence on the other line. I don't know why I'm still entertaining this conversation, but I check to see if the call is still connected.

It is.

I clear my throat. "Lose this number, Sebastian. If I never talk to you again, that'll be too soon."

I hang up before he has a chance to reply. Ugh! I throw my phone on the mattress and pull my bathrobe over my shoulders. I'll never go back to sleep now, so there's no point in trying. I can smell the coffee brewing in the kitchen, so I might as well head down there and get some. I storm out of my room and come to a grinding halt when I reach the top of the stairs. At the bottom, leaning against the wall, lazily sipping a cup of coffee, is none other than Beckett Armstrong.

He raises a single brow at me in a challenge. Oh, screw him. I'm not going to let him stop me from getting my cup of liquid gold.

"Excuse me." I give him a *get out of my way* look. "I need caffeine."

To my surprise, Beck steps aside, allowing me entry into the kitchen. I grab a mug from the cabinet, pour some French Roast into the cup, and add a healthy amount of milk and sugar. I can feel him behind me, watching my every move. After taking my first sip, I turn around to face him.

"What are you doing here?" I look at the clock on the microwave. "Don't you have work to do or somethin'?"

That's the thing about running a ranch. There are no days off. Not really. The animals depend on you to care for them. The best you can hope for is to be on-call one or two days a week and not be needed. That's what Beck's dad did while we were growing up. Beckett never was afraid of hard work, though.

He sets his mug on the counter before leaning against it, ankles casually crossed in front of him. He's no more than two feet away, and I'm fairly certain that was intentional. "You okay, Pres?"

"I'm fine." I lift my chin. "Now, answer my question. Why are you here? Why are you drinkin' my parents' coffee instead of your own?" I look around. "Speaking of... where are they?"

Beck inclines his head toward the window that overlooks the front of the house. "They went for a ride to catch the sunrise."

"That still doesn't explain why you're here at six-thirty on a Saturday morning."

He gives me his all-knowing smile. "I have a standing invitation to join your mom for coffee *every* morning. When I got here, she was just heading to the stables but told me to help myself like I always do."

My mouth gapes. "Wait... what? Why? Since when?"

His mouth kicks up in the corner. "Can I answer one question before you bombard me with twenty more?"

I set my coffee down and make a *hurry-up* gesture with my hand. "By all means."

"Since I got back."

I narrow my eyes. "I haven't seen you in the house once in the three weeks I've been here."

"That's because your mom asked me to give you some space."

"And that's no longer the case?" When Beck shakes his head, I add, "Why's that?"

He searches my eyes for a moment before replying. "Because I'm done giving you space, and I told her as much. You've had more than enough by now, don't you think?"

I rest my elbows on the counter behind me. "Shouldn't I have a say in this?"

Beck's gaze drops, and when I look down, I see why. The belt on my robe loosened just enough to reveal the thin tank top I wore to bed. Of course, my traitorous nipples are saluting him again. I pull my robe closed and tie the belt in a double knot, which only seems to amuse him.

I snap my fingers in front of my face. "My eyes are up here, Beckett."

"I'm well aware, *Presley*." His full lips form into a

cocky grin as he taps his temple. "Every inch of you is stored up here. Well... almost every inch."

I huff, completely ignoring the implication about my breasts. That comment should piss me off because there was nothing gentlemanly about it, but my stupid hormones disagree. The moment the words left Beck's mouth, I had to stop myself from leaning into him so he could feel me up like a horny teenager. After listening to Sebastian spouting insults and threats earlier, the last thing I should want is for anyone to touch me. Lord, my head's a mess of contradictions right now.

"Whatever. If you won't leave, I'll take my coffee in the bedroom."

Before I get the chance to walk away, he asks, "Who were you talking to earlier?"

Did he hear my conversation with Sebastian? I wasn't exactly quiet now that I think about it. Crap. How am I supposed to explain that?

"What do you mean?" I've learned that when all else fails, denial is your friend.

"Was it him?" A muscle jumps in his cheek. "Your husband? I couldn't hear much of what you were sayin', but it didn't sound like a pleasant conversation."

So much for denial. I should've known he wouldn't let it go so easily.

"That's none of your business, Beckett. *Nothing* I do or say is any of your business."

I tell myself not to fidget under his intense scrutiny. "What if I want to *make it* my business?"

"What happened to, *I don't want anything from you, darlin'?*" I lower my voice mockingly on that last part. "Besides, I don't think your girlfriend would appreciate that very much."

"Things change. Including the fact that I don't have a girlfriend. Technically, I haven't had one of those since you."

When Beck went chasing after Nicky last night, the possibility that they'd reconcile was nagging at me. I snort to disguise the relief I feel, reminding myself I shouldn't care one way or the other.

"Pretty sure Nicky would see it differently."

Beck nods once. "And *that* was part of the problem."

I pinch the bridge of my nose. "Can we please cut through all the bull? If you have somethin' to say, Beckett, just say it."

"Where's your wedding ring?"

I shrug, eyes falling to the floor. "Your guess is as good as mine at this point."

"Did you leave him? Is that why you came back?"

My eyes fill with tears, but I manage to hold them in. "Yes."

"Why?"

My head snaps up. "Why *what?*"

Beck's face falls, probably because I'm about to lose the battle with my tears. "Pres."

I flinch when he reaches a hand out. I've hated being touched for so long, it's a habit. My actions have absolutely nothing to do with the man before me, but the look on his face says he thinks it does.

"What was *that?*"

"I told you yesterday not to touch me, Beckett. That hasn't changed." When denial fails, try diversion. That's another thing I've learned during my marriage.

He considers that for a moment. "And that's all it is?"

I raise my eyebrows. "What else would it be?"

Beck studies my face, his intense focus making me fidget. I swear he's trying to ferret out every single thought I've ever had.

"What are you hiding, Presley?"

I swallow, trying my damnedest not to react. "What makes you think I'm hiding something?"

His brown eyes drill into me. "Because I got *really* good at reading people while I was in the Navy. And like it or not, I know you. I have no doubt you're hiding something pretty damn significant."

I shake my head. "You *don't* know me, Beck. Not anymore. Just like I don't know you."

He hasn't stopped staring at me, looking at me like he used to when we were kids. Like his proprietary claim on my heart is infallible. Like he's one-hundred percent confident I'm his, and I'll always be his, no matter what life throws our way.

If only that were true.

I'm not sure how much time passes before Beck stands to his full height and takes a few steps backward. "That's where you're wrong, Pres. I may not know what's gone down in your life since you left, and vice versa, but I know *you*. I *see* you, whether you want me to or not. You can't hide whatever it is that you're holdin' onto forever. When you're ready to talk, you know where to find me."

"Don't hold your breath," I mutter.

The infuriating man simply winks before stepping onto the porch. I watch out the kitchen window as he walks away, wondering what the hell I'm going to do about him. Avoiding Beck would take some serious effort, and quite frankly, I don't think I want to. I've been lugging around secrets and shame for so long, I didn't realize how tightly wound that made me until now. And the reason I've come to that realization is that when Beck was standing here next to me just now, for the first time in forever, I felt like I could breathe. I felt safe. Strong. *Free.*

Not once did I censor my words in fear of being struck. I didn't worry that I was less than perfect standing here in my bathrobe with no makeup and messy hair. The disgust I'd feel when using my body as a vessel to mollify someone else's rage was nonexistent. My integrity was firmly in place instead of being sacrificed to feed a brutal man's ego. Everything that made me anxious daily just disappeared. At least for those few moments. I don't think people realize what a luxury those things are until they've had them stripped away. I know I certainly didn't. After everything I've endured, I am well aware of how truly precious it is.

The brief reminder of what life feels like when you're not always walking on eggshells reaffirms that I did the right thing by leaving Sebastian. The road ahead might not be easy, but I feel better equipped to handle it. Maybe it's this ranch, maybe it's the people, hell, maybe it's just the fact that I'm not living under the same roof with him anymore. Whatever the reason, the fact remains that I'll no longer allow Sebastian to control me. I'll no longer let *anyone* control me.

Chapter Twenty-Nine
Beckett

"I hate to tell you this, buddy, but you're fucked."

Tommy glares at Chase Bradshaw. "You think you're so goddamn funny, Bradshaw. Not everyone's woman wants to run off to Vegas to elope."

Bradshaw grins. "Aw, don't be mad, sweetheart, just because I didn't have to sell a kidney on the underground market to pay for my wedding."

Carson laughs. "I still can't believe you asked if you could forgo the fancy dinner. Dude, you're never getting pussy again."

Everyone but Tommy laughs at that.

"Yeah, yeah," Tommy grumbles. "Laugh it up, assholes. You just wait until—"

I curse as our Humvee goes airborne.

Everything happens in slow motion. I don't know how much time passes before my ass is skidding across the ground. My ears won't stop ringing. There's chaos all around, flames licking at my skin, but all I can focus on is *the buzzing in my ears as I inch away from the heat. It's so fucking hot. I'm leaving a trail of red as I scoot my body forward. I'm still trying to make sense of what's happening when I bump into something. Correction: not something. Someone.*

I recoil when I realize what I've grabbed. My eyes come into focus, my hand coated in my brother's blood. When my gaze lands on his face, Tommy's lifeless eyes are frozen open in abject terror. I don't need to check for a pulse to know that he's gone. The entire lower half of his body is missing. Probably somewhere near the blast site—I'm not sure how far we were thrown. My head falls as spots dance across my vision. My vision blurs in and out, but all I see are his dead eyes staring back at me.

As my eyes open and close, Tom's broad nose narrows. His dark skin pales. When my lids open again, round hazel eyes that I'd know anywhere are looking back at me. Full lips that I spent countless hours kissing are now moving, but I can't hear the words. I can only read her lips as she pleads with me to save her. I scream her name, trying to inch closer, but it's no use. I can't move. I'm losing consciousness. The last thing I see is Presley mouthing the words, 'Beckett, don't let me die.'

"Fuck."

I jackknife into a sitting position and run a hand through my damp hair. I haven't had a nightmare that vivid in months, and I've *never* had one with Presley in it.

Christ, just when I thought they couldn't get any worse.

I climb out of bed and go through the motions of taking a hot shower to ward off the bone-deep chill that always accompanies a flashback. By the time I'm dressed and done eating breakfast, I'm still feeling restless, unable to shake off the dream. Thankfully, it's Sunday, so I'm on-call while the ranch hands take care of the animals. One of the mares is due to give birth any day now, so I need to stick close by, but I could really use some time to decompress, and I know just the perfect way to do it.

First, I need to talk Presley into it.

I walk down to the main house and get there just as her parents are leaving for church.

Mrs. J smiles when she sees me. "Good morning, Beckett. Did you come to join us for the early service?"

She knows that I lost my faith a long time ago, but it hasn't stopped her from trying.

"No, thank you, ma'am. I was about to go for a ride. Came to see if Presley wanted to join me."

They both raise their brows, but it's Mr. J who speaks first. "I think that's a great idea, son." He points a stern finger at me. "But if she says no, don't push it."

I nod. "Yes, sir."

He pats me on the back. "I take that back. Push her a little. I think it'd be good for her to take the old girl out."

I give him a crooked smile. "I'll do my best."

"Go on now." Mrs. J gives me a little shove. "You know where everything is."

"That I do." I nod. "Wish me luck."

They both laugh as they get in the truck. I let myself into the house and look around.

"Pres? You in here?"

She doesn't answer, so I check the kitchen and family room before heading upstairs. As I get halfway up, the reason she's not answering becomes obvious. The shower in the hallway bathroom is on. I tell my dick to ignore the fact that Presley is naked right behind that thin piece of wood and head down the hall to the last bedroom. The door is cracked, so I push it all the way open and stand there in shock.

It's like I jumped in a time machine that spit me out right in this very spot. I don't know why I'm so surprised, considering nothing else in the house has changed, but this room is *exactly* the same as the last time I saw it. There's a queen-sized bed in the middle of the room with the same purple and white quilt her grandmother made for her sixteenth birthday. The oak dresser and desk are still set against the opposite wall, matching nightstands on each side of the bed. Her cheerleading pom-pom is still wedged between the mirror above the dresser and the wall, its blue and yellow strands flopping over the reflective surface. Damn, the room even smells the same, like that honey and orange blossom lotion she favored.

There's a corkboard over the desk with miscellaneous pictures and show ribbons tacked to it. I step closer and glance at the photos. There are a few of Presley with her parents or Clayton, Pres riding Mag, Pres showing Mag, and... shit, I haven't seen this thing in forever. I trace my finger over the image of Presley looking like my teenage wet dream. She's wearing her tiny cheerleading uniform, hair pulled up high, tied with an oversized navy bow. I'm right next to her, dripping with sweat from the game, with my flattened hair plastered to my forehead, but Presley didn't seem to mind. She's curled into my side as close as she can be, beaming at the camera. God, we were so fucking happy. We were *always* so fucking happy until the one day it all went to hell.

"I love that picture."

"Shit."

I'm surprised she was able to sneak up on me. My hearing isn't nearly as good as it used to be, but I can usually sense when someone's at my back. I've been trained for it, for fuck's sake. I think being in this room is throwing me off my game. When I turn around and get my first glimpse of Presley, I have to focus on not gaping like an idiot. She's leaning against the doorframe, wrapped in a fluffy white towel, long wet locks hanging over her shoulder. Her hand is clutched where the towel is knotted at her breasts, which only draws my eyes to them more. My fists clench as I fight the urge to wipe the stray droplets away.

"What are you doing here, Beckett?"

It takes me a second to realize she said something. "Your folks let me in. I'm about to head out for a ride and wanted to see if you'd join me."

Her delicate brows draw together. "On a horse?"

I smile. "Well, I suppose we could take my truck

somewhere if you wanted... or maybe a quad. But I'd prefer the horses."

Presley shakes her head. "I don't know if I remember how to ride."

I laugh but quickly cut it off when I figure out that she's not joking. "Wait... you're serious? When's the last time you rode?"

Surely they had stables somewhere within driving distance from New York City.

Her greenish-gold eyes fall to the floor. "A little over twelve years ago? The last time we went, whenever that was."

My jaw does drop this time. "How is that possible, Pres? You *love* riding."

"Loved," she corrects. "I didn't leave the city much when I lived up north. And if I did... well, let's just say my husband isn't a fan of the country, or anything remotely resembling country living."

I grind my teeth together at the mention of that bastard. Standing in this room, Pres wearing nothing but a towel, it's too easy to forget things have changed. Sure, she said she's leaving him, but nothing is ever set in stone until she no longer has his name.

"Beckett?"

"I'll let you get dressed." I motion to the door, so she gets the hint and steps aside. "If you want to give it a try, I'll meet you out there. I'll probably head out in about thirty minutes." I give Pres a wide berth and start heading down the stairs.

"Wait."

I pause mid-step and look over my shoulder. "Yeah?"

She gives me a soft smile. "I'll meet you out there in fifteen."

"Yeah?"

Presley nods. "Yeah."

Well, okay then. I guess we're going riding.

Chapter Thirty
Presley

I spot Beckett as soon as I walk into the stables standing in front of Magnolia's stall. It looks like he's just finished tacking her up. I approach slowly from the side, extending my hand. I smile as Mag leans into my touch, and a soft, snorting sound escapes her. I still can't believe she remembers me after all these years. She was always a bit skittish around new people, but when I took her for a walk the other day, there was no apprehension whatsoever. Her ears were relaxed, her tail was swinging, and she wouldn't stop rubbing her head against me. When I brought her back to her stall, I could swear she was disappointed we didn't go for a ride, but I think she forgave me after I gave her a good rub down.

"Hey, girl, it's been a while, so I'm going to need you to take it easy on me, okay?"

Beck watches us for a moment before stepping back

to grab the other saddle. "Give me just a few, and I'll be ready to go."

He opens the gate three stalls down and takes a moment to greet the horse before slipping the halter over its head. Once it's secure, Beck leads the animal out and ties her to the hitching post.

"Presley, meet Moonshine."

I lift my brows. "Moonshine? As in the light from the moon or the liquor?"

He grins. "What do you think?"

I shake my head. Beck's dad loved making apple pie moonshine, and Beck and I had been known to sneak some on occasion. We'd sit out by the pond, slowly sipping it throughout the night. Sometimes we'd talk for hours. Other times, Beck would bring his guitar and sing songs, intentionally screwing up the lyrics to make me laugh. Then there were the times when we were so busy loving each other with our bodies, we didn't have time for words. I duck my head, trying to hide my smile, but I know he sees it.

I stroke Magnolia's neck and mane as I watch Beck giving Moonshine's glossy black coat a good once-over with the brush before cleaning out her hooves. Once she's all saddled and ready to go, we lead our horses out of the stable.

Beck holds out Mag's left stirrup. "Hop on, Pres."

I take a deep breath, loop my fingers under the rein, and grab the horn. Beck doesn't release the stirrup until my foot is firmly in place, and I'm pulling myself up.

I blink a few times, shocked that it only took one attempt. "Whoa, that was much easier than I was expecting."

"Told you. Just like riding a bike. You look good up there."

I chuckle. "It *feels* good up here, but there's no need to be cocky, Armstrong."

"We both know that's not true." Beck mounts his horse like a pro and winks.

My cheeks warm, and I get this strange flutter in my stomach. It takes me a moment to realize I'm blushing.

Beck laughs when he gets a good look at my flush. "Nice to see that I haven't lost my touch."

Beck gives Moonshine a little nudge, and she starts off on a walk with Magnolia and me following. Wow, this *is* like riding a bike. I'm not about to go barrel racing, but I think I can handle a slow ride.

I give him a wry look. "You know... if this friendship thing is going to work, you can't be doin' that."

"Doin' what?"

I flick my finger between us. "The flirting. If you want to be friends, you need to back off on the flirting."

He laughs. "I never said I wanted to be your friend, Pres."

"Oh." I bite my lip, unsure of how to respond to that.

Beckett shakes his head. "I meant that I don't want to settle for being your friend. I want it all. No point in trying to deny that any longer."

"Beck," I groan. "I'm not... we're not... I haven't even filed for divorce yet. I can't think of anything beyond getting past that right now."

"So, I'll wait." He maneuvers the horse, so he's on my right. When I give him an inquisitive look, he says, "I lost the hearing in my right ear a while back. It's easier for me if you're speaking on this side."

My brows draw together. "How did that happen?"

His shoulders lift. "IED."

I wait for him to say more, but he doesn't. "Um... you can't just tell me something like that and not explain. Is that why you're no longer in the Navy?"

Beck nods. "What's there to say? One minute we were driving, and in the next we got up close and personal with an explosive."

I gasp. "How did you make it out of that? Did anyone die?"

I'm aware being in the military poses a safety risk, but knowing this man came so close to death doesn't sit well. What if he didn't survive? What if the last time I ever saw him was the day I walked away from him?

He looks away. "You're not the only one with shit they don't like talkin' about, Pres."

I consider that for a moment. As curious as I am about what happened, I respect that he doesn't want to relive it by sharing the details with me, so we ride in silence for about fifteen minutes before I realize where Beck's taking me. My breath hitches when the pond comes into view. I shift my weight deep in the saddle, lean back, and tighten Mag's rein, signaling her to stop.

My parents' house hasn't changed one bit, but it's the exact opposite here. The trees surrounding the water are fuller and taller. Instead of a narrow, worn-out cedar dock, there's one twice its original width with a large side deck at the end. The side deck has a small gazebo built into it with a hammock hanging in the middle. I can just imagine lying beneath the canopy to escape the hot summer sun, birdsong and croaking frogs providing the perfect soundtrack for you to drift off into a nap.

"Wow. How long has this been here?"

"About five years," he answers.

Beck dismounts, leading Moonshine over to a wooden hitching rail—also a new addition—and ties her up. I follow his lead and do the same with Magnolia. Being here stirs up all sorts of conflicting feelings. I'm in awe—it's even more beautiful than I remember—and I'm hit with the warmth of nostalgia. Many beautiful memories were created in this very spot. Yet, as I think about the last time I was here... when Beck and I made love, knowing it was goodbye... I'm overwhelmed by sadness. He and I used to talk about getting married at the edge of the dock. Building a house here and raising children, watching them making their own memories. The fact that none of those things will ever happen fills me with profound regret. I'm on autopilot as I walk across the wooden planks, running my finger along the gazebo's railing. There are built-in benches on the inside, so I drop down on one, looking out at the water, dabbing at the tears forming in the corner of my eye as I soak it all in.

Beck takes a seat beside me. "There was a mission. We were riding in the Humvee, scoping out an area; fairly routine stuff. One of our brothers—this guy named Tommy—was planning on getting married when we got back to the States. His fiancée wanted this really extravagant wedding, and we were giving him shit about how much it was going to cost. He was talking to Andrea—that's her name—earlier in the day, and she was going on and on about dining options, asking how he felt about steak and lobster." His lips form into a faint smirk. "She was *not* happy when he asked if they could serve chicken nuggets instead. Anyway... one minute, we were all laughing about Tommy being in the doghouse, and in the next... we weren't.

"I have flashbacks sometimes. Mostly while I'm asleep, but every once in a while, something will trigger a memory, like a sudden loud noise. They only come in bits and pieces—a lot of smoke, this extreme heat that I can somehow still *feel*. Blood... so much fucking blood. The one part that's always crystal clear is Tommy. As I was crawling on the ground, disoriented, ears ringing, in more pain than I could've ever imagined, bleeding heavily from the shrapnel that lodged itself into my leg... I found him." Beck turns his head in my direction. "*Half* of him. I reached out to Andrea afterward... maybe two months later. She told me that she'll never forgive herself for the fact that she hung up on him without saying 'I love you' like she usually did at the end of their calls. They grew up together, were high school sweethearts. Almost every memory she had was with Tommy, and suddenly, she had to figure out how to survive without the one person on earth who made her whole." He turns back to the pond, eyes unfocused. "Puts things in perspective, you know?"

I nod, my eyes blurry from tears. "Yeah."

"When I came back here... sitting around trying to cope with the mess in my head wasn't doing anyone any favors. And then my dad died, which turned up the noise to deafening volumes, no pun intended. Colby suggested I try the whole *fake it until you make it* approach, but I've always thought that was shit advice. Instead, I decided to face my problems head-on. Forced myself out of bed every day and worked hard. Kept busy. If the day went to hell, I'd get up the next morning and try again." He gestures to the dock. "This was my first project. I chose it because this spot haunted me more than any other place on this ranch. I was determined to make it a place that brought me peace again. It took me a lot longer than I would've liked to finish it. I had already taken over my dad's position at that point, so I could only work on it on days when I was on-call."

"Did it work? Do you feel at peace when you're here?"

"Close enough. I'll come out here when I'm having a rough day. Sometimes, I'll fish, but mostly, I'll lie in the hammock and just *be*. This seems to be the only place where I can successfully do that."

I don't question it when Beck reaches for my hand and twines our fingers together.

"I told myself that if you were happy with him, I wouldn't interfere. I was so fucking angry that you married another man, and I won't ever pretend to understand it, but we were young, Pres. We both made mistakes. Maybe you should've never left, but maybe I should've fought harder to keep you. It took me a long time to realize that, but I do now.

"The fact of the matter is, you're back, and I'm tired of being the guy who's always pissed off at the world. I don't want old scars getting in the way of my future happiness. I don't want to figure out how to live life without you again. I barely survived it the first time; I don't think I could handle it a second. *You're my person,* Presley. You have been since the moment we met. Your absence didn't change that, even though sometimes, I wished like hell it would.

"I know you have your own demons, and you have shit to wade through, but whatever's troubling you isn't going to dissuade me. If you need time, I'll give you time. But unless you can honestly say you don't want me, too, that I'm not the one person on earth who makes you feel whole, I need you. I need you to be open to the possibility of us being together again, whenever that may be."

I wipe the tears streaming down my face with my free hand. "Too much has happened, Beck. If you knew... you wouldn't be saying these things. You wouldn't want me. I don't just have baggage. I have the entire carousel."

Beck shifts his body toward mine. He swipes a thumb across my cheek, wiping away the wetness. "And you think I don't have my own issues? Darlin', I've got issues and then some. My mind can be a fucked-up place. I still see a counselor sometimes when things get really bad. But I get up every morning, work hard, and focus on surviving one day at a time. It's all I can do, but I'm tired of doing it alone, Presley, and I'd bet you are, too. When I said I wanted all of you, I meant it. I want the good and the bad. So, we should be askin' ourselves, why can't we focus on healing together? What's stopping us from doing just that? Life's not worth livin' if we're just surviving."

I shake my head. "It's not that simple. God, Beck, I wish it were, but it's just not."

"So, *make it* that simple. Stop thinkin' about whatever's going on back in New York. Focus on the here and now. Focus on how you feel being on this ranch again." Beck jerks his head toward the horses. "How you feel when you're near them. How you feel when you're near *me*. You'll never know if it'll work if you don't try, Pres."

I think about everything he's said. There's so much heartache to overcome. So much trauma. Can I really push that aside and focus on the present? I look around, remembering all of the good times this place has seen, wondering if I can ever feel that kind of happiness again. It seems so farfetched, but I do think Beck's right about one thing. I won't ever know if I don't try, and the last thing I need is more regret.

I squeeze his hand. "I can't make any promises... but... I'll try."

Beck's face lights up in a grin as he bumps his shoulder into mine. "Yeah?"

I nod, infusing as much conviction into my reply as I can manage. "Yeah."

Chapter Thirty-One
Presley

"Hey. Can I get a beer?"

"Hey, yourself." I smile, popping the top off a Coors and setting it in front of Beck. "What are you doing here?"

"Came to see you." He takes a long drag from the bottle, never once looking away. "That okay?"

"Sure." I prop my hand on the edge of the bar, leaning into him. "I mean, I'm working, so I can't chat with you all night, but things have been slow since the dinner rush ended."

"Hey, Pres, can you—" Clayton notices Beck as he returns from the storeroom and lifts his eyebrows when he sees how close we're talking. "Hey, Cowboy. To what do we owe the honor of your presence on a Monday night?"

Beck flips my brother off, making me chuckle. Clayton told me Beck *hates* that nickname, and therefore, Clayton being Clayton, uses it as often as possible. "I didn't realize I was limited to certain days."

"You're not." Clay gives him a knowing smirk. "I'm just surprised, that's all. Although I suppose I shouldn't be, all things considered."

Beckett's forehead is lined with creases. "What's that supposed to mean?"

Clayton looks around at the other patrons before returning his gaze to Beck. "I think you know *exactly* what I mean. Although, if you'd like, I'd be more than happy to explain in front of all these people."

My eyes widen. "Clayton."

My annoying brother laughs. "Relax, kiddo. I'm just fucking with him. I think it's great you two are getting along. If you'll excuse me, I'll hang out on the other end of the bar so I can pretend I don't overhear anything that would offend my delicate sensibilities."

I smirk. "I'm pretty sure you and I have very different definitions of *delicate sensibilities*."

Clayton gasps loudly and presses an open palm over his heart, channeling his inner Southern Belle. "Why, Presley Anne, bless your heart. I have no idea what you're talkin' about. I am an angel, sent straight from the heavens to do God's work. I wouldn't dream of misbehavin'."

There is nothing ladylike about my snort. "Clayton, you and I both know there aren't many things you enjoy more than misbehavin'."

"Don't you know it," he says, dropping the act. "It's what makes life worth livin'."

Beck and I exchange a loaded glance. I'm sure he's thinking about our conversation by the pond yesterday, too. I couldn't stop replaying it in my head all night, and it's the first thing I thought of when I woke up this morning. When Derek's wife, Melissa, called to discuss filing for divorce, I didn't feel the dread that I usually feel when thinking about Sebastian. Melissa's going to prepare the paperwork and let me know when my soon-to-be-ex-husband's been served. I should probably be nervous about Sebastian's reaction, but instead, I'm excited that I've taken the first step to put the last twelve years behind me.

I can't keep focusing on things that are out of my control; Sebastian's temper is one of them. He's going to do what he's going to do, and I'll just have to cross that bridge when I get to it. For now, I'm going to focus on finding little pockets of joy in my day however I can, and I have a feeling the man before me is going to be a big part of that.

"Yeah... I don't need to see *anyone* looking at my baby sister like that, least of all the man who's practically a brother to me. It's kind of creepy when you think about how incest-adjacent the whole thing is." Clayton shudders and inclines his head to the left. "If you need me, I'll be over there."

I shake my head. "You're an idiot, Clayton."

"Love you too, Pres," he calls over his shoulder.

Beck smirks. "Don't let him fool you; he's happy to have you back. We all are."

Of course, the moment the words leave his mouth,

the one woman who's definitely not happy I'm back, walks in. When she sees Beck and me, she glares and tugs on the arm of the man behind her, dragging him to a booth in the back.

"Who's your hot date, Nicky?" Clayton shouts. "Aren't you going to introduce us?" He laughs when she raises her middle finger in the air without looking back.

Clay walks back over to where I'm standing. "Well, that didn't take long. I thought she'd give it at least a week before she started spreading those long legs for someone else."

I whack my brother with a dishtowel. "Clayton, don't be so crass."

I watch Beck carefully, seeing if he's bothered by the fact that the woman he'd seen for two years has moved on so quickly. There are no outward signs, but I don't know if I can read him as well as I used to.

"You okay?"

Beck lifts his brows. "Why wouldn't I be?"

I shrug. "It's okay if you're not, you know. You spent two years of your life with her."

He takes another pull from his beer. "Pres, I think you're overestimating the situation. It wasn't like that."

I cross my arms over my chest. "What's that supposed to mean?"

Beck swallows. "It means it wasn't like that."

"What my good pal here is tryin' to say," Clayton offers, "is that he and Nicky never did much talkin' during the time they spent together. There was no substance behind it. She was just a warm hole to sink his dick into."

I gasp at the same time beer goes spraying out of Beck's mouth. "Christ, Clayton. Really? I was trying to be a goddamn gentleman."

Clay holds up his hands in surrender. "I'm just telling it like it is, buddy."

I take deep breaths, telling myself to calm down. Obviously, I know Beck had slept with Nicky, likely many, many times. Still, the visual my brother just planted in my head is something I could've gone my whole life without. And the worst part is, this town is too small to avoid her altogether, especially if I'm going to be workin' here. This is the only place in town that serves alcohol. It's where most people around here go for dates because the next closest option is thirty minutes away. I thought I could do this, but being faced with the drama head-on, I'm not so sure anymore.

I wipe my sweaty palms on the half apron I'm wearing. "I'll be right back."

Beck gets up from his stool when I start walking away. "Pres—"

I hold my hand up. "I'm fine, Beckett. I just need a minute."

"Thanks a lot, asshole," I hear Beck mutter behind my back because, of course, he's following me.

He catches up to me right as I'm pushing through the door to Clayton's office. I spin around when I hear him lock the door behind us.

"Beckett, I told you I needed a minute. What part of that do you not understand?"

"I told you I'm done giving you space, Presley."

I park a hand on my hip. "You also told me you'd give me *time*, which is what I just asked for."

His jaw tics. "Not when you get that look in your eye like you're gettin' ready to run."

I sigh as I prop my butt against the edge of Clay's desk. "I'm not running away. I just... needed a minute to think."

"What happened back there, Pres?"

I pinch the bridge of my nose. "It's stupid. I'm being stupid."

"Hey." Goose bumps form on my arms when he pulls my hand away from my face. He waits until I look up before speaking again. "I don't want to hear you say things like that. Now, tell me what happened back there."

I shrug. "When Clay... what he said... it made me picture things I never wanted to think about. I know I have no right to be bothered by it, but it still leaves a sick feeling in my stomach."

Beck cringes. "If I could take it all back, so you'd never have to deal with things like this, I would."

I shake my head. "That's my point, Beckett. *You shouldn't have to.* You had every right to date whoever you wanted. My insecurities are just getting the best of me."

"Pres." He places his hands over each side of my jaw and presses his forehead against mine. "You have *nothing* to be insecure about. You're all I see. You're all I've *ever* seen. Nicole, or anyone else for that matter, was a futile attempt to take my mind off of you."

"Yeah... well... some habits are hard to break."

Beck pulls back and searches my eyes. "What'd he do to you?"

I avert my eyes. There are so many different ways to answer that question, and none of them are pleasant.

"Maybe this was a mistake, Beckett."

His entire body stiffens.

"What you and I had was over a long time ago. Maybe trying to recreate that is wishful thinking. I'm a mess, and I don't know if I'll ever fully get back to the girl I was."

He puts slight pressure on my jaw, prompting me to look at him. "Listen to me, Presley. What we had is not over. It was—"

"Beck, I can't—"

"Fuck it," he growls right before slamming his mouth over mine.

I squeal in surprise, which Beck takes advantage of by sliding his tongue into my mouth. The moment that happens, a switch is flipped, lighting me on fire. I throw my arms around his neck, pulling him into me. My memory didn't do this man's kissing skills justice. The soft velvety slide of his tongue against mine, the way he pulls back just enough to bite softly on my lower lip before diving back in again. The love and adoration that's suffused into every lick, every nibble, every groan are all-encompassing. The way his muscular body feels pressed against mine awakens a hunger inside of me that I've only known with Beckett. No matter how close we are, it's never enough. My need for this man is both electrifying and terrifying. How am I supposed to learn how to stand on my own two feet again when my very existence feels dependent upon his?

"Beckett," I pant. "Stop."

I've been so conditioned to having my pleas denied, the fact that Beck freezes immediately sends another shockwave to my senses. He helps me into an upright position—I hadn't even realized I was bent backward over the desk—then slowly removes his arms from around my back.

"What's wrong?"

I touch my fingers to my swollen lips. "What happened to taking it slow?"

His full lips curve into a cocky grin. "You wouldn't stop trying to think of excuses why this can't work, so I had to knock some sense into you somehow. It's the first thing I could think of."

I shake my head. "That can't happen again, Beck. I'm not ready. I'm still married. I haven't even filed for divorce yet. I'm going to... I've started the process... but I'm not there yet."

His face falls. "You're right; I'm sorry." I know I should look away as he discreetly adjusts the rather large problem in his pants, but I can't seem to do so. "But next time you try convincing yourself that this won't work, think about what just happened. What happened with Nicole and me doesn't matter. What happened with you and that bastard doesn't matter. What *does* matter is that kiss we just shared. It proves that we're not over, Presley. We were *never* over. You're lying to yourself if you think otherwise."

Chapter Thirty-Two
Presley

I give myself a few moments after Beckett leaves, but I know I need to get back out front before people start talkin'. I check my reflection in the little mirror on the wall and smooth down my hair. Once I'm presentable, I head back out and join Clayton behind the bar.

"Where's Beckett?"

Clay smiles. "Oh, you mean the guy who just walked out of here with nothing more than a half-assed wave and a shit-eating grin? A grin that matches yours, I might add."

I narrow my eyes. "Quit stirring the pot, Clayton."

"I'm not stirring the pot. I'm simply making an observation. Now, if you're done with your *break*, it's gettin' a little busy in here, and I could use some help."

Old Man Caruthers plops down on the stool in front of me to prove Clayton's point. "Hey there, pretty lady. Can I get a Jack and Coke when you get a moment?"

"On it," Clayton says, grabbing the soda dispenser and the bottle of whiskey. He sets the drink on the bar. "Now, remember, your beautiful wife says you only get one of these, so don't even think about asking for another."

Mr. Caruthers harrumphs. "Damn meddling woman. Always worried about my goddamn health."

"It's because she loves you so much, she wants to keep you around for as long as possible." I give him a flirty wink. "You can't blame her for that, right?"

"Yeah, yeah," he grumbles into his glass. "What about you? I heard you've ditched that husband of yours and moved back to Hope Springs."

"News travels fast," I say dryly. "Lucky me."

He flashes a big yellow-toothed smile before barking out a laugh. "Girl, you can't take a shit in this town without everyone knowin' about it. I bet you didn't have that problem up north."

"No, I did not."

But I had plenty of other problems.

Mr. Caruthers takes the final gulp of his drink and pins a ten-dollar bill beneath the glass. "Well, anyway, it's nice havin' you back, Presley. I'll be seein' you around."

Becca, one of the three servers working tonight, leans on the bar and whispers. "Uh, Clayton, I think we have a problem on seventeen."

Clay and I both look up to the table in question. I'm not entirely surprised she's referring to Nicky's table.

"What's she doin'?" Clay asks.

Becca looks over her shoulder. "She's only had two drinks since she's been here, but I suspect she indulged in a little pre-gaming beforehand. She keeps making unsavory comments about..." Her eyes slide in my direction. "Well, let's just say she's fast approaching cut-off, and I'm thinkin' she won't take that so well. Her date seems even worse."

"I'll take care of it," Clay promises. "Presley, call Colby for me, will ya? His cell number's by the phone. Tell him we might need some help convincing this guy he shouldn't be driving himself home."

I nod and do what he's asked. As I'm relaying the information to the sheriff, I watch Clayton approach Nicky's table. They exchange words, and from the looks of it, they're not all that pleasant. Her date stands up and puffs his chest out, trying to look intimidating, but my brother has six inches and at least fifty pounds on him. I see Colby's police cruiser pulling in front of the doors right as the man storms outside. Clayton and Nicky are still getting into it, their volume becoming increasingly louder. I consider intervening but think better of it. The only thing I'm bound to do is make the situation worse. Clayton motions Theo, one of the other servers, over. The two men discuss something briefly while Nicky is going off on Clayton, calling him all sorts of names.

"All right, that's enough, Nicky." Clay grabs her by

the elbow and starts weaving her through the tables.

"How many times do I have to tell you, dickbag? It's *Nicole!*"

"Sorry about the foul language, ma'am." Clayton winks at an older woman scandalized by Nicky's language. "Don't worry, folks, we'll get this all cleared up in no time. You each get a drink on the house for your troubles. C'mon, Nicole. Let's go have a chat in my office."

Theo sidles up to me behind the bar. "Damn, she's not taking the whole breakup very well, is she? I don't think I've ever seen her be *nice* per se, but ever since Beckett dumped her, she's like a swarm of Yellowjackets in a potato sack."

That's an interesting—yet freakishly accurate—analogy.

Colby pops his head inside. "Everything okay in here?"

I nod in the direction of the hallway leading to Clay's office. We can hear Nicky screaming from all the way over here, and if I'm not mistaken, she's throwing things. Poor Clayton. I'm sure this isn't the first time he's had to deal with an unreasonable drunk, but adding a woman scorned on top of it is just askin' for trouble.

"I think Clayton's got it handled, but it might not be a bad idea to check."

The sheriff smirks. "Nah, I'm sure he knows how to handle Nicky just fine. It'll be good for him."

My eyebrows rise. "You're not scared of Nicole, are

you?"

He laughs. "Hell, yes, I'm scared of her. That woman is scary. Very, *very* scary. Give Clay my condolences."

"Well, okay then. You have a good night, Sheriff."

"You too, Presley. Say hi to Beckett for me." He tips his hat with a wink as he walks out the door.

My chest tightens, and sweat beads my brow when a loud crash comes from the office. I know Clayton would rather die than raise a hand to a woman, but the noise triggers a memory of a man with fewer morals. I flash back to when Sebastian threw me into a glass coffee table, and it shattered from the impact. A large chard had pierced my side, and I really should've had stitches, but Sebastian wouldn't let me go to the hospital, so I had to make do with a butterfly bandage. Maybe if I had split my face open, he would've been more concerned about scarring, but since the cut was on my torso, he couldn't care less. He'd put a possessive hand over the jagged pink line as he was rutting into me sometimes. Looking back, I think he was proud of his mark on me as if it was his own personal brand. In a way, I suppose all of the scars he left behind are.

I blink away the awful memory as Clayton appears in the doorway, with a screaming Nicky thrown over his shoulder. "Pres, I don't suppose you'd mind keepin' an eye on things around here, would you? I need to take this banshee home before she breaks everything in my office."

Nicky's clenched fists are pounding on my brother's back as her long, black hair brushes against the back of his knees. "Clayton James, I swear to all that is holy, if you don't put me down right now, I will rip your balls from your body and feed them to you! Then, I'll repeat the process with your dick!"

Theo cringes. "Damn."

Clayton seems unconcerned by the colorful threat. "Keep it down, woman. People are eatin' here. They don't need to hear about your strange fetishes."

When Nicky screeches, I see why my brother chose that particular mythical creature.

"Yep, I'm good. Are you sure you're safe driving with her acting like that? Maybe we should get Colby back here."

"Yes!" Nicky shouts. "Call the sheriff! Tell him I'm being kidnapped by this jackass!"

"Nah, I'm good," Clayton insists. "I'll be back as soon as possible."

Nicky raises her head as they're heading for the door. Her face is cherry red from all the blood rushing to it. That doesn't stop her from glaring at me with all her might and delivering a parting shot. "Beckett might screw you six ways from Sunday, but he'll never love you, Presley. He's too messed up to be capable of lovin' anybody anymore."

"I said, keep quiet, damn it," Clayton grunts as he adjusts her weight over his shoulder and ducks down low enough to get her out the door without clocking her head on the doorframe. "Call if you need anything, Pres!"

When the door swings shut behind them, my eyes

wander across the bar to find every single person staring in the direction Clay and Nicky just went. They all blink rapidly, some with their mouths still hanging open from the spectacle. It takes 'em a moment to realize the show's over.

"Those two really need to bang each other's brains out and get it over with." Becca sets her tray on the bar. "Can I get two Crowns straight-up and a Bud Light Lime, hun?"

I pull out two glasses and start filling the order for her table. "Who should screw each other's brains out?"

She looks at me like I'm an idiot. "Your brother and Nicole. They've been dancing around each other for years."

I frown in confusion. "But..."

Becca smiles. "But she wasn't technically single? Oh, sugar, I'm talking *way* before that. This has been going on for many, many years. I'm fairly certain they hook up whenever she's not datin' someone else, but they keep it low key."

No way. I would've known about that, right? I know Nicky and Clay fooled around when we were younger, but that was back when Nicky was a tolerable human being. Clayton can't stand her now, and from what I've seen, the feeling's mutual.

Becca laughs as I set the drinks on her tray. "Don't underestimate the power of a good hate fuck. Just ask him about it. Maybe he'll come clean with you, considering you're related and all."

Oh, don't worry; I plan to.

Chapter Thirty-Three
Beckett

"Where are we going, Beckett?"

I look at Presley out of the corner of my eye as I switch the blinker on. "We're almost there."

The construction crew just finished paving the new driveway for the lodge. I wanted Pres to have the full experience the first time she saw it, which is why I'm taking her down this route instead of riding across the property. She gasps when the building comes into view. Only the framework is done so far, but it's obvious it will be larger than the average house around here.

"What is this? My parents didn't tell me they were building a new house."

I shift my Ford into park and kill the engine, but I leave the high-beams on so she can see better. I'd prefer doing this when we had daylight, but I had to work past sunset, and I didn't want to wait any longer to show her.

"Technically, it's a lodge."

"For what?"

"Get out, and I'll tell you."

Presley meets me at the front of the truck. "So? Spill."

"We're starting a program—an equine-therapy program for people suffering from PTSD, to be more specific. Unfortunately, insurance companies won't cover an expense like this, but we've secured some private funding for veterans and victims of abuse, which will be earmarked for people who can't afford to pay out of pocket. They'll come here for a retreat-like experience, but it'll be focused on helping them develop coping skills that will allow them to function better when they get back home. Horses have been proven to be effective therapy animals, so the program is being designed where the guests will have daily interactions with them. The new indoor arena is going to be part of it."

Presley stares up at the bones of what'll eventually become an impressive structure. I can practically see the thoughts racing through her head, but it takes her a good minute before she says anything.

"This is incredible, Beckett." When she turns to me, her eyes are glassy. "Really, *truly* incredible. Who thought of this?"

I adjust the brim of my ball cap. "Uh... I did. I mean, the concept, in general, isn't new, but I'm spearheading the whole thing. Your folks have been incredibly supportive from day one, though."

Presley's eyes bounce between mine like she's having some sort of internal debate. I grab her hand and place it on my chest. She used to always do that when we were younger... place her hand over my heart to feel its beat. She said it soothed her.

"Talk to me, Pres."

Her tears spill over before she quickly brushes them away. "Lord, I feel like I'm always crying around you. I really need to stop doing that."

"Honey, if you need to cry, then cry. Don't hide from me. You're safe with me. No matter what, Pres, you'll always be safe with me."

Presley's blonde hair spills over the side of her face as her head drops to my chest. Her body starts shaking violently, right before the most gut-wrenching keening sound escapes her lips, and she completely loses it. Shit, what did I say that caused this?

"Shh, Pres." I smooth my hand through her hair. "What'd I say? I didn't mean to upset you."

"It's not you." She hiccups a sob. "I think what you're doing is amazing, Beckett. Absolutely amazing."

My brows draw together. "Then, why are you crying?"

"I don't... I can't..." She loops her arms around my waist and squeezes.

I take a deep breath and run my hand along her back. "It's okay, you don't need to tell me. Just let it out, darlin'."

And she does. When her legs become unsteady, I carefully lower both of our bodies to the ground, draping her over my lap, so she's not sitting directly on the dirt. I've seen this woman cry many times over the years, but nothing like this. Not even after we lost the baby. I don't think I've ever felt more helpless in my life. These tears... they're pure, soul-shredding agony. It's like she's exorcising every demon she's ever had all at once. Eventually, her tears dry up, but she makes no move to leave.

"Can I do anything?"

She tucks her face into the crook of my neck. "You're doin' it, Beckett. Just be here with me."

"The forecast is callin' for rain tonight. What do you say we move this inside?"

"I know it's probably getting late, but I don't want to leave you right now."

"I didn't say you had to." I slide my finger under her chin, raising her face up to me. "We can go back to my place if that's okay with you. I'll take you home whenever you're ready."

Presley nods. "Okay."

I scoot her off my lap so we can stand and help her inside the cab of the truck before rounding the hood and hopping in on the driver's side.

Presley flips the visor down and looks at herself in the mirror. "My God, I'm a blotchy mess."

I pull her hand away from her face and weave our fingers together. "You're gorgeous, Pres."

She ducks her head shyly and looks out the window. We make the short drive in complete silence, all the way until she steps through my front door.

"Wow."

Presley looks around, taking in the improvements I've made over the last few years. The cottage is small, just over a thousand square feet, and I've knocked down a couple of walls to create an open floor plan, so most everything is in view as you walk in the front door. The kitchen cabinets have been painted an off-white to complement the new marble countertop. There's now a raised breakfast bar where a couple of industrial stools sit, though only one of them is ever occupied. It's just me, so I never bothered with a dining table, although there is a built-in bench by the front window if I ever need another dining space.

I refinished the hardwoods throughout the entire house, staining them a rustic gray color, and replaced all the doors and trim with a white maple to match the shiplap on the walls. The wood stove was replaced with a more modern unit set in the middle of a floor-to-ceiling brick surround with a living edge mantle. The low plaster ceilings were ripped out, creating a vaulted effect with beautiful exposed beams. You can't see the sole bathroom from here, but that, too, has been completely gutted. I smile when I think about how much she'd love the oversized clawfoot tub. Presley always had a thing for country chic design, which is pretty much what I've done here. Her parents technically own this house, but they've allowed me to treat it as my own. They offered to fund the renovations, but I declined. When you're deployed, hazard pay adds up when you have nothing to spend it on. Plus, my housing expenses are covered with the job, so I don't have to worry about those either.

"More projects?" she surmises.

I nod. "More projects."

Presley's delicate brows lift. "Not exactly a bachelor pad."

I laugh. "Were you expecting empty beer cans and pizza boxes?"

She smiles bashfully. "Maybe."

"You wanna see the rest?"

"Very much so."

I show off the bathroom where Presley reacts exactly how I predicted, then I show her my office-slash-guest room, also known as my childhood bedroom.

"Wow, look at that. Your room doesn't look like a teenager threw up in here like mine does."

"Well, technically, this isn't my bedroom anymore." I nod to the doorway at the end of the hall. "I moved into the primary."

Presley gets a sad smile on her face. "I'm sorry about your dad, Beckett. If I had known—"

I shake my head, cutting her off. "It's okay. Even if you had, I probably wouldn't have been very receptive. He passed only a few months after my discharge." I tap my temple. "Not a lot of positive thoughts going on up here back then."

She hangs her head. "I still wish I knew. I'm sorry."

I pull her into me, unable to stand not touching her anymore. "It's okay, Presley. Really."

I can feel her jaw stretching against my chest as she yawns. "Sorry, it's been a long day... and I think all the dramatic waterworks earlier made it worse."

"You want me to walk you home?"

She lifts her head and looks me in the eye. "How would you feel about me stayin' here?"

My eyes widen, and I have to tell my dick to calm the fuck down. "What do you mean?"

Pres grins. "Get your mind out of the gutter, Beckett. Being naked is not on the agenda."

I return her smile. "There's plenty of things we could do fully clothed."

She gives me a wry look. "Nothing dirty is on the agenda. Sleep and nothing but sleep is what I'm offering. I'd like to just be near you, but if you think it'd be too difficult, or awk—"

"Stay, Pres. You can take my bed. The mattress is more comfortable. I'll sleep in the guest room."

Presley glances into my bedroom. "Oh, no, that's okay. I don't want to kick you out of your own room."

I narrow my eyes. "Why did the mention of taking my room make you clam up just now?"

Her eyes widen. "What? I didn't—"

"Stop being so cagey, and just tell me what's really on your mind, Pres."

She groans. "Fine. It makes me feel icky. It hasn't even been a week since you ended things with Nicole, and I just think it'd be weird if I slept in the same bed where she recently slept." Presley glares when my lips twitch. "What could I possibly be saying that you'd find funny?"

"Because you're *feeling icky*, as you put it, for no reason. Nicole—or any other woman—has never been in that bed. Besides your mother, you're the only woman who's ever been inside this *house.*"

Presley's mouth forms into an O. "How is that possible? You were... doing *whatever* with Nicky for two years, Beckett."

I shrug. "I don't know... it just didn't feel right. And for the record, the *whatever* hasn't happened since I found out you were back almost a month ago. Trust me, Nicole didn't like not being able to come here. It caused more than a few arguments, and she's actually showed up on my doorstep unannounced a time or two tryin' to invite herself in. But I wasn't willing to cave. The thought of bringing anyone else into this place felt... disrespectful, I guess."

"To my parents?" She frowns. "You felt weird bringing another woman here because I'm their daughter?"

My head slices slowly to the left, then the right. "No, Pres. Your parents were never a factor."

"Then, wh—"

"*You*, Presley. It felt disrespectful to *you*. To the memories. I know that makes me seem pathetic, or whatever, but—"

I completely lose my train of thought when Presley presses her lips against mine. I groan, sweeping her into me, pinning her against the wall as I own her mouth. My lips travel down her jawline to the nape of her neck, inhaling her sweet orange blossom scent as I go. My cock is ready to punch through my zipper, but I do my best to ignore it and focus on her. I continue south, over her collarbone, pausing when I reach the swell of her breasts.

"Beckett," she pants. "Don't stop. It feels so good."

I pull back to look her in the eyes, to make sure there's no hesitation in them. When I see none, I raise her arms above her head and remove her T-shirt. When I get my first glimpse of Presley's breasts covered in nothing but a lacy bra, I swear I almost come in my pants like a fourteen-year-old boy.

"Fuuuuck."

Presley follows my line of sight. "They're not real. They're…"

I place my index finger over her lips until she stops talking. "I don't care, Pres. You're the most beautiful woman I've ever seen either way."

She bites her lower lip. "I know I said no nakedness, but do you… do you want to see them?"

"Is that a real question?" I give her an incredulous look. "Honey, I want to see every part of you, but only if you *want me to see*. Don't do it for me."

"It's been so long since I've felt…" Her chest rises and falls as she takes a few deep breaths. It takes extreme concentration to maintain eye contact, but I manage it for the most part. "Never mind, that part doesn't matter." Presley reaches behind her back and fumbles with the clasp of her bra. "I trust you, Beckett.

I've *always* trusted you, and because of that, I *want* you to see me."

For some reason, I get the impression this is about much more than being naked in front of me. I don't want to push her, though, so I let Presley take the lead. When her bra straps slide down her arms, it takes every ounce of willpower I possess not to take her into my arms, kissing and touching her everywhere.

Presley reaches for my hand, and when I grab hers, she walks backward until we're crossing the threshold into my bedroom. My fists clench in anticipation when she pops the button on her jeans and slides the zipper down.

"I'm not ready to... I can't make love to you, Beck. Not yet. But I want you to see *all* of me. Can you be around me like this without having sex? Would that be okay?"

I give her a single nod in reply, too afraid if I reply verbally, I'll shout something stupid like, "Fuck yeah, it is!" and ruin the moment.

I watch as Presley slowly shimmies her jeans down her long legs and steps out of them. Next, she loops her fingers under the straps of her cotton panties, hesitating for only a second before those end up on the floor, too. I bite my knuckles as I take her in from head to toe. She's bare below the waist, which surprises the hell out of me, but also turns me right the fuck on. Even more surprising? The next words that come out of her mouth.

"Please touch me, Beckett."

I tilt my head to the side in question. Didn't she *just say* sex was off the table?

Presley seems to read my mind because she adds, "I want to remember what it feels like to be touched by someone who..." She takes a deep breath. "Please don't make me explain right now. I can't... I'm not ready for *everything* yet, but... the way you used to touch me... I need to feel that. I really need a reminder of what a loving touch feels like, so if that's something you'd be interested in... I'd very much like that. So? Would you like to touch me?"

I cup my hands around her jaw. "Honey, I don't think I've ever wanted anything more."

Chapter Thirty-Four
Presley

When Beckett kisses me this time, there's so much more at stake. I don't know where I got the courage to get naked and ask him to touch me, but what I told him was the absolute truth. I desperately need to know the touch of a loving hand. I need solid, physical proof that I can enjoy sex again... that I can feel pleasure. That I won't always be so messed up. I'm terrified that I won't be able to go through with this. That I'll freak out, and Beck will quickly figure out precisely what Sebastian has put me through. But I know I need to try, and there's no better candidate for the job. I fell in love with Beckett Armstrong before either one of us knew what that meant. Time and distance haven't changed that, no matter how hard both of us have tried to pretend otherwise, and there's no one I trust more.

"Lie back, honey. Let me take care of you."

The soft mattress cradles my body as I scoot back

on his bed. For some reason, I find it incredibly erotic that I'm completely nude, and Beck is still fully clothed. Don't get me wrong; if I have my way, I'll be seeing much more of him tonight, too, but right now, I need to focus on my senses and live in the moment.

"God, Pres, I don't know where I want to start first."

Our eyes meet as he stands at the foot of the bed. "Just touch me, Beckett. I don't care where. I just want to feel you."

He flashes a sexy smirk that sends the butterflies in my stomach soaring. When Beck's large hands begin trailing a path up one leg and then the other, I squirm in anticipation with every inch he gains. I gasp and arch my back when his lips touch my inner thigh, right above my knee.

"Beckett," I pant.

He groans before running the tip of his tongue along my skin. Instinctively, I widen my legs, giving his broad shoulders more room to settle between them.

"Can I taste you, Pres?" Beck places an open-mouthed kiss just a little higher than the last one. "Would that be too much?"

The second the question leaves his mouth, I imagine his dark blond hair moving between my thighs, and I can feel my body readying itself for him. My nipples stiffen to an almost painful degree, and the ache in my core is demanding more.

"Please." My need is so great, it's the only response I can manage. A one-syllable word followed closely by an embarrassingly loud whimper. At the first swipe of his tongue, I add, "Oh. My. *God.*"

Beckett releases a soft chuckle as he places my legs over his shoulders. "I'll take that as a good sign."

I nod furiously. "Very good sign. *Very, very good sign.* Keep up the good work, sir."

He barks out a laugh right before lowering his mouth once again, all humor instantly fading. Beck kisses, and licks, and sucks my hot flesh, stoking the fire inside of me more and more, until I'm on the verge of free-falling off a magnificent cliff. It's been so long since I've had an orgasm, even longer since I've had one to this degree, so when it hits me, I'm incapable of controlling the screams or the pleas. I beg him to keep doing this forever and ever, to never stop because things like work, and breathing, and eating are *so* over-rated. Beck softens his tongue and continues licking me through the aftershocks of my climax. I think we're both surprised when another orgasm hits me seemingly out of nowhere, only seconds later. This one is much shorter but just as powerful. I don't even realize I'm weeping until the tears drip down my face onto the bedding.

"Holy shit, you're good at that." I throw my arm over my face. "So, so good at that."

I can feel Beckett's lips curving into a smile as his mouth travels over my pelvic bone, to my abdomen, and finally to the underside of my breasts. Much to my dismay, I stiffen when he palms one of them.

He instantly retreats. "Is this not okay?"

God, why can't I just be normal and enjoy this? I had no problem a few minutes ago when Beck was going down on me. I couldn't help it, though. The moment he touched my breast, I was sucked into a void where Sebastian controlled me again. I don't hate my boobs; I actually love what I see when I look in the mirror. I was adamant about keeping a natural shape and size for my frame. The surgeon did a fantastic job of honoring my wishes. But I do hate what they represent. I hate that I associate any touch —even if I'm just washing in the shower—with Sebastian. He'd have these moments where he'd fixate on my breasts. He'd paw them, twist my nipples until I'd cry out in pain. Suck on them or bite them until marks were left behind for days. Slide his dick through them until he painted my face with his semen. He'd essentially use my breasts as a tool to debase me as often as possible. To remind me that I was his to do with as he pleased. Maybe I'm not as messed up over receiving oral because Sebastian rarely did that.

I take a deep breath, reminding myself to focus on the present. Focus on the beautiful man before me and how amazing he just made me feel.

I prop myself up on my elbows and look him directly in the eye. "It was a knee-jerk reaction. I want you to touch me, Beckett. *Everywhere*. Just... be patient with me, okay?"

He frowns, undoubtedly trying to read between the lines. When he makes no effort to move, I reach for his hand and place it back over me, holding his gaze the entire time.

He groans. "Pres."

I put pressure on his fingers, curling them into my skin. When his calloused palm abrades my nipple, I gasp, but not in pain. "Touch me, Beck."

Erase my bad memories with some good ones.

Beck nods before slowly running his finger along each curve, down each dip and valley, before circling my areola and repeating the process on the other side. He watches my face the entire time, clearly searching for any signs of distress, which would be incredibly unnerving with any other man. But Beckett Armstrong is no ordinary man. God, the amount of control he's exerting right now proves that in spades. I know his body is demanding relief, but his concern for me outweighs any physical needs. He may not know why I'm so jumpy, but he's smart enough to understand how important this moment is.

When he slowly lowers his head and swirls his tongue around my peaked tip, my head falls back on a breathy sigh. I moan shamelessly when he does the same to the other. Beck takes his time, loving on me, reminding me that my *entire* body is fully capable of pleasure once I get past the roadblock in my mind. When his hand glides down to my sex, toying with that bundle of nerves while he simultaneously creates suction on my nipple, any walls I had remaining are obliterated. Stars burst behind my eyelids as I come apart for the third time under his gentle touch. After the tremors wane, Beckett trails soft kisses along my neck, over my jaw, before once again fusing his mouth to mine. I can taste my arousal on his lips, and for some reason, it only heightens the intimacy of this moment.

Beckett pulls back and wipes some damp hair away from my forehead. "You good?"

"I'm *great.*" I smile, running my finger down the bridge of his nose, pausing at his lips for a moment. "I never thought I could feel that way again. Who knew being proven wrong would've been the best thing that's happened to me in a long time?"

Beck's head falls into the crook of my neck. "Presley, you can't say cryptic shit like that and expect me not to have follow-up questions."

I run my hand along his back, cursing the shirt he's wearing. "Beck, you're wearing too many clothes. I want to feel your bare skin against mine."

He lifts his head, narrowing his bourbon eyes. "Are you trying to distract me?"

"Depends." I shrug. "Is it working?"

His lips twitch. "Honey, you're naked. I'm *already* distracted. But I still have questions. *A shit ton* of questions."

"Not tonight, Beckett." I reach between us and pull on his belt buckle. "Let me touch you. Feel you. I want to take care of you like you just did for me."

Beck climbs off the bed and begins unbuckling his belt. "I can't believe I'm sayin' this, but I don't want you to return the favor. Not because I don't want you, because, fuckin' A, honey, *I want you,* but that's not what this was about." He flicks his finger between us as his pants drop to the floor.

"Then, why are you taking your clothes off?"

Beck pulls his shirt off in that sexy one-armed way and tosses it behind him. "Because you asked me to, and I'm not stupid enough to waste an opportunity to be close to you."

My God, it's even better than I imagined. All of his muscles seem larger, the ridges on his abdomen are deeper, and the way his waist tapers into that sexy vee makes my mouth water. His legs are strong, defined muscles sculpted by the heavy lifting he does each day. My eyes travel to the erection that's trying to escape his black boxer briefs, and I lick my lips, thinking about what's behind that cotton.

He looks to the ceiling for some divine guidance before pointing a stern finger at me. "And *that* is exactly why I'm keepin' my underwear on."

A shocked giggle spills from my lips when I realize what just happened. I was downright ogling the man, thinking about climbing him like a tree.

"You know, it's not exactly good for a man's ego when you laugh while he's standing before you practically naked."

That makes me even more hysterical, so much so that I'm clutching my side. Before I know what's happening, Beck's on top of me, pressing his cotton-covered erection against my core. I moan as it creates another wave of arousal.

Beck curses before falling to my side and yanking

the covers over us. "Well, that backfired, didn't it? It's late. Go to sleep, Pres."

I rest my head over his heart, running my fingers through the thin patch of hair on his chest. "What if I don't want to go to sleep?"

"Tough shit."

I smother my laughter into his chest. We never did turn on the lights when we came in here. There's still plenty spilling in from the hallway, but it's not bothersome enough to get out of bed and flick it off. Despite my earlier sass, I am actually tired, especially after having three mind-blowing orgasms. As I listen to the rhythm of Beck's heartbeat while he strokes the back of my hair, I drift off into the most restful sleep I've had in over a decade.

Chapter Thirty-Five
Presley

I wake to the sounds of Beck moving around in the kitchen. I listen for a few moments, smiling when he curses as the unmistakable smell of burnt food permeates the air. I gather the comforter around my body and pad down the hall to see what he's up to.

"Good morning. Why didn't you wake me?"

He smiles. "You looked so warm and cozy under the covers; I didn't want to disturb you."

I lean against the wall, taking in all the golden skin on display. "Isn't it a little dangerous to cook around grease with so few clothes on?"

Beckett scoffs. "I have clothes on."

"I can't imagine a pair of boxer briefs will offer much protection against a grease splatter. But, if you want to risk burning such a sensitive area..."

Beck grabs the nearby pot holder and shoves it down the front of his underwear. "There. Problem solved."

I laugh at the ridiculous oval-shaped bulge. "I sincerely hope you plan on washing that before you hang it up again. I'm pretty sure things that touch your junk aren't supposed to go near your food."

He raises an eyebrow. "If I recall correctly, you were begging to touch *my junk* just last night, and you're about to go near your food."

I roll my eyes. "And here I thought you were a gentleman."

Beck crosses the kitchen and cages me in against the wall. "If you want a gentleman, Pres, I'm more than capable of delivering." He presses his hardness—and the potholder—into me, which is equal parts arousing and amusing. "But if you want *really fucking dirty...* I'm more than happy to provide that service as well."

I shiver. "Beckett, I cannot have a serious conversation with you while that thing is down your pants."

He nibbles on my earlobe and dips beneath the blanket to palm my butt. "So, take it out."

"What happened to no reciprocation?"

He drags his tongue down the nape of my neck as one of his hands dips between my legs. "That was before I spent the entire night rock hard pressed up against your ass. Right now, I wouldn't be opposed to a little *tit* for tat if you're up for it. You might want to check for an indentation on your ass, by the way. I wasn't kidding about having the boner from hell all night."

I start to laugh, but it's choked off when his finger teases my entrance. "Beckett."

He places a soft kiss on my shoulder when the comforter falls down just enough to expose it. "This feel good, Pres? Do you want me to keep going?" He dips the tip of his thumb inside before pulling out and dragging it higher. "It sure feels like you do, but if I'm wrong, you just say the word, honey."

My toes curl when his thumb begins making lazy circles over my clit. "Don't stop."

The moment Beckett's finger slips inside of me, I shove my hand down the front of his shorts, remove the damn potholder, and fist his length.

"Fuuuuuuck, Pres." He pulses in my hand as I flick my thumb through the bead of moisture at the tip.

Beck and I develop a rhythm—his finger pumps in and out of my body while my hand moves up and down his shaft. Just as a delicious ache is forming low in my belly, the screech of the smoke alarm echoes throughout the room.

"Shit!" Beckett shouts, pulling away and looking at the smoke rising from the pan. He turns off the burner, switches the fan to high, and opens some windows. "Shit. Goddamn fuck fuckity smoke alarm!"

I pull the comforter around me more securely and head to the front door. While I'm swinging the door back and forth, trying to fan some fresh air into the room, I see my father's truck coming up the drive.

I slam the door shut and plaster my back to it. "Crap! My dad's coming!"

"What?" Beck exhales in relief when the smoke alarm finally shuts up.

"My dad!" I repeat. "He's coming up the driveway, and I'm naked!"

He laughs. "Well, then go get some clothes on."

"Beckett!" How can he be so nonchalant about this? "I'm naked. The sun's barely up. It reeks like sex in here, and I'm betting that scent is even stronger on your hand! *And my dad's coming!*"

The infuriating man leans against the wall and crosses his arms over his chest. "Honey, you do remember we're thirty years old, right?"

I growl. "*And I'm a married woman!* I'm married, and I'm standing naked in your house, first thing in the morning, looking and smelling like sex!"

His expression instantly darkens as he clenches his jaw. "Right. How could I forget such an important detail like the fact *you're married to another man?* I'll try my best not to make that mistake again."

My face falls. "Beckett, I didn't me—"

"*Go get dressed, Presley.* I'll take care of your dad."

"You two do realize that half the windows are open, and I can hear everything you're sayin', right?" My head swings in the direction of my father's voice. "Don't worry about me; it sounds like you kids have some things to sort out. I was just headin' out and heard the smoke alarm. Wanted to make sure everything was all right. I'll talk to you later."

I can feel all the blood rushing to my face in mortification as I hear my dad's truck kicking up gravel. "Oh, God."

Beckett grabs the pan off the stove, tosses it in the

sink with a loud clank, and grips the edge of the counter with his back turned to me. I can see his muscles tensing as he takes labored breaths.

"Beck—"

He spins around, fists clenched and nostrils flaring. *"I said, get dressed, Presley! Now!"*

My blood immediately turns cold when I see the look on Beckett's face as he's yelling. My feet can't carry me back to the bedroom fast enough. I slam the door, lock it behind me, and put my hands on my knees, telling myself to calm down. Unfortunately, that doesn't stop the tears from pouring down my face as I begin to hyperventilate. I fall to the floor, chest aching, gasping for air. I whimper when I hear the doorknob jiggle.

"Pres, open the door."

My forehead moves from side to side on the hard floor, but I can't speak. I'm nauseated as my lungs wheeze, and hacking coughs wrack my body. Black spots dot my vision.

"Presley, goddammit, open the door!" The knob jiggles harder, and something slams into the wood, making me jump. "You're scaring the shit out of me. Don't make me break this damn thing down."

I wail, lost to the panic, trapped in a loop of awful images that won't stop flashing through my head. I curl into a ball and rock back and forth, begging a God I no longer believe in to make it stop. Another series of curses and bangs before the door to the bedroom blasts open, with a furious man standing in the middle. I immediately scramble for safety.

"Presley, damn it, stop moving!"

When he grabs at me, I kick my legs, landing a solid blow somewhere that makes him grunt. I look around, frantically trying to find an escape route. The window would take too long, so my only hope is getting past him and out the door. Unconcerned about my nudity, I hop up and over the bed and start sprinting for the door, arms flailing when I see him coming at me from the side. The wind is knocked out of me when he tackles me to the ground, but I keep fighting. I can't let him win. I won't ever let him win again.

"Get off of me!" I scream at the top of my lungs, digging my nails into his arms. When that doesn't work, I clamp my teeth down, pulling back when my mouth fills with the metallic taste of blood.

"Jesus Christ, that fucking hurt! Presley, what's the matter with you? Calm the hell down."

"I said, *get off me!*" I keep squirming, refusing to give in, refusing to let him beat me down again. I know if I do, I'm dead. He'll kill me for sure this time.

He lies on top of me, using his weight advantage to immobilize me. "Honey, you gotta calm down before you really hurt yourself. It's *me*, Pres! *Beckett!* Baby, you're scaring me. You need to snap out of it." He tightens his hold. It feels like there's a boa constrictor wrapped around my lungs. "Please, Presley, snap out of it. Tell me what to do to make it better. I'm so sorry you're going through this. I'm so fucking sorry, Pres.

Just please, fucking come back to me. I need you. I need you, baby. *Please.*"

I don't know which part finally makes it register. Once my mind clears, and I realize who I'm with, I release a shuddering breath, which is easier said than done with over two hundred pounds on top of you.

"Beck... can't breathe."

"Shit. Sorry."

He immediately sits back, which allows my lungs to fully expand. I lie on the floor with my eyes closed, trying to regulate my breathing. I know Beckett is staring at me. I can *feel* it, especially when he releases a choked curse. He's probably cataloging every little scar on my back from the lash of Sebastian's belt. The razor-thin marks on my hips from my own pathetic attempts to distract myself from the agony I felt on the inside. The *fucking initials* carved right above my back-side, so my psychotic husband could see his name on me every time he took me from behind.

I carefully angled my back away from Beckett last night, but now he's seeing me in all my shameful glory. There's no sense in trying to hide my body from him now. I'm sure all the little pieces clicked together while I was in the process of having a meltdown. The only man I've ever truly loved is going to know that I broke his heart and ran straight into the arms of a devil. Beck's going to see how weak I was to stay with a man who tormented me daily simply because it gave him a sick sense of satisfaction.

The marks on my body are nothing compared to

the ones you can't see. And now, thanks to my epic panic attack, Beck is intimately familiar with those invisible scars. He's well aware the girl he fell in love with no longer exists. That my mind is so warped, there's no turning back. I can't believe I snapped like that. Nothing like that has *ever* happened to me before. Usually, when Sebastian would come after me, I would retreat to this special place in my mind where I felt suspended from reality. I was always fully aware of what was happening, but I had somehow figured out how to numb myself against the horror of it all. I guess I'm not so numb anymore, am I?

The mind is a tricky thing. The longer I'd been away from Sebastian, the more hopeful I became. I actually believed the old me was coming back. I felt in time, I'd be okay. Just this morning, I thought I could even be worthy of Beckett's love. His forgiveness. But if my freak out earlier taught me nothing else, it's that I'm too damaged. I'll never be the same, I'll never be able to have a normal relationship, and now Beck knows that. He knows I'm not worth the effort.

"Pres."

I hear him shifting behind me, right before he covers me with a blanket. See? That right there proves how disgusting he finds me.

"You don't have to say it, Beckett. I know."

"You know *what?*"

"That I'm pathetic. That I'm crazy. That you're better off without me in your life. If you can just give me a few minutes to get dressed, I'll be on my way, and I won't bother you again."

"Well, clearly you *don't* know because I wasn't going to say any of those things. I would never even *think* any of those things."

"It's okay; you don't need to spare my feelings." I gingerly sit up, careful to keep the blanket wrapped tightly around me.

"Presley, look at me." When I make no move to do so, he adds, "Please, honey. Just look at me."

When I finally get the courage to turn around, I find Beck sitting back on his heels, his eyes bloodshot and glassy. His spine is straight, his fingers are spread, palms down on his knees. I cringe when I see the teeth marks on his forearm, little droplets of blood pooling in them.

"I didn't... I didn't mean to bite you. I didn't realize it was you. I'm sorry."

"I know, Pres. It's okay." His tone is even. Soft. "Do you need a glass of water?"

Now that he mentions it, my throat feels like the Sahara. "Um... yeah, that would be nice."

Beckett nods. "I'll be right back."

I take advantage of his absence to dress as quickly as possible. Thankfully, at some point this morning, Beckett must've picked my bra up from the hallway floor and brought it in here. He's just coming back with a tall glass of water as I'm pulling my jeans up my legs.

I take the glass from his extended arm. "Thank you."

I tilt my head back and drink. I had only planned on

taking a small sip, but I wind up gulping down the entire thing. Beck wordlessly offers to take the empty glass from me and sets it on the dresser.

He nods to the bed. "Do you want to have a seat? Or if you'd prefer, we can go out to the living room."

I sigh. "Beck, I appreciate what you're trying to do, but you don't need to baby me. This would be a lot easier if I just left."

"Honey, if you want to go back to your folks' house, I'm not going to stop you. But I *will* follow you, and I will wait as long as it takes until you're ready to talk to me."

I've already burdened my parents enough. The last thing I'd want is for them to know about what just happened, so I sit on the edge of the mattress, rubbing my temples, trying to alleviate some of the tension. "What exactly do you want to talk about?"

Beck takes a seat on the floor directly in front of me. His back is propped against the dresser, and his long legs are stretched out in front of him. This room isn't huge, so if I stretched my foot out just a little bit, we'd be touching.

"Have you ever talked to a professional, Pres?"

I frown. "About what?"

He never breaks eye contact. "About what he did to you. Have you ever talked to a professional—or anyone, for that matter—about it? Or have you been bottling this up inside yourself, suffering in silence?"

My eyes fall to my lap. I suppose there's no point in denying it anymore.

I lift my chin. "Beckett, I have at least a dozen injuries that never healed properly because I wasn't allowed to go to the hospital. When would I have been permitted to go to therapy?"

He's careful not to react, but I can see the shadows lurking behind his eyes. "It doesn't need to be a therapist. It could be a support group or a trusted friend. You had friends in New York, didn't you?"

I give him a sad smile. "No."

Beck's forehead lines with creases. "Not a single friend the entire time you lived there?"

I shrug. "There were a few in college... but as you know, I left after the first year. From that point on, anyone I had contact with was connected to Sebastian somehow."

"How long have you been living with this, Presley?"

I shake my head. "You really don't want the answer to that."

He swallows. "I wouldn't have asked if I didn't want to know. I know our situations are completely different, but one thing I've learned from all my shit is how valuable having a safe space to talk is. How meeting people who understand what you're going through can help validate that you're not as isolated as you feel sometimes. Why do you think I've been working so hard to get this program up and running? It's because I've learned firsthand how powerful a support system is. As fucked up as my head is right now, I guarantee it would be much worse if I was still trying to keep it all bottled up. If you won't talk to me, that's okay. But you need to talk to *someone*."

I think back to the first time Sebastian hit me. We were on vacation in Sint Maarten. I had never seen a more beautiful place; I believe I had referred to it as heaven on earth. We'd lie on the beach during the day, go boating, or sip cocktails by the pool, which I thought was particularly fun because I was only twenty at the time. We'd dine on exotic cuisine, then spend the next several hours in bed. Back then, I was caught up in our whirlwind romance. All of the exciting places I'd gone and the things I'd seen. It was a welcome distraction from everything I'd left behind in Georgia.

Then, about five days into our two-week vacation, Sebastian started behaving strangely. He'd snap at a waiter for no apparent reason. Disappear for hours at a time, only to come back drunk and disheveled. He blamed it on stress from work and claimed he just needed some time to cool off. On our tenth day in the Caribbean, which was coincidentally our first wedding anniversary, Sebastian had a big all-day celebration planned, but that morning, he got an email from work that upset him. To this day, I don't know what it was about, but he said he needed to take care of an *issue*. He didn't want my day to be ruined, so he encouraged me to spend the day on the beach, promising he'd be finished by dinner, then we could spend the rest of the night celebrating.

I hadn't seen or heard from him all day. I ordered room service for dinner in our private villa and ate it on the couch, watching some reality TV show. When ten o'clock rolled around, and I still hadn't heard from him, I became angry. When Sebastian finally returned three sheets to the wind about an hour later, I gave him a piece of my mind the second he walked through the door. When he backhanded me so hard, I stumbled into the wall, I was shocked. He immediately apologized, begged for my forgiveness, and promised he'd never do it again. I think I was so stunned, I believed the lie. When he kissed me tenderly, telling me how beautiful I was, how lucky he was that I chose him, I actually started questioning my sanity. At one point, I thought I had imagined the whole thing. That maybe I had dozed off waiting for him to return, and he was just waking me from sleep with his sweet kisses.

The next night when we returned to our villa for the evening, he had accused me of flirting with a waiter. That evening, when we had sex, he was rougher than he had ever been before. He was vulgar and demanding, calling me his dirty little whore, which I'd later learn would become his favorite term of endearment for me. On our final day on the island, Sebastian had woken me up by straddling my chest and pumping his erection, aiming it at my mouth. That was the first time he told me that my *wifely duty* was to serve my husband, however and whenever he pleased. That if I couldn't satisfy his needs, there were plenty of other women who would. In retrospect, I recognize the manipulation for what it was. Still, back then, I was young, and I was so determined to create this fairy tale life where heartache didn't exist that I was blinded by it. So, I let him use me and demean me because I thought that's what my husband needed to be sexually satisfied. I had convinced myself I'd learn to enjoy it eventually.

"Pres, you still with me?"

I blink out of the memory to find Beckett closer now, kneeling in front of me.

"Sorry. I spaced out."

"How long, Presley?"

I sigh. "Just over ten years."

Beck's sharp intake of air causes me to look up. His eyes are closed, and he's taking deep breaths. He hasn't said a word, but they're filled with questions when he opens his eyes. Beckett lifts one of my hands and kisses each knuckle individually. "It kills me to see you hurting like this. Will you please consider talking to someone? A lot of therapists take virtual appointments if that'd make you more comfortable. If you'd like, I can get you the names of the people we're working with for the lodge."

"Why are you being nice? You were so angry with me just a little bit ago."

"I'm not angry with *you*," he corrects. "I'm frustrated with the situation."

I hang my head, resting it on the top of Beckett's. "I hate feeling so weak. I hate even more that you're witnessing it. After everything I did... I don't deserve your kindness."

He wraps his fingers around each one of my calves,

kneading the muscles. "I already told you. We were young. We both made mistakes. And as far as you being weak? I'm calling bullshit on that. The strength it must've taken to survive what you did, for as long as you did, is incredible, Presley. You just need to figure out how to be at peace with the past so you can look toward the future."

"Hey, Beck?"

"Hmm?"

"I'd very much like your help findin' someone to talk to."

His warm breath blows on my hands as he exhales. "I'd very much like that too, darlin'."

Chapter Thirty-Six
Beckett

I don't think I've ever felt so homicidal in my life, and considering the shit I've seen on missions, that's saying a lot. I thought I had been exposed to some of the sickest motherfuckers I'd ever known. Men who would use children as suicide bombers against American troops. Men who saw nothing wrong with kidnapping and repeatedly raping a fifteen-year-old girl because her father had screwed them over on a weapons deal. I had zero qualms about their deaths because the world is a better place without them. One thing I will give them credit for is they made no attempt to disguise their true selves. You knew what you were getting yourself into when dealing with them.

But someone like Sebastian Winters—fuck, I can't even say his name in my head without wanting to hit something—he's an entirely different breed of evil. He presents a perfectly polished image to the public—the same image that no doubt lured Presley in—but, behind closed doors, he repeatedly tortured a woman he swore to love for over *ten fucking years*. Those marks on her... *fuck*. When I saw the SW carved into her back at the curve of her spine, I damn near exploded out of my skin. That motherfucker *branded her*. It wasn't enough to destroy her spirit; he had to stamp his name on her like she was fucking cattle. If Presley didn't need me so badly right now, I'd be on the first plane to New York to hunt that bastard down.

Presley stirs in her sleep, murmuring something too low for me to hear. Christ, why would anyone intentionally hurt this woman? She's so inherently good and pure of heart, which is hard to find these days. Why would someone want to soil that? I knew Pres went through some shit, but I had no idea it was this bad. After she calmed down earlier, we talked for a while until she got so worn out she needed a nap. She only told me bits and pieces—and I sure as shit wasn't going to push her for more than she's ready to give—but the few details I have, prove how resilient she is. Presley thinks that she's weak, but I think she's quite possibly the strongest person I've ever met. I know she believes there's nothing left of the girl she used to be, but that's not true. I can see it, I can *feel it*, but it's definitely buried deep.

"Beckett, what are you doing over there?"

I push off the doorframe and take a seat next to her on the bed. "Just thinking."

She leans into my touch when I softly pet her hair. "What time is it?"

I dig my phone out of my pocket and check the time. "Just after two."

Her eyes widen. "I slept for five hours?"

My lips turn up on one side. "You clearly needed it."

Presley frowns. "Why aren't you workin' right now? Have you been here the whole time?"

I nod, smoothing the crease between her brows. "Don't worry about that; I've got it covered."

I called Mr. J after she fell asleep and explained how I didn't feel right leavin' Presley today. She said her parents know some details about what she'd gone through, but she didn't want them to know about her panic attack earlier, so I kept it vague. Her dad's a sharp guy, though, so I'm sure he could read between the lines. He told me to take care of his baby girl, and he'd make arrangements to cover my work for the day.

"Beckett, I don't want to get in the way of your job."

"I said I've got it covered, Pres." When she chews on the corner of her lip, I pull it free from her teeth. "Tell you what. How about you come with me to check out the progress on the arena?"

She sits up, suddenly more alert. "Really?"

"Sure. Why not?"

She swings her feet out of bed and stands.

Fuck me.

Pres wanted something more comfortable to sleep in, so I gave her one of my old tees. Sadly for my dick, I didn't consider the effect seeing her in my clothes would have on me. She used to always wear my shirts when we were younger, but she was swimming in them, so she'd tie the cotton in a knot, exposing a sliver of her toned abdomen. I used to find every excuse possible to touch that small patch of skin. This time, my shirt's hanging halfway down her thighs, but somehow, it's even sexier. I have to avert my eyes when I'm treated to a glimpse of her perfectly sculpted ass cheeks as she bends over to grab her jeans off the floor.

I groan and discreetly adjust the persistent bastard in my pants.

She looks over her shoulder at the sound. "What's wrong?"

I wink. "Nothin' at all, honey. Just enjoying the view."

Presley gifts me with a small smile, and the tightness in my chest loosens just a little. I'm trying to figure out how to approach this whole thing, so I took a gamble on the flirting, which she seems to appreciate. It's my most natural state with her—always has been—so I'm hoping the familiarity will help soothe her. I'll make sure she knows I'm here if and when she's ready to talk, but I'm thinkin' some sense of normalcy will be good for her.

Presley approaches me and loops her arms behind my neck. I'm still sitting on the bed while she's standing, so she leans down just a bit to place a kiss on my left cheek. Her hair creates a curtain around us and tickles my cheek as she leans into my ear.

"Thank you, Beckett."

"For what?" I pull her onto my lap, her legs hanging off the side.

"For being the greatest man I've ever known." She pulls back with a smile. "Please don't tell my father I said that."

I laugh. "Your secret's safe with me, honey. Though, I don't know how much truth there is behind that statement."

She trails her index finger along my stubbled jawline and traces the same path with her lips. "It's *my* truth."

I run a hand along her back as she moves down to my neck. "Pres, you keep that up, and we'll never make it to the arena."

She sighs dramatically. "Oh, fine. Geez, what's a girl gotta do around here to get some?"

I laugh, lightly tapping her ass as she stands. "Arena first. If you still want to ravage me after, I'm all yours."

"Are you?" She tilts her head to the side. "Are we really doing this, Beckett? All my... stuff doesn't make you want to run for the hills?"

I get off the bed and take her hand. "Darlin', I've been yours since we were five years old. If I'm runnin' anywhere from this point on, it'd be *to* you." I place a kiss on the underside of her wrist. "You set the pace, Pres, however long that takes. I'm just happy going along for the ride."

She wraps her arms around my waist and rests her head over my heart. "Do you really think I'll get to the point someday where I don't feel so screwed up?"

"If you stop tryin' to do this all by yourself, I do."

Presley tilts her chin up. "When I'm with you—barring that episode this morning—it's the closest I've felt to normal in a long time."

I give her a crooked smile. "Then I guess you're stuck with me."

She chuckles, walking backward out of the bedroom. "C'mon, Cowboy. Let's go see that arena."

"Oh, no. Don't you start that, too."

Now she's really laughing. Fuck, she's beautiful when she does that. "Why not? I think it's adorable."

I narrow my eyes. "Honey, adorable is one of the last words I'd want you to use to describe me. Handsome, sexy as fuck, *extremely well-endowed*—all of those things are golden. *Adorable* or Cowboy, not so much."

Presley gives me a sassy wink. "I think I'll stick with Cowboy because I think it's *adorable*."

"Fucking Clayton," I grumble, holding the front door open for her.

"Can we take the four-wheeler?" she asks the moment we step outside.

"You sure? It'll be muddy."

While it didn't rain too heavily last night, there's still a decent amount of standing water, and the forecast is calling for more. We've got a few hours if we're lucky before it starts again.

"Yeah." She takes the hair tie from her wrist and piles her blonde locks on top of her head. "I have no issue with a little mud. So, unless you're worried about ruining your outfit"—she makes a twirly motion with her index finger—"then, I say we go for it."

I laugh. "Okay, wiseass, the quad it is."

We make the short trek to the machine shed and climb on the ATV. Once we clear the immediate area, I gun it, flying across the pasture. Presley's musical laughter has me smiling the entire time as we drive along an old path we used to take back in the day. When we get to the arena, I park the quad and kill the engine, waiting for Presley to climb off before I do the same. It feels like someone took a fucking defibrillator to my heart when I get my first glimpse of her.

Presley's hair is a tangled mess, completely fallen out of the bun, her face and arms are splattered in mud, and her eyes look a little crazed. She looks feral, almost, and for some goddamn reason, I find that incredibly hot.

"What?" Presley looks down at herself. "Why are you looking at me like that?"

I give her a leisurely once-over. "Because this whole dumpster fire thing you have goin' on is making me hard."

Her eyes widen before she belts out another laugh. "You're disturbed, Beckett."

I band an arm behind her back and pull her closer. "No doubt, honey. But I'm still thinkin' about dirtying you up even more."

Pres pulls out of my grasp. "Nuh-uh. Arena first, ravage later. Remember?"

"I should really get my priorities in order."

She shakes her head and gestures to the steel-framed building in front of us. "Are you going to show me this thing, or what?"

I slide the door open and motion for her to go ahead of me. "Ladies first."

Presley walks inside and surveys the area. "It's huge! It seems much bigger from the inside."

"We wanted it to be large enough to accommodate our regular lessons and the therapy program. Your dad went with the whole, *go big or go home* mentality and doubled the recommended size."

Presley smiles. "Why doesn't that surprise me?"

I grin. "What do you think?"

She turns in a complete circle. "I love it. Do you currently have a lot of people enrolled in lessons?"

"Nah." I shake my head. "We're maxed out on boarding, so riding lessons have taken a back seat. I need another trainer, which is easier said than done."

Presley's eyes wander around the arena again before coming back to me. "Could I help? I mean... I'd need to get a little more comfortable with the other horses first, but I'd love to start teaching lessons again."

"Yeah?" I smile, really liking the idea of Presley being in her element like that. Doing something that'll make her happy.

She nods. "Yeah. I think it'll be good for me."

I band my arms around her from behind and rest my chin on her shoulder. "I think so too, Pres."

Her body relaxes as her back molds to my front. "Are we crazy, Beckett?"

"I'm gonna need you to be a little more specific, darlin'."

Pres moans when I place a kiss on the spot where her neck meets her shoulder. "For thinking this could work? You and me, I mean. That we can just go back to the way things were with all the other garbage we have surrounding us."

I turn her around and cup her delicate jaw in my hands. "I don't want to go back to the way things used to be. I want the person you are *now*, Pres, and I'd hope you can say the same about me."

Her eyes bounce back and forth. "I do."

"Well, then, we'll figure out the rest as we go, one day at a time."

"I just feel like everything's happening so fast."

"Remember, you set the pace, Pres. If what happened last night was too much too soon... we hit the brakes."

She gives me a shy smile. "What if I want to step on the gas?"

I couldn't help the cocky grin that stretches across my face if I tried. "You sure as hell won't hear me complaining."

Her lips twitch. "Good to know."

I grab her hand, telling my dick not to read too much into that. "C'mon, let's get back before the sky opens up."

"Hey, Beckett?"

I lift my brows in question. "Yeah?"

Presley squeezes my fingers. "I'm drivin'."

I laugh. "You think so, huh?"

She reaches into my pocket and snatches the keys. I could stop her if I wanted to, but I don't.

She holds the keys up and smiles victoriously. "Oh, I *know* so."

Chapter Thirty-Seven
Presley

"We're a mess, but that was so worth it!"

I kick off my boots and socks on Beckett's front porch while he does the same. I took several detours on the way back and drove the ATV through every single mud puddle I could find. It's been ages since I've done something so carefree, I couldn't resist.

Beckett lifts a section of my hair. "I never considered what you'd look like as a brunette, but you could definitely pull it off. You know, minus the glops of mud."

I roll my eyes. "You think you're so funny, don't you?"

"I have my moments." His mouth kicks up in the corner as he opens the front door. "Now, get your sexy ass in the bathroom, and try not to leave a trail along the way."

"You're bossy today, aren't you?"

Beck winks in reply and follows me into the bathroom. Reaching behind the shower curtain to turn the spray on, he says, "Give the water just a minute to heat up before you hop in." He grabs a fluffy towel from the bottom of the open vanity and sets it on the counter. "Holler if you need anything."

"Stay." I manage to get the word out right before he leaves the room.

He pauses mid-stride and looks over his shoulder. "Pres, I don't know if that's such a good idea."

I lift my borrowed T-shirt over my head and drop it to the floor. "Beckett, please. Stay."

He swallows hard when his mocha-colored eyes fall to my breasts. "Honey, my willpower is shit right now. I don't trust myself to be in the same room with you if you're not wearin' any clothes. I want you too much."

"So, take me." I don't know who this bold woman is or where she came from, but I think I'll keep her. "Get cleaned up with me, then *take me*. Show me how much you want me."

"Pres." Beck shakes his head. "I don't think that's a good idea after what happened this morning. You need time."

I peel my wet jeans off my legs. "What I *need* is a reminder of what you feel like *inside of me*. Loving me. Touching me."

Beckett curses when my bra joins the pile of clothing on the floor. "But, this morning—"

"I need you *more* because of what happened this morning." I pull my underwear down, the last piece of material I had covering me. Beckett's eyes flash with heat, but he's still resisting. "I know you said they didn't bother you, but I need you to *show me* that my scars—both inside and out—don't repulse you. I need to know—"

I squeal in surprise as Beckett closes the gap between us in one long stride and takes my face in his hands. "You listen to me, Presley. *Nothing* about you could ever repulse me. I hate that you had to go through the pain of getting those marks on your body, but they don't make you any less beautiful, inside or out. If anything, they highlight how stunning you are. Those scars prove that you're a survivor. A warrior. That bastard tried to break you again and again, but you kept fighting, and you found the strength to walk away. I know that in itself was scary as hell, but you did it. You persevered when the odds were stacked against you, and you continue to do it each day you get up and try to find your footing again."

I fist his shirt. "Show me, Beckett. *Love me.*"

He swipes his thumbs over my cheeks, back and forth, searching my eyes. "Honey, I never stopped loving you."

God, this man. I don't know why I'm being gifted this second chance with him, but I'm done wasting time because I'm worried about what other people might think. Yes, I'm still technically a married woman, and some might feel this is wrong. But as far as I'm concerned, my marriage was over the first time Sebastian laid his hands on me in anger. I've done what I can to finalize the process by leaving New York and hiring an attorney. Now, it's just a matter of getting the legal part in order. I refuse to miss out on another day to be with the love of my life. We've both lost so much over the last twelve years. It's time we start makin' up for that.

I lift up on my toes and kiss the underside of his jaw. When I get to his good ear, I whisper, "Make love to me, Beckett."

I pull back and walk slowly to the tub, maintaining eye contact the entire time. I leave the curtain open so Beck can see me as I tilt my head under the flow of water. Once I'm satisfied I have the majority of the mud rinsed out, I grab the bottle off the shelf, spreading the eucalyptus-scented shampoo through my hair. As I tilt my head back again to rinse, I smile to myself when I hear Beckett groan as he watches my erotic peep show. My back is arched, my chest is pushed forward, and my sudsy breasts jiggle as I run my hands through my long hair. I know exactly the kind of picture I'm making right now, which is precisely why I'm doing it.

"You're killin' me here, Pres."

I grab some conditioner and finger comb it through my hair. "So, put us both out of our misery and get in here."

Next up is the soap. I take my time, working the bubbles over my skin, making sure not a trace of dirt remains. I pay special attention to my breasts, imagining it's Beckett touching them instead of me. Doubt starts creeping in when he still doesn't make a move to join me, but then I realize there's empowerment in putting myself on display like this. And one glance at Beck tells me he knows that, too. I can see how desperately he wants to touch me by the rigid set of his jaw, the way his eyes track my every move, and the way his fingers continuously flex. Plus, there's the obvious erection in his pants. But he's allowing me to have this moment as if he instinctively knows how much I could use the confidence boost.

His restraint is unmatched, and if I didn't want to feel his touch so badly, I'd be impressed. As it stands, I'm achy and needy, and my patience is wearing thin. I decide I need to do something that'll prove to Beckett I'm ready. That while my self-esteem has taken countless blows over the years, I believe him when he says I'm beautiful. That I'm safe. That I'm loved. Beck's eyes round when I trail my hand down my abdomen, heading straight for my core. I pull my lip between my teeth as my fingers slide through my slick, soapy flesh, igniting the sensitive nerves. I've never touched myself in front of anyone before; hell, I can't remember the last time I even felt the desire to do this alone. I was too young and shy when Beckett and I were first together, and with Sebastian... well, he preferred me submissive, and he didn't care if I came or not.

But at this moment, with Beckett, I want to own my pleasure. I want him to witness every second of it —see the exact moment I take my power back. When I vow to put myself first sometimes. When I remind myself that it's perfectly healthy to have desires and there's nothing shameful in what I'm doing. As a deep ache forms in my belly, signaling my impending release, my eyes close, and my head falls back to the tiled walls. I move my fingers faster, giving my body just the right amount of friction it needs. When I come in a spectacular fashion, it's with Beckett's name on my lips. As my tremors wane, I realize he's here with me, in the tub. At some point, when I was consumed by bliss, he managed to remove his clothing and join me.

I open my lids with a lazy smile. "If that didn't convince you to get in here, I was fresh out of ideas."

Beck's eyes twinkle with amusement. "That was the hottest fucking thing I've ever seen." His large hands span my hips, and I'm surprised to find I'm not worried about him feeling the grooves on my skin. "I want you so goddamn bad it hurts, Pres."

I give his length one long stroke from root to tip and kiss each corner of his mouth. "Then wash that mud off and meet me in the bedroom, Cowboy."

He narrows his gaze in mock annoyance. "The only reason I'm letting you get away with that is that you're naked."

I step out of the tub, closing the curtain, and wrapping the fluffy towel around my body. "Don't make me wait long, Beckett."

I laugh when I hear him scrubbing furiously, trying to wash up as fast as possible. I've barely stepped foot into the hallway when Beck switches the water off and starts coming for me in all his wet, naked glory. A shocked gasp falls from my lips when he bends at the knees and flips me over his shoulder.

"Beckett Ryder Armstrong!" I brace my hands on his lower back, trying to push myself up. "Put me down!"

I laugh when he dumps me unceremoniously on the bed, but my amusement quickly fades when I feel his cock pressing against me. I stretch my neck to meet him halfway as he leans down for a kiss. Beck's hips settle between my thighs as our lips and tongues move in perfect harmony. When he pulls back, his gaze never leaves mine as his hand goes to where the towel is tucked between my breasts. Beckett wastes no time unwrapping me like the most precious gift as I give him a subtle nod. My nipples pebble under his stare, begging for his touch. I'm hyper-focused on every breath, every shift of the mattress. The raindrops hitting the roof. A sharp gasp rushes out of me when Beck's warm, wet mouth surrounds one pink tip while he gently rolls the other between his thumb and fore-finger. I run my hands along his back, down the corded muscles of his arms. A deep sound rattles in his chest when I angle my hips up, seeking friction.

Beckett's lips continue their descent until he's placing soft kisses over the scars on my hips. I wait for the shame to hit as it usually does when I think about self-harming, but it doesn't come. My brain is too busy wondering where Beckett's mouth is going to go next. I jolt in surprise when he separates my lower lips with his thumbs before gently sucking my clit into his mouth. He eats me like a man starved, licking and sucking and nibbling me into a frenzy. When he inserts one finger and then two, I lose control. I'm riding his hand so hard, the headboard is slamming against the wall, thump, thump, thumping in the same staccato as the wet sucking noises our bodies are making. My hands claw his thick hair as I shred all inhibitions, caring about nothing but the pure ecstasy this man is giving me.

He continues pumping his fingers in and out as his mouth moves back to my breast. This time, when he pulls my nipple into his mouth, mimicking what he just did down below, I shout obscenities, telling him how good it feels, how I can never get enough. I'm straight-up fucking his hand at this point, not caring one bit how crazed I must look. I can feel my orgasm just out of reach, and I'd do damn near anything to get there.

"Beckett, please."

"I know, baby," he coos. "Just hold on."

When he presses the pad of his thumb to my clit, applying the perfect amount of pressure, I unravel completely. Explosively. After I come down, Beck sits back on his knees, gently massaging my leg muscles. I'm sweaty. Loose-limbed. Dying for more. I whine when he leaves the bed, walking toward his dresser.

He opens the top drawer and retrieves a giant box of condoms, giving me a sheepish smile as he removes the plastic shrink wrap. "Call it wishful thinking."

I smile, wishing I could tell him we didn't need condoms because I'm on the shot. I'd love to feel him with nothing between us, but considering Sebastian's extra-marital affairs, it wouldn't be the responsible thing to do until I get my test results back. The last thing I'd want is for Beckett to suffer the consequences of my husband's infidelity. Thank goodness I had the foresight to ask for an STI panel when I went to the clinic for my shoulder check-up. I lick my lips as Beck fists his erection, pumping it a few times before opening the square foil and sliding the condom in place.

"I'm all yours, Pres. Tell me how you want me."

His words shouldn't feel foreign in my head, but it's been so long since I've been given a choice, I find myself flipping through my mental catalog of sexual positions, wondering which one I should pick. When it hits me, I sit up, gesturing to the space beside me.

"Sit up against the headboard."

Beck gives me a crooked smile as he heeds my command. I chose this position not only for its intimacy but also because it puts me in control of the situation. There is nothing about this that will resemble any encounter I've had with Sebastian. I hope there will come a time when the awful sexual experiences I've had over the last decade won't cross my mind, but I know it'll be a while before that happens. And this first time is so important, such a pivotal moment in breaking free from the mental prison I've been locked in, that I need it to be just right.

"No pressure, right?" I mumble under my breath.

Beck tilts his head in question, but I shake mine,

imploring him to drop it, which thankfully, he does. That's one significant change I've noticed about him. Before, he had the ultimate hero complex. He felt compelled to fix everything; refused to let something go if he thought he could make an impact. But now... he seems to understand that sometimes a person just needs to work through their own shit, that they need to prove to themselves that they can make it through to the other side. I can tell he still feels the urge to step in, but he has a tight leash on it.

Beck reaches for my hand. "C'mere."

I place my palm against his and allow him to guide me to his lap. Once I'm straddling him, only inches away from taking him inside of me, I have a brief moment of panic.

I press my cheek against Beckett's and take a deep breath. "I'm nervous. Why am I so nervous? We've done this too many times to count."

He lifts my chin toward him with his finger. "It doesn't matter. The only thing that matters is this. You and me. Right here. Right now. Focus on this moment and nothing else. Do you think you can do that?"

I close my eyes and find my center. When I open them again, I see nothing but the man before me. The rest of the world has gone black. "Beckett?"

He raises an absurdly sexy eyebrow. "Yeah?"

I smile. "Kiss me."

He gives me a lopsided grin. "Gladly, honey."

Chapter Thirty-Eight
Beckett

I plan to ease in slowly. I really do. But the moment Presley positions herself against me, it's like gravity. I'm helpless to stop the fall. With a few shallow thrusts, I'm buried to the hilt, standing at the motherfucking gates to heaven.

I break our kiss, my head falling to her shoulder on a groan. "Fuck, Pres."

"I know," she pants, rising up to almost the tip, before swiveling her hips and plunging back down again.

Christ.

I've never felt anything like this before. No woman has ever been able to match the hold Presley has over me, but this is beyond that. I feel like I'm in a fucking trance as I watch her hips rise and fall. Her rosy nipples call out to me like a siren, and I can no longer resist the temptation. While Pres takes me in deep like it's her sole purpose in life, I bury my face in her tits, dying for a taste. She screams in pleasure, and her pussy clenches when I pull a pink tip into my mouth, simultaneously swirling my tongue and applying suction. Since she seems to like that so much, I do it to the other side for a minute before I sit up to watch the pure rapture dance across her face as she rides me.

Seeing Presley using my body to get off—and there's no mistaking that's exactly what she's doing right now—is the sexiest fucking thing I've ever experienced. Being with her was always incredible, but even that pales in comparison to this. Maybe it's because she's known so much pain in the years we were apart, she appreciates pleasure more. Maybe her wings have been clipped for so long, she remembers the freedom in flight. Maybe it's simply because this magnetic attraction we share is much more powerful than it's ever been, and it's futile to resist.

Whatever the reason, seeing her like this is a thing of beauty, like watching a phoenix rise from the ashes. Presley knows what it's like to suffer the unimaginable, and because of that, she's evolved. In the midst of all the darkness in her mind, she's created her own source of light, refusing to be caged any longer. This fierce woman has collected all her broken pieces and formed them into a magnificent mosaic. The transformation is stunning, and I'm so fucking honored she chose me to be a part of this. That bastard tried to destroy her, but the only thing he succeeded in doing was making her stronger. Presley doesn't need me—or anyone for that matter—to be her salvation because she's found it within herself.

In a flurry of moans, teeth-clashing kisses, and colliding hips, I fall more in love with this woman than I ever thought possible. When she comes apart in my arms, I trail kisses down the elegant slope of her neck, the feel of her rapidly beating pulse beneath my tongue. When her movements become choppy, I take over, bracketing her hips with my hands, thrusting into her from below.

"God, Beckett," she says on a breathy sigh. "I forgot how good it could feel. I can't believe I've...oh, God, just don't stop."

I set an unyielding pace, driving us to new heights, something neither one of us has ever experienced before. When Presley explodes one last time, I follow quickly behind, chanting her name over and over as I spill into the condom. We take a moment to stare at each other in wonder, to acknowledge this new dynamic of ours. She sighs when I brush some damp hair away from her face, planting a kiss on her temple. Neither one of us says a word, but the undeniable truth sits between us. We both know there's no turning back after this. That neither one of us can return to the way things were. This beautiful, resilient woman and I are in this for the long-haul, and anyone stupid enough to come between us will most certainly regret it.

I prompt Presley to climb off of me before I soften

too much and step into the bathroom to take care of the condom. When I return to my bedroom, she's under the covers, her long blonde hair spilling over the pillows.

I lean against the busted doorjamb and take her in. "You look good in my bed, Pres."

She smiles. "I bet the view's even better up close."

"Is that an invitation?"

Her eyes fall to my dick. "You're lookin' a little cold there, Beck. It's nice and warm under the blankets."

I laugh. "Don't start somethin' you have no intention of finishing, darlin'."

Presley raises her delicate brows. "Who says I have no intention of finishing? I plan on *finishin' all night long*. If you think you can keep up, that is."

I grab the box of rubbers off the dresser and cross the room in two long strides. Climbing into bed with her, I say, "Oh, I can keep up, all right." I press my growing erection into her thigh to punctuate my statement.

Pres moans, arching her back as she rubs against me purposefully. "God, Beck. How do you do it?"

"Do what?" I pepper kisses along her jaw.

"Make me feel so alive. So wanton." She gasps when my hand slips between her thighs. Fuck, she's still soaked. "I never thought I'd feel this way again."

I'm sure she's sensitive, so I'm careful to keep my touches feather-light. "I could ask you the same. I've never wanted anyone like I want you."

She frames my face with her hands, turning me toward her. "No, you're not getting it, Beckett. I haven't felt *any* kind of desire in a long, long time. I didn't even feel the need to touch myself. I thought that part of me was dead, and I was honestly okay with that."

I move my hand to her back so I don't distract her. If she's going to say something like that, I need her to explain before letting my imagination get the best of me. Pres had more than a healthy appetite when we were first together. I understand her reluctance to be intimate with that abusive fuckface she married, but to lose her desire entirely? To not be concerned about its disappearance? Something had to have happened to cause that.

"Why, Pres?" I draw figure eights on her lower back, directly over those fucking initials. Knowing Presley, she's especially sensitive to that particular scar, and I need to prove to her that it doesn't bother me. Not in the way she's worried about, anyway.

"I learned to use sex as a tool, and in doing that, it became a matter of self-preservation rather than satisfaction. Sebastian was... when he'd get in that zone, I knew that if I didn't offer up my body, he'd take his rage out on me with his fists. It seemed like the lesser of two evils at the time. During... he wasn't exactly kind, which made my interest dwindle even more until there was nothing left."

"Presley, did he... were you forced?" I hold my breath, waiting for her answer. In the time it takes her to respond, I've reminded myself five times I cannot flip my shit in front of her, no matter how horrifying her answer may be.

She gives me a sad smile. "No. As much as I hate myself for it, I went to him willingly." Pres looks away, staring at something over my shoulder. "Except for the last time."

I'm trying to remain calm, but it feels like my blood is literally boiling. I'm vibrating with unspent energy, which I really need to get in check before I scare the shit out of her. I climb out of bed and practically rip my dresser drawer off the track when I pull it open to grab a pair of boxers. I'd rather not have my dick hanging in the breeze while I'm trying to avoid going nuclear. I clasp my hands on top of my head and pace the small space in between the bed and dresser, taking deep breaths.

Presley sits up in bed, clutching the blanket to her chest. "Beckett? You okay?"

My eyes swing to hers. "No, I'm not fucking okay!" Damn it, too loud. I take another deep breath and try again, this time lowering my volume. "How can I be okay with something like that? The more important question is, are *you* okay? When did this happen? When—"

"Right before I came back." She clears her throat. "When I first got here... did my mom ever explain why she wanted you to stay away from the house?"

I shake my head in reply, doing the breathing exercises I learned during counseling. In for four counts, out for eight. In for four... out for eight.

She tucks her hair behind her ear. "I was in bad shape, Beckett. I thought Sebastian was actually going to kill me. He'd never taken it that far before, probably because I didn't usually fight back. But that night... I found out he was having an affair. I don't know why that set me off like it did, considering everything else that's happened over the years, but I refused to back down. I felt so betrayed—which is ridiculous when I think about it—and I flew off the handle. While I was yelling at him, he got this manic look in his eyes that I'd never seen before. It's like he was looking right through me, so on instinct, I ran, but I never even made it to the elevator. Anyway..." Presley pulls her knees up to her chest under the covers. "While he was... I refused to give him the satisfaction of a reaction. I didn't want him to have any more of my tears. So, when he was done, he beat the crap out of me until I blacked out. I'd never seen him lose complete control before that night. When I woke up, he was gone. I was pretty out of it—the doctor said a concussion will do that to you—but I knew that if I didn't take the opportunity to leave at that exact moment, I'd never have the chance again. I somehow managed to get dressed and make it down to the lobby, but the effort must've taken too much out of me because they told me I passed out. I woke up again in the ambulance, but I was still too groggy to remember much."

I lean against the dresser, curling my fingers around

the edge. "What did the police do when you told them what happened?"

Presley gulps. "I didn't tell them anything."

"What?!" I scrub a hand down my face. "Why the hell not?"

Her hazel eyes narrow. "You don't get to judge me, Beckett."

I pinch the bridge of my nose. "I'm *not* judging you. I'm *curious* why you'd let him get away with that when you had the chance to report it. Surely, the hospital documented all your injuries. He should be behind bars, Pres."

She shakes her head. "It won't happen. He's too powerful. He has too much money, too many connections, and he's too damn manipulative. *Millions* of people adore him, Beck. He's their savior. Sebastian is a smooth talker, and he's well-practiced at deception. The charges would never stick. The only thing an accusation like that would do is make me a target for the media."

I finally feel like I have enough control over myself to be near her again. I sit next to her on the edge of the mattress and weave our fingers together. "Honey, you don't know that. You can't let him get away with this."

Pres sighs. "I've made peace with it, Beckett, and I need you to respect that. Karma will bite him in the ass one day, hopefully, sooner rather than later. I'll be happy if I can get this divorce to go through without any problems. My attorney said it should be pretty simple since I don't want anything from him. Provided he doesn't contest it, that is. I just want to be done with that part of my life so I can move on."

I don't like the idea of him getting away scot-free, but I decide to let it go for now. If Presley doesn't press charges, I just might need to personally teach that motherfucker what it's like to be pounded on by somebody bigger than you.

I cup my hand around the back of her neck and press our foreheads together. "I really wish I would've said something that day. Maybe none of this would've ever happened."

I can feel her frowning in understandable confusion. "The day I left?"

"Well, that too. But I was referring to the time I saw you in New York."

She rears back. "I'm sorry, but *what?* When did you see me in New York?"

I run my finger along the crease between her brows. "Right after your engagement was announced." Her eyes widen. "I talked Clayton into giving me your address, and I took the first flight out."

Presley shakes her head. "I don't understand. We never saw each other in New York."

"That's not entirely accurate," I correct. "*I* saw *you* getting out of a car with him. I had this big plan. I was going to beg you not to marry him, to come home with me, but I couldn't do it. I was fucking miserable without you, but you seemed genuinely happy. I didn't understand how that could be true, but I saw it with my own eyes. I knew I had to let you go. Now, I really wish I would've been more selfish."

The green in her eyes brightens with unshed tears. "It was all an act, Beckett. I was trying to convince myself I could be happy with him, but I never was, not even in the beginning. I *never* loved Sebastian. I almost left him at the altar, but I thought the damage between you and me had already been done. I was afraid to be alone with nothing but my depressing thoughts. I was incredibly sad, and it was eating me alive, so I had talked myself into staying with him. That was before I knew who he really was. I thought I'd be a fool to walk away when he was seemingly so perfect." She wipes her tears as they spill over onto her cheeks. "God, I've made too many stupid decisions out of fear."

Fuck.

A part of me is relieved she never really loved him because that confirms what we had was the real deal. But the other part is filled with regret for all the things she and I left unsaid. All of this could've been avoided if we learned how to communicate better. I slip under the covers and coax Presley into lying down next to me.

"Pres, I need you to promise me something."

She sniffles. "What?"

I brush my hand along the side of her torso. "I don't want to make the same mistakes. If you're struggling, or if something's on your mind, I need you to talk to me. I mean full disclosure, no matter how hard it is, or if you think it'll upset me. Can you do that?"

Presley searches my eyes. "Can *you?*"

I brush the back of my hand over her tear-stained cheek. "Yeah, honey, I can. Because the alternative... the possibility of losing you again, isn't a road I want to go down."

She outlines my lips with her index finger. "Me neither, Beckett."

Chapter Thirty-Nine
Presley

"I have good news."

When I saw my divorce attorney's name on my caller ID, I became instantly nervous, but her positive tone is alleviating some of my anxiety.

"What kind of good news?" I cross my fingers.

"I just received a call from your husband's attorney. He's not going to contest the divorce."

My eyes widen. "Seriously?"

"There is one condition." Now her tone is more ominous. Great. I can't wait to hear what Sebastian wants.

"And what would that condition be?"

"You need to sign an agreement swearing you will not release any details regarding your husband's affair."

"Done."

Melissa sighs audibly. "Presley, that's not all. The agreement also covers what you learned about Sebastian's... *character* during your marriage."

I frown. "Meaning what exactly?"

"You cannot tell anyone about the abuse, which means you can't file for an order of protection. You can't press charges. *Ever.* If you do, Sebastian will have every right to sue for damages, which could be significant."

"Done."

"Presley, thin—"

"I said, *done*, Melissa. I appreciate your concern, but I don't want anyone to know what I went through, especially not the public. I just want this to be over as quickly as possible. My family already knows what an asshole Sebastian is, so he'd have to deal with that. But they would never say anything if I asked them not to."

She's silent for a moment. "Okay, I'll respond, telling them we accept their terms. Depending on how backlogged the courts are, things should be final in sixty to ninety days."

I can handle three months. After that, I'll be a free woman, and I'll never have to think about Sebastian again.

"Thank you, Melissa."

"It's my pleasure, Presley. I'll be in touch about the paperwork."

"Okay. I'll talk to you then."

I hang up the phone and let out a heavy sigh. I don't even realize I'm crying until I hear my mama's voice.

"Honey, what's wrong?"

My eyes slide to her. "I'm not crying because I'm upset. I'm... relieved. Sebastian isn't going to contest the divorce. I'll officially be a free woman in sixty to ninety days."

"Oh, honey, I'm so glad to hear that." She takes a seat next to me on the couch and grabs hold of my hand. "Speaking of bein' a free woman... I told myself I wouldn't pry, but your daddy mentioned you were at Beckett's house the other mornin'... and you didn't come home again last night." She gives me a knowing smile.

Ugh, why is this so uncomfortable? I'm thirty years old, for Christ's sake. I should be able to talk about sex without blushing.

I raise my eyebrows. "What are you asking?"

"Does that mean you two have reconciled?"

"I think it means we're trying. Ideally, I'd like to keep quiet about it until the dust settles with Sebastian, but I know people 'round here are already talkin'. They think it's too soon or—"

My mom wraps her arms around me and pulls me into a hug. "Never mind those squawking birds, Presley. You and Beckett deserve happiness, and if you have it because you've found your way back to each other, it's nobody's business but yours."

"It feels almost too good to be true, you know? One second I'm convinced I'm doing the right thing, and everything will work out, and in the next, I'm questioning *everything*. I'm trying not to be so negative, but I've been living in this state of heightened anxiety and doubt for so long, I can't seem to stop myself from falling into old habits. I've made lots of bad decisions throughout my adult life, Mama. Awful, *terrible* decisions. What if jumping into a relationship with Beckett so fast is another one?"

"Presley, I've said this to you once before, but I think it bears repeating. You and Beckett have a once-in-a-lifetime kind of love. There's a reason why it's not called twice-in-a-lifetime. You and that boy feed each other's souls; you always have. How can you go wrong with that, especially when you're both nursing so much pain? I think finding your way into each other's arms again is God's way of makin' things right. It's his way of nourishing your minds and your hearts back to health."

"Mama, you know I don't believe in God anymore. How could I?"

She pushes some hair away from my face. "That's okay, baby, because I believe enough for both of us. I've been prayin' this day would come, and it has. I'm sorry y'all had to go through so many trials and tribulations, but you and Beckett are back where you're supposed to be, surrounded by people who love you. The rest will fall into place."

"But what exactly is 'the rest'? I don't know what I want to do with my life. I went from living here, to my dorm, to a penthouse with Sebastian, and now back here again. I love this ranch, Mama, and I appreciate you and Dad welcoming me back after I behaved so poorly, but at the same time, being here feels like I'm going backward. I don't know what independence feels like. I don't want to be this weak, scared woman anymore, and I feel like I'm never going to get out of that holding pattern until I branch out on my own. Don't you think at this point in my life, I should know what it's like to not be so dependent on other people?"

My mom shakes her head. "I can't answer that for you, Presley."

"I've been thinking about renting a place of my own, maybe one of those new apartments right outside of town. I have enough money left from selling my rings to pay for at least a few months of expenses and maybe an older used car." I give her a soft smile. "Beck said he could use some help with riding lessons, so with that and what I'd be makin' at the bar, I think I could manage it."

The more I think about it, the more convinced I am it's the right thing to do. It'd give me balance. I'd still be here a lot, I'd be around the horses, but I'd also have my own place to go home to at night. I'd know what it's like to support myself.

"Sweetheart, if this is something you feel you need to do, then I'd say do it. But may I suggest an alternative to the apartments?"

I nod.

"Do you remember Daryl and Eloise Wilson? Well, they have a small cottage at the back end of their property that they rent out. It's newly vacant, and I believe they're still looking for someone to lease the place. It's fully furnished, and it'd be much nicer than livin' in an apartment building with thin walls."

The Wilsons live about five miles from here. I never

told my mother this, but Beck and I were looking into renting that cottage once we graduated high school. It's tiny, but the main house is on the opposite end of their twenty-acre property, so privacy wouldn't have been an issue. Beck and I loved it. It would've been perfect for the three of us.

God, the baby.

I haven't thought about that in a while. I rub at the sudden tightness in my chest. Who would've thought after all these years, my grief would still cause physical pain? Maybe if I saw a therapist back then, it wouldn't be so bad, but who knows? I can't imagine not feeling this ache in my heart when I think about our child. I don't understand why in this day and age, but there seems to be a stigma with a miscarriage that says you should suffer your loss in silence. Hell, I felt that way at first, too. But over time, I've learned that it doesn't matter if you were eight weeks into gestation or eight months. When you experience a loss like that, it's not just about the life itself. It's about the utter sense of failure you feel. The constant guilt, thinking you did something wrong that caused it or didn't do enough to prevent it. It's all the hopes and dreams and possibilities that will never have a chance to come to fruition.

"Pres, honey, are you okay?"

I clear my throat. "Yeah. Sorry, I spaced out. Do you have their number?"

"I do. I'll tell Eloise to expect your call." My mom looks at me thoughtfully. "Did Beckett tell you about the new lodge yet? Or the program we're startin'?"

I nod. "He did. I think it's amazing you guys are doing that."

"Maybe he could use your help there, too."

I shrug. "Maybe."

I need to get my own head sorted out before I try helping anyone else fix their problems. My phone buzzes from its place beside me. When I look down, I have an incoming text from Beckett. When my mom sees his name on my phone screen, she winks and silently excuses herself.

> Beckett: Don't make plans tonight.

I smile as my thumbs type a reply.

> Me: What if I already did?

> Beckett: Cancel them because you have plans with me now.

> Me: Awfully presumptuous, don't you think? What if I don't want to have plans with you?

> Beckett: Trust me, honey. You WANT what I have planned for you.

> Me: If these plans have anything to do with a certain underwhelming appendage of yours, I'll pass.

Beckett: You and I both know there's
NOTHING underwhelming about me,
Pres. And now you'll be getting a few
extra reminders tonight. 😏👅🍆🍩

Just like that, after a few flirty texts, my mood is lifted. I don't know how he does it.

Me: Let's pretend I'm on board with this
plan of yours. What should I wear and
what time should I be ready?

Beckett: Dress comfortably. I'll see you
at eight. 😉

Me: Yee-haw, Cowboy. 🤠

Beckett: 🤦

I laugh.

Me: Love you, too, babe.

I gasp when I realize what I just did. Holy crap! I didn't mean to just blurt it out like that, especially not in a text. Gah! Why am I so awkward? A grown-ass woman should not have these issues. I groan when I see the text bubbles pop up and disappear. And pop up and disappear again. Finally, when Beck's message comes through, the pressure is lifted off my chest.

Beckett: I love you, Pres. Always have.
Always will.

I smile down at my phone as I read his message a few more times. There may be a lot of things up in the air for me right now, but there is one thing I'm absolutely certain of.

Beckett Armstrong is still one swoony bastard.

Chapter Forty
Presley

"Man, talk about a blast from the past."

Beckett pats the tailgate of his truck. "What are you waiting for? Get up there."

I smile to myself as I kick off my shoes and climb onto the bed of his truck. There are a bunch of blankets stacked together for padding with an oversized sleeping bag and fluffy pillows on top. Beck even backed the truck up to our pond, and there's a little cooler that I presume is filled with snacks. It's the exact same setup we used as teenagers.

I tuck my legs into the sleeping bag, but I'm sitting against the cab. "What are you planning to do with me now that you've got me here?"

His white teeth gleam under the moonlight as he flashes a panty-dropping grin. "Mmm. We'll get to that. But first, there's this." He holds up a small flask.

My lips quirk. "What's in there?"

The truck bed bounces under Beckett's weight as he climbs up. "See for yourself."

I take the flask from his proffered hand and twist the cap off. My eyes burn when I get a little whiff of its contents. "Is this what I think it is?" I take an experimental sip and immediately start coughing. "Yep, it sure is."

He laughs as he grabs the steel container from me and tips it back for a long swig. "You're out of practice, Pres. It's supposed to go down smooth."

"Not many opportunities for drinkin' rocket fuel in New York."

"Where's the fun in that?" The moon is full and reflecting off the pond, so I can clearly see his wink.

My eyes and nose are still burning, but when he offers it back to me, I take another small sip. "Did you have a reason for bringing me out here besides gettin' me drunk?"

Beckett tilts his chin up to the sky. "It's a warm, starry night, and I had a feelin' it's been a while since you've caught a good time."

I chuckle under my breath. "Did you forget about the *good time* we had this morning? *And* last night?" I pass the moonshine back over.

"No, darlin', I definitely haven't forgotten about that."

I incline my head toward the lunch cooler in the corner. "What's in there?"

"Water, jerky, cheese, fruit. Quick sustenance if we need to refuel."

"How long are you plannin' on keepin' me out here, Mr. Armstrong?"

Beck playfully nips at my neck, making me laugh. "As long as it takes to do all the dirty, dirty things."

To my utter embarrassment, a full-body shiver courses through me, and of course, Beckett notices.

I reach my hand out. "Give me that."

He laughs as he hands the flask over. "Don't drink too much, Pres. I have plans for you."

I give him a wry look. "Yes, I know. Dirty, dirty plans, apparently."

"Are you complaining?" Beckett leans over and carves a line of kisses down my jaw.

I shake my head. "Nuh-uh."

"Good." I can feel his smile against my skin. "Because I plan on takin' my time loving you tonight."

I smile. "Before we get to that portion of the evening, I wanted to talk to you about some things."

"What kind of things?"

"Well, for one, I heard from my divorce attorney today."

"And?"

"*And* he's not going to contest the divorce. I need to sign an agreement that I'll keep quiet about his affair and *other* things, but if I do that, Sebastian will walk away."

Beck's brows draw together. "So, he's essentially bribing you for his cooperation. That's bullshit, Pres."

I shake my head. "It doesn't matter, Beckett. I'll be free. That's more important to me."

"You can still be free," he insists. "And he can rot in prison where he belongs."

"I've explained this already. They'd never prosecute him. I just want him gone from my life, Beckett, and this is the fastest way to do that." I sigh. "Can I please move on to the next thing? I don't want Sebastian to ruin our night."

Beck takes a swig of moonshine and passes it back to me. "What's the next thing?"

"I was talking to my mom earlier about standing on my own for once. I can't do that if I'm sleeping in my childhood bedroom every night."

"You're more than welcome to sleep in my bedroom every night where we can do some *very grown-up* things." He winks.

"I will happily spend lots of time with you in that bed, but if I'm there every night, it kind of negates the whole independence thing I'm going for." I roll my eyes playfully. "Anyway... my mom mentioned the Wilsons' cottage is up for rent, so I'm going to call them in the morning."

Beckett searches my eyes for a moment. "Is this something you really need, Pres?"

"It is, Beckett. I'm thirty years old, and I've never lived on my own before. I need to know what that feels like." I weave our fingers together with my free hand. "But you're welcome to come over and keep me warm at night, any night. Just... maybe not *every* night. Do you understand where I'm comin' from?"

He nods. "I do. I won't pretend I don't want to share

a bed with you every night, but I understand *and respect* your desire to do this."

"Thank you."

Beckett takes the alcohol from me and screws the top back on. The moment he drops it, his mouth is on mine. I moan as one of his hands sinks into the back of my hair to hold me in place. The only time our lips break apart is when we have to pull away to remove our shirts. One by one, our clothing is tossed aside. Each time more skin is exposed, Beckett makes due on his promise to take his time, kissing and caressing every inch of me that's bared to him. At some point, we burrowed under the sleeping bag with me lying on my back and Beck on top of me, careful not to crush me with his weight.

When he fumbles to retrieve a condom from his wallet, I say, "Wait."

He freezes immediately. "Are you okay?"

I nod reassuringly. "Yes. I want this, Beckett. I want *you*." My eyes flick to the foil square in his hand. "But we don't need that if you don't want to use it. I'm on the shot... and when I went for my shoulder check-up, I had them test me, just in case. The last result came back today, and I'm good. I'm STI free. So, if everything's good on your end, and you trust me, I—"

Beck cuts off my incessant rambling with a hard kiss. "I trust you more than anyone else on this planet, Pres. And I'd love nothing more than to take you bare. I haven't... you're the only person I've been with like that. Ever."

I don't know why that statement makes me so weepy, but I have to choke back a sob when he says it. "Then love me, Beckett, with nothing between us."

I give him one long stroke from root to tip before placing him at my entrance. I'm more than ready, so when he shifts a little and pushes forward, he slides right in.

His head drops to my shoulder. "Fuck, *so* good."

I gasp when he deepens the angle. "Perfect."

Sweat dots my skin as Beckett goes deep and long, toe-curling pleasure slowly building inside of me. When my body reaches the point of no return, I dig my nails into his back and cry out his name as I'm overtaken by bliss. A few seconds later, Beck's muscles stiffen as he, too, finds release. He places soft kisses along the nape of my neck and my temple before pulling up just enough to look me in the eye.

Beckett leans into my palm as I rest it over his cheek. "I meant what I said earlier. I didn't mean to just blurt it out in a text message, but I do love you, Beck. I never stopped. I just... I need you to be patient with me. If I seem hesitant sometimes, it's not because I don't want to be with you. I want that more than *anything*. But I've spent most of my adult life doubting my thoughts... my worth." I laugh humorlessly. "I questioned pretty much *every-thing*. So, even though I'm sure that I'm right where I belong, sometimes, I might need a reminder."

"I know, darlin'." He turns his face into my hand and

kisses my palm. "You know what I think we should do?"

I release a breathy sigh as he withdraws from my body. "What?"

He sits back on his knees. "Go skinny dipping."

I release a shocked laugh. "Beckett! It's October. And we've been drinking."

"So?" he challenges. "It's also eighty degrees. Just a quick dip; we'll be fine. And if we get cold, I have ways of warming you up."

I sit up with him. "Well, in that case, what are we waiting for?"

Beckett smacks a hard kiss on my lips. "There's my girl."

I'm laughing the entire time we're running down the dock. As I watch Beckett cannonball into the pond, I smile to myself, thinking about how lucky I am, having this second chance with him. Maybe my mama was right. Perhaps there is a God after all.

"And now it's time for the entertainment portion of the evening."

I smile. "I don't know... I think the last couple of hours have been pretty entertaining."

When we got out of the water—which was way too cold, thank you very much—Beckett went straight to work warming me up again. Afterward, he told me to get dressed because he had another surprise for me in the gazebo. Beckett reaches for something in the corner, but it's too dark for me to see until he switches on a small battery-powered lantern.

"Have a seat, Pres." He takes the spot to my right, holding an acoustic guitar.

"You still play?"

Beckett nods. "Not as much as I used to, but I'm not too rusty."

I sit up, excited to hear him play again. "Play something that makes you think of us."

He thinks about it for a moment before taking the pick out of the strings and positioning the guitar on his lap just right. I smile when I hear the opening notes to one of my favorite Dierks Bentley songs. This tune was released years after I left, so there's no way Beck could've known how much I love it. Sebastian hates everything country, so I could never listen to my favorite music around him. Thankfully, he wasn't around a lot, so I didn't have to give it up entirely while I was in New York.

When Beckett starts singing the first verse, the breath whooshes out of me. Beck's voice sounds almost identical to the original artist. They have that same deep, raspy tone that makes all your girly parts take notice. Dierks is my absolute favorite country artist because of that sexy, gritty voice. Now I have to wonder if that's no coincidence. Like maybe my subconscious recognized the similarities, even if it wasn't obvious on the surface. Huh. Funny how that works, isn't it? Beckett bumps his shoulder to mine when he gets to the verse about being mean enough to stare the girl's demons down. He looks right at me as he sings about hard times putting the shine into diamonds. God, this song could have been written about us. I love it even more now.

When he strums the final note, I practically jump on top of him and press my lips against his. One kiss quickly escalates, and before I know it, Beckett is inside of me again, masterfully playing my body like he just played that guitar.

Damn swoony bastard.

Chapter Forty-One
Presley

Alight breeze blows as I approach Mr. Armstrong's grave, whipping my long hair into my face. I've meant to get here sooner, but his son has been keeping me busy. These last few weeks with Beckett have been amazing. We spend every possible moment together when we're not working, and sometimes Beck will even hang out at the bar when I'm behind the counter slinging drinks. We're not outwardly flaunting our relationship around town, but we're also not hiding it. I've accepted that people will think what they're going to think, and there's nothing we can do about it.

We may not know all the details about each other's lives while we were apart, but my brother was right when he said Beck and I are still the same where it counts. The events during those twelve years may have shaped us into more guarded, cautious people, but that inexplicable bond we formed at an early age is stronger than it's ever been. Everything with Beck is just so easy. Natural. Comfortable, but not in the boring sense.

Our connection isn't the only thing that's stronger. Our need for one another is at a fever pitch. Maybe we're subconsciously making up for lost time, but we can barely keep our hands off each other. In the month since Beck and I reconnected physically, he's never failed to take my body to new heights. Sometimes we make slow, passionate love. Other times, we're mindless and frenzied like animals. But whether he takes me soft or hard, I never once doubted my own safety or his love for me. I enjoy exploring my limits and curiosities with him, and his patience with me in that regard is extraordinary.

"Hey, Mr. Armstrong. I'm sorry for not coming sooner." I lower myself to my knees and run my fingers over his headstone, clearing some dirt away from the letters engraved into it. "I don't know if you're watching over Beckett or not, but just in case, I'll bring you up to speed. We're together again, and I'd like to think it's for good this time. You see, Sebastian, the man I married in New York, turned out to be a horrible person. He hurt me... many, many times until I finally had the strength to leave. Beckett's been so patient and understanding about the whole thing. He's showing me every day that good people do exist and that I deserve their kindness. I don't know how I survived so many years without him. Truth is, that's all I was doing. Surviving, I mean.

"Your son reminds me why life is worth livin'. I'm

hopeful about the future for the first time in a long time. I feel loved and accepted for who I truly am, not who someone wants me to be. I wish you could be here to witness all the good he's doing. As you know, Beck also had his share of awfulness in his life, but he's taking that experience, and he's doing something productive with it. Something that will help others who've been in similar situations. I don't know why I was granted this second chance with him, but I promise you, I will never make your son regret it. I will love him with my whole heart and soul.

"He asked if I wanted to teach riding lessons again. I haven't started yet. I'm still gettin' to know the new horses, learning their temperaments, and stuff. But it feels right, you know? It feels like this is what I should've been doing all along. I think somehow, Beckett knew that. You probably remember, but we were always so freakishly attuned to one another, and that hasn't changed one bit. I hate that you're gone, but I love seeing him taking charge of everything like you used to. My father still refuses to retire completely— the stubborn goat he is—but I think he's getting closer to that point now that he knows the ranch is in such good hands. You know, maybe one day Beck and I will be running the place together.

"Clayton still helps out here and there, but he has no desire to dedicate that much time to it. Mama says since he bought the bar, he's really been focusing on that, and she can't fault him for it because it makes him happy. God, listen to me, just rambling on. I'm making up for lost time, I guess. I'm sorry I didn't know about your passing until recently. I'm sorry I didn't get to see you again before you left us. But I meant what I said earlier. You can rest in peace, knowing Beckett is wholly loved and appreciated like he should be. I won't let you down."

I take a few moments of silence, my skin warming under the unseasonably warm temperatures. Southern Georgia usually has mild weather in the winter and fall, but almost ninety degrees at the end of October is a bit much. Maybe I got used to the colder temps up north, and I'm just not as tolerant as I used to be. Right before I get ready to say my goodbye, the hairs on the back of my neck stand at attention. I can't shake the feeling that I'm being watched, so I look around the cemetery to see if anyone is there. Sure enough, leaning with his booted foot propped against an old Spanish moss, Beckett is watching me have a one-sided conversation with his father. With a blush staining my cheeks, I stand up, brushing the grass away from my knees. Since it's so warm, I went with a pair of cut-offs and a tank top today. It shows a lot more skin than I'm used to these days, but by the way Beckett's eyes darken as he watches my approach, I'd say he approves.

"Hey, you."

He kicks off from the tree and pulls me into a hug. He doesn't say anything for a good minute; he just holds me and nuzzles his nose into my neck. "Hey. How long have you been here?"

"Twenty minutes, maybe. How long have *you* been here?"

"Just a few."

I look over toward the parking lot, wondering why I didn't hear the familiar roar of his truck engine as he drove up. "Where's your truck?"

"Parked along the road." Beck jerks his head toward the gates. "I was making a supply run, so I have the trailer hooked up to it."

Ah, that explains it. This is a fairly large cemetery, but the parking lot is tiny—it only has ten spots in two rows of five. There's no way Beck's truck would've had room to maneuver with a trailer hitched to it.

"I'm guessing you came here to visit your dad?"

Beck nods. "Yeah. It's been a while."

I shift on my feet. "Well, I won't keep you. I have to get back anyway because I'm working with Clay tonight. I'll see you later?"

He wraps his strong arms around me again and kisses my cheek. "Thanks for comin' here, Pres. It means a lot."

I trace my finger down his jaw. "You don't need to thank me, Beckett. I'm happy to do it. I'm just sorry it took me so long."

Beck brushes some damp hair away from the side of my face. "I love you, Presley James."

"I love you too, Beckett Armstrong." I press up on my toes and kiss him softly on the lips. "You want me to stop by when I get home tonight?"

He nods. "Always."

"Well, okay then, Cowboy." I laugh when he narrows his eyes and pinches my backside. "I'll see you tonight. By the way, I won't complain if you're waitin' for me in your birthday suit."

Now he laughs. "Well, I aim to please, darlin'."

I make a shooing gesture. "Go talk to your dad, Beckett. I'll see you tonight."

I don't turn back to check, but I can feel his eyes on me during my entire walk to the parking lot, so I put an extra sway in my hips. I hop in my new-to-me CJ7 and crank the engine. As I'm pulling out, Beckett lifts one hand in a wave, so I blow him a kiss in return right before I drive through the gates.

God, I love that man.

————

"Hey, Theo, has it been busy?"

Theo looks up from his spot behind the bar. "Hey, Pres. Pretty slow right now, but it's been hoppin' most of the night."

"Where's Clay?"

He jerks his head toward the hallway. "Workin' on the books."

"Let me go stash my purse in the back, and I'll be right out."

He nods in reply.

When I open the door to Clay's office, I'm frozen in shock.

"Damn, Nicky," my brother groans from his position at her back. "Why is your pussy my favorite? You're an honest-to-God witch, aren't you?"

Nicky stretches even farther over the surface of the desk, gripping the edge with her talons. "Just shut up and fuck me, Clayton. I'm not interested in your riveting conversational skills."

I cringe as the sound of skin slapping on skin gets louder. "Oh, that's right. You just want me for my dick."

"And your tongue," she pants. "As long as you're not usin' it to talk."

Maybe if I wasn't singing along to the song blasting loudly through the speakers, I would've noticed the noises coming from behind the door before I opened it. Maybe if Clayton and Nicky weren't so busy screwing each other on top of his desk, they would've noticed me and took cover. Maybe if I wasn't so stunned, I wouldn't still be witnessing this shit show from the doorway. I suppose I should be thankful they're both still mostly dressed, and behind the desk, so my view is limited, but my brother's thrusting hips are something I could've gone my whole life not seeing.

I finally shake out of my stupor long enough to cover my eyes and back out of the room. "Ugh, sorry. I'm leaving."

"What the hell?" Nicky screams right before I shut the door. "Get the hell out of here, Presley!" I hear some shuffling before she yells again. "Oh, my God, you idiot! You didn't lock the door?"

"You didn't give me much of a chance when you waltzed in here and shoved your bare ass in my face!"

More moving around. "Where are you going? I wasn't done."

I startle when the door flies open, and Nicole storms out with a murderous glare on her face. "Fuck you, Clayton James! We're *so* done! I don't know what the hell I was thinkin'." Her evil eyes flick to me. "I don't want to hear a word, Presley."

I plaster my back against the wall as she runs off, listening to the telltale sounds of my brother buckling his belt, cursing under his breath. Oh my God, why couldn't I have just tucked my purse beneath the bar?

"Pres, it's safe to come in now."

I shake my head, but he probably can't see me. "Nope. I'm good out here." I can smell the sex wafting from the room, and I have no desire to go in there anytime soon.

Clayton curses again before the floorboards creak as he walks across the room. He leans against the door-jamb, scrubbing a hand down his face. When he looks up, at least he has the sense to look embarrassed.

"What're you doin' here?"

I give him an incredulous look. "It's seven. I'm here for my shift. Just wanted to drop my purse in your desk drawer like I always do."

Clay looks confused. "It's seven already? Shit. We were goin' at it longer than I thought."

I scrunch my face. "Gross, Clayton. I don't need to know that. If you want to talk about your sex life, I'm sure there are plenty of other people who'll listen."

His eyes widen. "You can't say a word, Pres, not even to Beck. She doesn't want anyone to know."

"Yeah, I'm sure the last person she'd want to know about this is Beck." I scoff. "What the hell were you thinkin', Clayton? Nicky? Really? You could do so much better."

He thunks his head against the doorframe and closes his eyes. "I'm in love with her, Presley."

I mime unplugging my ears. "I'm sorry; there's no way I heard you correctly."

His periwinkle eyes flicker to mine. "Trust me, if I could turn these damn feelings off, I would've done it years ago, but I fucking can't."

"But..." I shake my head and try again. "I don't understand, Clayton. How long has this been going on?"

He stretches his neck from side to side. "Off and on for... what? Thirteen, maybe fourteen years now?"

"*What?!*" My jaw drops. "How? Why? *Why her*, Clayton? She's the devil incarnate!"

Clayton releases a heavy breath. "There are things about her that you don't know, Pres. There are things about her that *no one* else knows. It's not my place to tell, but let's just say Nicky's life isn't what she leads people to believe. There's a reason she's so..."

"Unbelievably bitchy?" I helpfully supply.

He gives me a wry look. "Yeah. That."

I lightly tap the back of my head on the wall. "God, Clayton. Of all the people."

"I know," he agrees. "Just please... forget you ever saw anything tonight. Okay? And don't say a word."

I sigh. "I'm not going to lie to Beckett, Clayton. You can't ask me to do that. Not when we're just getting back on track again."

"Pres—"

I hold my hand up. "The best I can do is I won't outwardly volunteer the information until you get your crap sorted out. But if he asks... I won't lie."

My brother thinks about that for a minute. "Thanks, Pres."

I give him a good once-over, taking in his messy hair, the unevenly buttoned shirt, and the bright red lipstick smeared across his mouth. "I'm gonna get to work. Maybe you should take a look in the mirror before you come back out." He catches my purse when I toss it to him. "Put that in your desk for me, will ya?'"

Clayton nods. "I'll be out in a bit."

I start walking away. "Take your time."

Theo gives me a strange look when I return to the bar. "Everything okay back there?"

I clear my throat. "Yeah, fine. My brother and I were just having a chat, that's all."

Theo lifts a dark brow. "That chat didn't have something to do with the angry woman marching out of here a few minutes ago, did it?"

"Trust me, Theo. It's best if you just leave it be."

"Oh, I know." He laughs. "Doesn't mean we're all not curious. You'd have to be blind not to see it."

"If that's true, then clearly, I need to get my vision checked."

Theo smiles. "To be fair, Presley, you haven't been around. I've known Clayton most of my adult life, and whatever's been goin' on with those two isn't going to resolve itself just because they keep trying to ignore it. In fact, I'd go as far as to say it's probably makin' it worse."

Damn, could I have really been that clueless about my own brother? Theo's right, though. I haven't been around. Maybe if I did a better job keeping in touch while I was in New York, Clayton would've confided in me, but I doubt Sebastian would've allowed that. It's just one of the many things I wish I could change, but I can't. When my brother comes back out front, he implores me with his eyes to drop the subject. I decide to honor his wishes for tonight, but I'm definitely going to start being a better sister and paying attention going forward.

Chapter Forty-Two
Presley

I'm roasting.

I squirm away from Beckett's heavy arm, trying to put some distance between us, but I only have a full-sized bed in my new place, so there's not a whole lot of room left. The sheets are soaked. Beck's bronzed skin is shiny with sweat as he writhes and thrashes in his sleep. Obviously, he's having one helluva nightmare, but I'm not sure what the proper protocol is in a situation like this.

"Beck, honey, wake up. You're having a bad dream."

He still doesn't shake out of it, so I reach across the mattress and place my hand on his shoulder.

The moment I touch him, Beck's eyes snap open, and a guttural sound emanates from his chest as his arms fly toward me. He maneuvers our bodies until my back is pinned to the mattress. I squirm beneath him as his hands wrap around my throat and immediately start squeezing.

"Beckett." I gasp for air as his fingers tighten. "Please... can't... breathe."

His eyes are wide open, but they're vacant. He stares down at me like he's trying to eliminate a threat. Like I *am* that threat. My fingernails claw at his forearms as my vision goes blurry. His muscles are bunched as he squeezes even tighter, an angry vein popping out on the middle of his forehead. Ironically, I'm perfectly calm, but I know I need to somehow get through to him before losing the chance.

"Ple—" I sputter, trying to wake him before I lose consciousness.

The fight is draining from my body. My airway is constricted, and I'm not getting enough oxygen. As my lids begin to flutter, I can see the fog slowly lifting from his eyes. He's finally coming back from whatever horrible place his mind was trapped in. The second he realizes what he's doing, he releases me and jumps back, stumbling off the too-small mattress onto the floor.

"Fuck." His eyes run the length of my body, likely checking for damage.

I sit up, resisting the urge to rub my aching neck. "Beck, it's okay. I'm fine."

His brown eyes widen. "Are you fucking kidding me, Presley?! That's bullshit! I could've just killed you!" He stands up, pacing the length of the bed. He must've gotten up at some point in the night and put his boxers on because he wasn't wearing them when we went to sleep. "Fuck!" He pulls on the ends of his thick hair.

"Really, Beck, I'm—"

He points a finger at me. "Don't you dare fucking say you're okay. It's *not* okay, Pres! Me putting my hands on you in violence would *never* fucking be okay!"

"Beck, you were sleeping." I clear my throat, trying to smooth the grit out of it. "You were having a nightmare. You didn't know it was me. I know you would never hurt me on purpose. I trust you."

"That doesn't matter, goddammit. What if I didn't wake up in time, Pres? What would've happened then? You *shouldn't* fucking trust me! I don't fucking trust myself! Christ. You must be scared shitless right now."

My throat is aching, and yeah, for a moment, I was shocked, but I've no doubt that what just happened was the result of a horrible nightmare, maybe even a flashback. Being afraid never crossed my mind because I know Beckett Armstrong wouldn't hesitate to lay down his life for me.

I crawl out of bed and grab my robe off the hook on the back of my bedroom door. As I'm pulling it over my shoulders, I say, "I'm not afraid, Beckett. I know you didn't mean to do it. And you woke up in time. You didn't hurt me. I'm *fine*."

I don't think this is a good time to remind him I've been through much worse.

Beckett scrubs a hand down his face. "But I *could* have. I could have done so much worse than hurt you, Presley."

Beck looks wary as I approach him, but he remains still. "I love you." When only a few inches of space exist between us, I cup his jaw in my hands and lift up on my toes. "You love me. You would *never* hurt me. If something like that ever happens again, I know you would wake up in time. I'm not afraid of you, Beck." I kiss the corner of his mouth. "You're my safe haven. I could *never* be afraid of you."

I hold his eyes as I lower myself to the ground. "I would never be afraid of you, Beckett."

"Pres, what are you doing?" He tries to bat my hand away as I tug on the waistband of his boxers.

I give him a cheeky grin. "I know it's been a while since we've done this, but I think it's pretty self-explanatory."

He shakes his head. "Pres, you don't—"

While Beck's gone down on me dozens of times since I've been back, I've yet to return the favor. I used to love doing this to him, but like many things, Sebastian ruined the act for me. But right now, I can't think of any better way to prove to Beckett how safe and secure he makes me feel. I want to do this for him, but I also want to prove to myself that my almost-ex-husband is no longer in control. I refuse to give Sebastian that kind of power anymore.

"Shh." I trace my finger over the bulge in his underwear before slipping my fingers under the waistband and freeing his impressive length. "Let me take care of you, Beck."

Beck curses as I lean forward, swirling my tongue over his tip before taking him into my mouth. He gathers my hair with one hand, holding it back so he can watch me. "You're killin' me, Pres."

I moan, relishing the taste of his skin as I coax him deeper into my mouth, running my tongue along the underside of his cock. There's too much of him to fully take, so I develop a rhythm using my hand and mouth, and before long, Beckett's hips start rocking on their own accord. He thrusts into my mouth in slow, shallow movements, all the while telling me how much he loves me. How amazing my mouth feels wrapped around him. How he's the luckiest son of a bitch alive.

Beck's grip on my hair tightens as he groans. "Jesus, that's so good. I'm gonna come, Pres."

My fingernails dig into his ass, pulling him closer. I take him in as far as I can, increasing the suction as he surges into my mouth. When he's done, I pull away and sit back on my knees, Beckett's salty taste on my tongue. I smile, proud of myself for taking my power back and more than a little aroused. I choke out a surprised laugh when Beck scoops me up and tosses me on the mattress with a bounce.

"Beckett! What are you doing?"

His muscular body hovers over mine as he slowly unties the belt to my robe. He kisses down my neck, to my breasts, down the center of my abdomen. "I think it's pretty self-explanatory, Pres." He winks, clearly amused with himself for throwing my words back at me. I open my mouth to deliver a sassy retort, but the moment Beck's tongue swipes through my hot flesh, all conscious thought flies out the window.

My phone rings as I'm climbing into my Jeep after my shift at the bar. Every muscle in my body tenses when I look down at the caller ID and see Sebastian's name. I think about ignoring him, but it's been almost two months since our divorce paperwork was filed, and this is the first attempt he's made to contact me. My curiosity gets the best of me as I decide to accept the call. Since Bluetooth isn't an option on this old thing, I'll have to talk to him from *Dive Bar's* parking lot.

I take a deep breath as I press the button to answer. "What do you want, Sebastian? You're not supposed to be calling. I told you, if you had anything to say to me, you could do it through my attorney."

"Oh, but Presley, there's nothing *legally* stopping me from calling you, now is there?"

I frown. "That's beside the point. What do you want?"

"I wanted to have a little chat. How was your shift tonight?"

"What are you talking about?"

"Your shift at your brother's hick bar," he explains. "You just got off work, did you not?"

I suppress a gasp. "How do you know that, Sebastian?"

His dark chuckle makes the fine hairs on my arms stand up. "Did you think I was bluffing when I said I had eyes on you?"

Honestly, I did. I figured since I hadn't heard from

him in so long, he was just trying to intimidate me. How could I be so stupid?

"What's wrong, Presley? Cat got your tongue?"

"What. Do. You. Want. Sebastian?"

"I want you to stop being such a stubborn bitch and come home."

"I *am* home," I say through gritted teeth. "Our divorce should be final any day now, or have you forgotten that fact?"

"Ah, yes, another trivial attempt on your end to cut me out of your life. You didn't think that was going to actually work, did you?"

I hold my phone out for a second and just stare at it in shock. "Why *wouldn't* it work? The paperwork was filed with the courts. I signed your stupid agreement. Now, it's just a matter of waiting for the judge to sign off on it."

"Hmm... yes, that is typically how the process goes."

I pinch the bridge of my nose. "What's that supposed to mean?"

"Well, from what I hear, the courts are incredibly backlogged right now."

I shake my head. "That's not what my attorney said."

"Well, maybe you should check again because your petition won't be getting in front of a judge anytime soon."

I have to forcibly unclench my jaw. "I swear to God, Sebastian, if you di—"

"Speaking of God...you must give my best to my dear mother-in-law. Tell her she looked beautiful in that floral dress she wore to church the other day. It complemented your father's suit well."

Okay, that's too much of a coincidence. Sebastian definitely has someone watching me, and apparently, my parents, too. I nervously glance around the parking lot to see if I can spot anyone suspicious. Of course, no one is conveniently waving their arms around, saying, "Look at me!"

"Sebast—"

"Let's cut the shit, shall we, my dear wife?" he barks. "I'm done waiting for you to come to your senses. Maybe spreading your legs for that backwoods boyfriend of yours has made you even dumber than you were before, but make no mistake, Presley. You are *mine*. You will always be mine. It's time for you to come home and accept your punishment for being a two-timing slut. But don't worry; I'll fuck you so good afterward, you won't even remember his name. We have a lot of time to make up for, don't you think? And while we're at it, we might as well kill two birds with one stone. I took the liberty of canceling your upcoming appointment for a new birth control shot. I've decided it's time for us to start a family."

My jaw drops. "*Are you insane?!* That's it, isn't it? You've lost your mind, or maybe you never really had it to begin with. First of all, you still seem to forget that *you* were the one having an affair. Not me. The thought of starting a family with you—of bringing an innocent child into your life—makes me sick. I would *never* have a baby with you, Sebastian. Our marriage is over, and quite frankly, it was over long before I ever filed for divorce. Anyone I choose to be with from this point on is none of your concern."

I was always grateful that Sebastian's obsession with vanity extended to the fact that he didn't want me to get pregnant. As he so delicately put it, he didn't want me to get a fat ass. I had already met his evil half at that point, so I took it for the blessing it was.

"I see you've become rather spirited during your time in Georgia. I'm going to enjoy breaking you of that ridiculous notion."

I'm so angry and freaked out, I'm shaking. "You know what, Sebastian? Screw you. I don't need to listen to this."

I jab my finger against the screen, ending the call, right before I block his number. I can't do this right now. I need to think. I need to come up with a plan. Sebastian's obviously not going to just let this go like I was so foolish to believe. I need to speak with Beckett and see what he thinks I should do. I drive straight to the ranch, bypassing my parents' house and parking right in front of Beck's. We didn't make plans to see each other tonight, but Beck was obviously still awake because, by the time I get out of my Jeep, he's standing on the front porch waiting for me.

"Hey. This is a nice surprise."

The moment I loop my hands behind his back, my panic morphs into desperation. I know Beck and I will need to discuss Sebastian, but right now, I need Beckett's touch to remind me I'm safe in his arms. That no matter how many threats Sebastian makes, I'll be okay. That I'll never be a victim to his torment again.

He runs his hand down my back soothingly. "What happened, Pres?"

I jump up, crossing my ankles behind his back. "Kiss now. Talk later."

He doesn't need convincing. Beck seals his mouth over mine, walking blindly through the house until we reach his bedroom. We only manage to remove the bare minimum clothing before our bodies are joined together, seeking release at a frenzied pace. We strip the remainder of our clothes off piece by piece and take our time exploring each other's bodies the second time around. We make love for hours, until we're both sleepy and sated, curled in each other's arms. Right before I drift off, I feel Beckett slip out of bed.

"Where are you going?" I mumble.

Beck inclines his head toward the hall. "I'm going to sleep in the other room."

That jolts me awake. I sit up, clutching the comforter to my chest. "Why?"

His eyes dance across the room, looking at seemingly everything but me. "Pres, you know why."

I sigh. "Beckett, I thought we resolved this earlier. I trust you. Come back to bed."

He groans. "I can't, Presley. If I ever hurt you—accidentally or not—I'd be no better than that piece of shit."

"So, what?" I throw my hands up. "You're never going to sleep in the same bed with me again?"

"If that is what it takes..." Beckett rubs the back of his neck. "My nightmares... they've been much more frequent lately for some reason. I can't bear the thought of harming you. Why can't you understand that? Let's not fight about this, Pres. I'll come back to bed, and I'll make sure you're really asleep before I get up next time."

Okay, I know I'm being irrational. My emotions are likely still ragged from my conversation with Sebastian earlier, but I can't understand it. I mean... I get why he wouldn't want to hurt me, but I don't know why he doesn't feel the same conviction I do that he'd never actually do it, no matter how out of it he was. I just want Beckett to hold me. I want to feel safe, like only he can make me feel. But what I definitely *don't* want is to be lulled into a false sense of security, only to wake up cold and alone. I've been there, done that, too many times.

I hold up my hand to stop him when he moves toward the bed. "Don't bother, Beckett. I'm going home."

He blinks a few times. "What? Why?"

I throw my shirt over my head, not bothering to locate my bra. "It's been a long day, and I don't want to fight with you. Maybe I'm being overly sensitive, and I'll be more agreeable after getting some sleep, but I really need to leave right now. I don't want to say something I'll regret."

Beck grabs my wrist as I'm pulling my jeans on. "Hold up."

I shake out of his hold. "It's fine. I'm planning to spend the day at the stables tomorrow, so I'll see you then. I love you."

Beckett's body is carved and rigid like a statue as I kiss him on the cheek before walking out the door. On the short drive to my rental, I almost convince myself to turn back three times, but I remind myself that I need to stand my ground. I silently amend that thought the moment I step into my cottage and realize my mistake. I was so determined to be independent, I dismissed the warning signals that were triggered earlier this evening. And because of that, instead of sticking around and having a conversation with a man I know would never hurt me, I'm now standing in a room with the one who'd like to do the most harm.

Sebastian's bright blue eyes shine with malice as he flips the light on. "Hello, wife."

Chapter Forty-Three
Presley

"It took you long enough to get here, Presley. Where've you been?"

Sebastian raises a brow in challenge when I eye the door. Adrenaline is coursing through my veins, telling me to run, but how far would I really get? I dropped my keys the moment I realized I wasn't alone. If I took the time to retrieve them, Sebastian would tackle me in a heartbeat. I decide playing it cool is the best route to take. Maybe, if I can get him to let his guard down, I'll have a chance to escape.

"When did you get into town?"

Whiskey permeates the air of my small house. When I get a good look at him, it's clear he's been drinking for a while.

His lips curve into a cruel smirk. "I'll answer your question after you answer mine. *Where've you been, Presley?* I've been waiting for hours."

"Clayton asked me to stay late."

"Liar!" Sebastian roars, shooting off the couch. "Don't fucking lie to me, you whore! You were with *him*, weren't you?"

I casually hang my purse on the hook by the door, trying not to visibly shake as he gets closer. "Who, Sebastian?"

Sebastian's arm swings out so fast, I don't even realize his fist is coming at me until it makes contact with my face. I cry out as I'm knocked back into the wall from the force.

"Oh, I'm going to enjoy this," Sebastian promises, rolling up his shirt sleeves.

It takes a moment before my head stops spinning. When it does, rage fires up within me. This man has taken so much from me over the years: my body, my dignity, my happiness. I refuse to give him any more. My eyes dart around the room, looking for anything I could use as a weapon. When Sebastian sees me eyeballing the lamp, he gets a sinister smile as he pushes it off the table. The moment it hits the ground, we're plunged into darkness again. I decide to run for it before his eyes have a chance to adjust, but luck's not on my side because he easily predicts the move.

Sebastian grabs a fistful of my hair and shoves me to the ground. "Get on your knees where you belong, bitch."

My ears start ringing when he punches me a second time. Blood fills my mouth as the back of my head hits the floor. I groan, blinking through the haze. I refuse to let this man win. I would rather die fighting him off than ever tolerate his abuse again. I focus on breathing, rolling onto my side so I can push myself up.

"Where the fuck do you think you're going?" he yells. "I'm not done with you."

"Too bad." I spit a mouthful of blood on the floor. "Because I'm so fucking done with you, Sebastian."

"Who knew you were such a kinky slut? I mean, why else would you antagonize me like this? Do you *want* me to hurt you while I'm fucking you?" He releases a sinister laugh. "Because that can easily be arranged."

When Sebastian's fist flies forward again, I actually manage to dodge it this time. Not only that, but I kick his legs out from under him, causing his body to fall to the floor with a satisfying thud. I can't see very well in the dark, but I'm pretty sure I just shocked the hell out of him.

I run for my purse and grab my phone from the outside pocket. As I'm hitting the call button, Sebastian pushes me from behind, and my cell goes flying across the floor, into the attached kitchen.

"Nice try, Presley. Now, get the fuck on your knees and accept your punishment!"

"Fuck you!" I whirl around on him, slamming my knee into his balls as hard as I can. "*You* get on your fucking knees, you sick bastard!"

He goes down fast, moaning in pain. My eyes have adjusted in the dark, so as I spot my keys on the living room floor, I scoop them up and run for the door. I freeze when I hear the unmistakable sound of a gun cocking.

"I wouldn't do that if I were you, Presley." Sebastian's hot breath washes over me a second before I feel the cool barrel pressing against my temple. "Unless you want me to paint the walls with your blood." He grinds his erection into my back and moans. "Fuck, why does the thought of that make me so hard?"

"Because you're psychotic?" I'm sure the question was rhetorical, but I can't seem to help myself.

He presses the muzzle into me even further. "Watch your mouth."

I stare at the door no more than five feet in front of me, rolling my odds of escape around in my head. Sadly, in my current predicament, I don't think they're all that favorable. So close, yet so far.

I blow out a breath. "What do you want, Sebastian? It doesn't have to be like this. Why can't you just let me go?"

He bands his free arm around my torso, grabbing my breast. I clamp my teeth down on my tongue to avoid crying out.

"I already told you what I want, Presley. You're going to come back to New York with me, rescind the divorce, and we're going to pretend like this whole thing never happened."

"Just like that?"

I have no intention of going anywhere with this man, but I'm trying to buy myself some time to think.

"No, not just like that." Sebastian's head lowers until

his face is nuzzling my neck. His grip on my breast tightens. "Why *the fuck* do you smell like another man, Presley?" He releases his hold on me, only to spin me around and slam me against the wall. "Strip."

I blink away the spots in my vision. "Excuse me?"

"*Fucking strip!*" he screams. "You're going to strip, then you're going to get in the shower and wash his scent off you. Then, I'm going to fuck every one of your holes to ensure no trace of him is left behind. If you take it like a good girl, *then* we'll discuss going home. But if you fight me..." Sebastian takes the gun he was pointing at me and forces it past my lips. "Then, I'm going to blow your fucking brains out, right before I drive to your parents' ranch and do the same to your boyfriend. Hell, I might take out my dear in-laws, too, just for the hell of it. They did help keep you away from me, after all."

Bile rises up in my throat when I hear the truth in his statement. Sebastian has every intention of delivering on those promises. My eyes water, and I gag when he shoves the gun farther into my mouth.

"Are you going to be a good girl, Presley?"

I nod as much as I can with this thing in my mouth.

I gasp for air when Sebastian pulls the gun out. His arms straighten, aiming the weapon directly at my heart. "Now, fucking *strip*."

I know I only have one chance. I have to get it just right, or I won't make it out of this alive. I don't bother trying to hold back my tears. I want him to think I'm still the weak little lamb he tortured for so long. It's the only chance I have of pulling this off. My hands go to the hem of my shirt. I can see the whites of Sebastian's eyes as he watches while each new inch of skin is revealed.

Right before I lift the cotton over my breasts, I throw my arm out, flattening my hand and slamming the knife-edge of it through his elbows. Sebastian's gun slides across the floor as he loses his hold on it. We both lunge for it at the same time. Just as my fingers grip the cool metal, Sebastian sweeps his arm out, pushing it farther out of my reach.

"No!" I scream.

"You're going to pay for that, you fucking bitch! You'll be *begging* for death by the time I'm done with you."

My limbs are flailing wildly; anything I can do to prevent Sebastian from getting there first, I do it. He grunts and curses each time I make contact, but it doesn't stop him. When my fingers finally reach the gun again, I act on pure instinct.

I flip the safety off, loop my finger around the trigger, and twist my body to aim the barrel right at my husband's head. "Don't fucking move, Sebastian."

He sits back on his knees, laughing. The man is legitimately cackling, like having a gun pointed at him is the funniest thing in the world.

"Shut up!" I stand up, carefully keeping the gun trained on him.

"Presley, don't be stupid. You don't know how to

handle that thing. Now, put the dangerous weapon down before you hurt yourself."

I chuckle, flipping the overhead light on, so he can see my face when I inform him how very wrong he is. "You think I don't know how to handle a gun?"

One thing my dear husband doesn't know about me is that I am *well-trained* in shooting a gun. It's been a while, but any country girl worth her salt knows how. I can see the moment the doubt registers on Sebastian's face.

"Uh-uh, I wouldn't do that if I were you." I tsk as Sebastian starts to lunge for me. "You will have a bullet between your eyes before you can even blink."

Sebastian shakes his head. "I don't believe you."

"No?" I move the gun lower and shoot it right between his spread legs.

"What the fuck?" Sebastian screams, shielding his crotch with his hands. "You could've shot my dick off!"

I smirk. "Don't tempt me. You and I both know you'd deserve it."

He pales. "Presley, put the gun down, and we can talk about this."

"Really?" I quirk my head to the side. "Did you want to *talk* when you punched me in the face earlier? When you were beating the shit out of me time and time again back in New York? How about when you were *raping me?* The time for *talking* is over, Sebastian. Look who has the power in this relationship now. I bet this is pretty emasculating, isn't it?"

I think I might be a little punch drunk because I could swear I just heard a noise from my bedroom.

His icy blue eyes narrow. "You fucking bitch. You'll regret this."

I scoff. "Doubtful."

"It's over, asshole," a deep voice growls behind me.

Huh. I guess I did hear something.

I see Beckett coming up beside me, with his own gun pointed at Sebastian.

"You okay, Pres?" Beck gives me a brief once-over.

"Peachy."

He smirks. "Smartass."

A feral noise erupts from Sebastian. I look up just in time to see him lunging for Beck like a man with nothing to lose. "You bastard! She's fucking mine!"

Everything happens so fast. Sebastian and Beckett wrestle for control of the gun in a whirl of grunts and punches. I step back, keeping my Glock aimed at them, but I have no intention of firing unless I have a clear shot. I scream when Beck's gun goes off, having no idea if anyone was hit. In the next moment, Sebastian leaps on top of me, taking me to the ground. He looks crazed as he attempts to get the gun from me. Stars dance across my vision when the bastard headbutts me. We fight and fumble, both of our hands on the trigger at one point. I refuse to let go; I refuse to give in. One way or the other, this ends now. I will not allow this man to torment me any longer.

Sebastian headbutts me again, and this time, red streams across my vision as blood drips down my face.

Whether it's mine or his, I couldn't tell you. I cry out as he twists my wrist, trying to turn the barrel toward me. I don't know if it's through sheer force of will or pure luck, but I manage to turn it back toward him. He must realize he won't win because he stops fighting me for it, and instead, wraps his large hands around my throat. My gun is trapped between our bodies as my eyelids flutter. I know I don't have much longer. When this evil man throws all his strength into choking the life out of me, I know I've officially run out of options. I do the only thing I can to survive.

I pull the trigger.

Chapter Forty-Four
Beckett

The first thing I notice upon waking is the incessant beeping. Second is the fact that I hurt like a motherfucker. It takes a moment, but it all comes back to me at once.

"Pres," I mumble.

"Take it easy, Beckett." A warm hand squeezes mine. "I'm right here."

My eyes jolt open at the sound of her voice. Presley is right next to me, looking a little worse for wear, but I'll take it if she's able to sit up and talk.

"Are you okay?" I croak. Damn, my throat is dry.

"Am *I* okay?" Pres chuckles lightly. "Beckett, I'm not the one who was shot."

Fuck. I can't believe that asshole shot me.

"How'd I get here?"

"Ambulance." She lightly runs her finger over the top of my hand, careful to avoid the IV needle sticking out of it. "God, I was so scared when you wouldn't wake up. You lost a lot of blood, but the doctor said you'll be okay. The bullet didn't hit anything major."

I groan as a sharp pain stabs me in the abdomen. "Is he in police custody?"

I don't bother mentioning his name. We both know who I'm talking about.

Pres slowly shakes her head. "He's dead, Beckett. I... shot him. We never have to worry about him again."

I briefly close my eyes in relief. I hate that Presley knows what it feels like to take a life, but I'm not fucking sorry he's dead. "Did anyone give you trouble? Colby has to know it was self-defense. Nine-one-one dispatch was on the line listening to the whole thing."

When Presley called for help, an alert was sent to the sheriff's office, and Colby immediately contacted me. Colby wanted me to wait for him, but he was at least twenty minutes out, and there was no way I was going to leave her alone with that bastard a second longer than necessary. Thankfully, I was already on my way to her house because I didn't want to leave our conversation so unsettled.

"He does know." She nods. "I talked to him earlier."

"Well, look who's awake." A woman, who I'm assuming is my nurse based on the scrubs she's wearing, walks into the room. "How are you feeling?"

I attempt to answer, but my tongue sticks to the roof of my mouth. "Thirsty. Could I get some water?"

Presley digs into the bag at her side. "I got it." She uncaps a water bottle and holds it to my lips.

After I take a few swallows, I return my attention

back to the nurse. "How soon can I get out of here?"

She chuckles. "A little impatient, Mr. Armstrong?"

"Beckett," I insist.

"Beckett," she repeats. "If you recall, you were shot tonight, and you lost a significant amount of blood. I'll let the doctor know you're awake so he can come by and explain your injuries and what to expect from your recovery. How's your pain on a scale of one to ten, with ten being the worst?"

"About a seven." It's probably more of a nine, but I don't want to be heavily drugged.

"Okay. Well, it's time for new pain meds, so after I take your vitals, we can get that taken care of."

I tighten my grip on Presley's hand when she starts to get up. "Where are you goin'?"

Pres leans down to kiss my cheek. "I'll be right back. I just want to let everyone know you're awake, and I figured this was a perfect time while Elena is checking your vitals."

I'm guessing Elena is the nurse.

"Can't you call? I don't want you out of my sight, Pres."

She smiles. "Relax, Beck. I'm not going far. They're out in the waiting room."

"Who's they?"

"My parents, Clayton, and Colby. They've been here for hours waiting for an update. I'll be just a few minutes." She points a finger at me as she walks back toward the door. "Don't be cranky with Elena. She's been taking good care of you."

"We'll be just fine, honey. You go do what you need to do." Elena laughs, typing something into the computer against the wall. When Presley leaves, she says, "You're a lucky man. If the bullet would've been an inch to the left, it would've punctured your lung. Your guardian angel's been lookin' out for you."

I scoff. "I highly doubt I have one of those."

"Hmm." Elena checks my temperature, blood pressure, and oxygen levels before going back to her computer to log the results, I'm guessing. When she's done, she swivels on her stool and looks at me thoughtfully. "You look a lot like him, you know."

I frown. "Who?"

"Your father."

"You knew my father?"

She smiles fondly. "I knew David quite well. He was a good man."

I chew on her words for a moment while I take her in. Elena's probably in her late forties, maybe early fifties. She has kind eyes and a pretty face, and I could definitely see my dad being attracted to someone like her. But if they were dating, which I would assume based on how well she supposedly knew him, why in the hell would I have never met her?

She must see the questions running across my face because she speaks up again. "We were together for just about four years. Your dad knew I had no desire to ever get married again, but I loved him deeply. I would've happily spent the rest of my days with him."

"But..."

"Why haven't we met before?"

I nod. "Yeah."

"When you were hurt overseas, he said he needed some time to focus on you. We decided to take a break right before you returned home. We still talked regularly, but your dad thought it was best if I stayed away from the house until you were feelin' better. You weren't doin' so well, and he didn't want any distractions. Unfortunately, with him passing so soon after, you and I never got a chance to meet."

"I don't understand. Why would he keep your relationship a secret from me?"

Elena's eyes flicker to the doorway. "I believe it had something to do with the pretty lady that just left. He was afraid if you saw how happy he and I were... it would remind you of another time in your life. He was worried your head wasn't in a good place, and he didn't want to make it worse."

"That's..."

"Ridiculous?" she offers. "I can see why you'd think that, but I didn't think so. When you have kids, you'll understand. My two are in their early twenties, but they'll always be my babies. When they hurt, I hurt, and I'd go out of my way to make them feel better. Even if it meant sacrificing myself."

"Shit." I take a deep breath. "I wish he wouldn't have done that. You could've had more time together."

Fine lines bracket her mouth when she smiles softly. "I have no regrets, Beckett, and I'd venture to say neither did he. Like I said before, he was a good man."

"Am I interrupting?" Presley hovers in the doorway, looking between Elena and me in question.

"Of course not, dear. I was just finishing up. I need to go get those pain meds, so if you'll excuse m—"

"Wait," I call out before she can leave. "I don't want anything that will make me feel out of it."

She nods. "I'll talk to the doctor and see what we can do. I'll be back in just a bit."

Pres waits for the nurse to leave before taking a seat in the chair beside my bed again. "What was that about?"

"Apparently, Elena was my dad's girlfriend. *For four years*, until right before I returned from Afghanistan."

Presley winces as she raises her brows, touching the mark that fucker left on her. "Seriously? Wow. I could totally see them as a couple, though."

I nod. "Me too. She seems really nice."

"Speaking of relationships... I was doing some thinking while you were asleep."

"About?"

"Us. My need for independence."

I grab her hand. "What about it specifically?"

Pres shrugs. "I want to take you up on your invitation to move into your place if the offer's still good."

"Of course, the offer still stands, honey." I kiss her palm. "But why the sudden change of heart? You've only been at the Wilson's place a few weeks. Is it because of what happened tonight? You don't think you can go back there?"

She shakes her head. "I don't *want* to. Tonight made

me realize that life's too short to waste time continually doubting myself. I know I have a long way to go, but I feel counseling will help. It already has. I keep thinking about something my therapist said to me the other day. She asked why I kept denying myself the things that made me happy. And the thing is, I didn't have an answer for her. Nothing makes me happier than being with you. So, why should I sit around in my living room watching TV by myself just because I have some misguided sense of what I *should* be doing versus what I *want* to be doing?

"I'm in this for the long-haul, Beckett. I want to get married and build a house overlooking the pond like we've always talked about. I want to fill that house with babies who will grow up running around on the ranch just like we did. I want to be with you every step of the way as you get the horse therapy program up and running because I know how important it is to you, making it important to me. I want us to have the forever we've always dreamed of, and I want that forever to start now. So... what do you think?"

I rub a hand over my jaw to hide my smirk. "Honey, this might be the drugs talkin', but did you just propose to me?"

Presley's full lips curve. "I suppose I did. You got a problem with that?"

"Nah, Pres. Not at all. I'm plenty secure in my masculinity to handle a little role reversal."

She laughs. "Good to know. So, is that a yes?"

I smile. "Darlin', that's a *hell yes*."

Chapter Forty-Five
Presley

"**B**eck, quit bein' such a stubborn mule. The bride and groom hafta' kiss."

Beckett makes a face. "Gross."

"Oh, my goodness, look at you two!" My mama has a ginormous smile on her face. "What are you up to?"

I twirl in my pretty white sundress. "Beck and I are gettin' married out by the pond today! Clayton's gonna be our minister and everything! I gave him a dollar from my tooth fairy money."

She puts her hands on her hips. "Is that so?"

I nod, grabbing my best friend's hand. "Yup. Right, Beckett?"

He smiles. "Yep. Presley's gonna be my wife."

Mama's lips do that funny twitching thing. "Well, that's lovely. Presley, may I say you make a stunning bride? And Beckett, honey, you are the most handsome seven-year-old I've ever seen."

Beck smiles. "Thank you, ma'am."

"Thank you, Mama," I say at the same time.

She claps her hands together. "Well, I don't want to keep you from the weddin'. Just make sure you're back in time for supper, okay?"

"Okay," we both agree.

I grab Beck's hand. "Let's go. Clay's probably already there waitin' for us."

"Okay, but I'm still not doin' the gross kissin' thing."

I stick my tongue out at him. "Fine. We can hug. Deal?"

He shakes my hand like grown-ups do sometimes. "Deal."

I blink a few times as the memory fades, glancing at my reflection in the full-length mirror. Today, I may be wearing a different dress, but the groom and the location are the same as they were over twenty years ago. It's been eight months since the shooting. That was one of the scariest days of my life, but thankfully, everything worked out in the end. Not wanting to be apart for another minute, I moved in with Beck the day he got home from the hospital. A week later, even though I had technically already proposed, he dropped to one knee, held out the same ring he used when we were first engaged, and asked me to spend the rest of my life with him. A month after that, we broke ground on our new home. And just last month, we welcomed our first guests to the Hope Springs Equestrian Center for Healing. We've been insanely busy, but it's rewarding work, and we've done it together, so I have zero complaints.

I look out the window of our bedroom and see the guests taking their seats in the white folding chairs we had set out off to the side of the dock. I don't know if I'll ever tire of waking up to this view every morning.

"Honey, they're ready for you. Your daddy's downstairs waiting to escort you outside."

I meet my mom's eyes in the mirror. "Thank you, Mama. I'll be right down."

"You look beautiful, Presley." She dabs at the tears forming at the corner of her eyes. "More importantly, you look *happy*."

"Thank you. I can't imagine feeling any happier than I am right now." I smile. "I take that back. Once I finally become his wife, that'll be even better."

She smiles. "It's been a long time coming, honey. Your father and I are so proud of both of you."

Now I'm dabbing at my eyes. "Okay, okay, get on out of here before I start cryin' and ruin my makeup."

She laughs. "I'll see you out there, sweetheart."

When I get downstairs, my father is waiting inside the French doors that lead to our back deck. Beck and I wanted a simple ceremony, so we decided to forgo the tuxedos. The men in our wedding party are all wearing nice jeans, boots, and plaid pearl-snap western shirts. I'm wearing a sleeveless cream-colored dress, its layered chiffon falling to my ankles, and a pair of matching ballet flats. The top of my hair is pinned with a magnolia at the crown of my head, but the majority of my long waves are cascading down my back. An acoustic guitar melody begins as my father and I step outside and begin our slow march down the makeshift aisle.

My smile gets impossibly wide when I get my first glimpse of my groom, waiting for me under the wooden pergola he and Clayton made last week. It's positioned right at the entrance to the dock, our pond serving as the perfect backdrop. Beck's wearing a matching grin, his eyes never leaving mine during my approach. God, I can't believe this day is finally here. As much as I tried denying it throughout the years, I never stopped dreaming of marrying him, wanting to recite vows and trade rings in front of the people we love most.

"Who gives this woman to be wedded to this man?" our minister asks when we reach the altar.

"Her mother and I do." My father shakes Beck's hand before placing my palm into my soon-to-be-husband's.

"You may be seated," Clayton tells our guests. Yes, my brother's performing this ceremony, too, but this one will be legal thanks to the internet, unlike last time.

Beckett's eyes sparkle in the sunlight when we turn toward each other. *I love you*, he mouths.

"I love you too," I whisper back.

"Y'all ready for this?" Clayton asks us with a wink.

Beck and I both fight a laugh as we nod in reply.

Clay clears his throat. "Ladies and gentlemen, we are gathered here today to celebrate the union of Presley Anne James and Beckett Ryder Armstrong. Now, as everyone in this town knows, it took these idiots long enough to get here, but they're here now, so I guess we can't give them any more grief about it.

Don't worry though, because as soon as they say their I do's, you can start askin' when they'll be making babies, 'cause you know y'all are thinking it."

The audience laughs while Beck and I shake our heads at my brother's ridiculousness. I should've probably expected this when I asked how he felt about getting ordained online.

"Anyway... since they're only paying me a dollar to do this"—he fake coughs into his fist—"cheap asses"— another fake cough—"I told them they had to write their own vows, so we should probably move on to that part, right? Beckett, you wanna kick it off?"

More laughter from the guests and more head shaking from Beck and me.

"Why did we ask him to do this again?" Beck whispers to me.

"I heard that!" my brother says.

Beck's eyes cut to Clay. "You were meant to. May I get on with my vows now?"

Clayton motions to me. "Oh, sure, buddy. Go right ahead."

"Thanks for the permission," Beck says dryly. He takes my hand and places a soft kiss on my knuckles. "Pres, as your brother *so kindly* reminded us, it's taken us a long time to get here. We may have had some detours along the way, but in the end, we found our way back to each other, and for that, I couldn't be more grateful. I can't remember a time in my life when I didn't love you. I've said this before, but you're the one person on earth who makes me feel whole. You're my best friend, my confidant, my lover, and the future mother of my children. There's no one else I want by my side through the good times and the bad. We may not be kids anymore, but we still have a lot of adventure ahead of us, and I vow to be with you every step of the way. Loving you, making you laugh, and holding you when you cry. You're it for me, darlin'.'" He gives my hand a little squeeze to indicate the end of his speech.

"For the life of me, I can't remember what I had planned to say, so I guess I'll just have to wing it."

Beck winks and gives my hand an encouraging squeeze.

"Beckett, I knew from the moment we met, you would change my life. We already have so many wonderful memories together, but in a way, our journey is just beginning. We've had some hard times in our lives, together and separately, but one thing I've learned is while we both have incredible inner strength, we're stronger together. There's nothing we can't accomplish as a team. I fell in love with you before either one of us knew what that meant. When I gave you my heart all those years ago, I knew no one else could ever take your place. You're *it* for me, too. I promise that I'll never take you for granted. I'll never stop showing you how much I love you. I'm honored to be the woman standing by your side for the next fifty or so years." I take a deep breath. "Um... I guess that's it."

Beck's lips quirk.

"I'm not crying; *you're* crying!" Clayton mutters, rubbing his eyes. "I got some damn dirt in my eye."

Beck and I both look up at my brother and laugh.

"Maybe we should move onto the part about the rings?" I suggest.

Clay waves us off. "Yeah... sure. Do that. Where are the goddamn rings?"

My mom stands up, handing a simple platinum band to each of us. "Clayton Daniel James, language!"

Snickers erupt through the crowd while I place the ring on Beck's finger.

"Sorry, Ma." Clayton waits until Beck slides my band over my finger before speaking again. "Okay, we've got the vows and the rings. Now, I just need to ask, Beck, do you take Presley as your wife? To honor and cherish and all that jazz?"

Beck smiles at me. "I do."

"And Pres, do you take Beckett as your husband? To honor, cherish, blah, blah, blah?"

I chuckle. "I do."

My brother straightens his spine. "Well, then by the power vested in me, the great State of Georgia, and the online Universal Church of Love, I now pronounce you man and wife. You may kiss the bride." Clay points at Beck. "But keep your tongue out of it. Nobody needs to see that."

Beckett places his hands on my jaw and pulls me in for a deep kiss, much to my brother's dismay if the gagging sounds are any indication. Beck retreats when the catcalls begin and gives me a soft peck on the lips before pulling away completely.

"Ladies and gentlemen, I give you Mr. and Mrs. Armstrong!"

Beckett takes my hand as we make our way down the aisle together, our guests' applause following us into the house. The moment the double doors are closed behind us, he backs me against the wall.

"We're married." I sigh softly when he places trailing kisses along my neck.

"We are. How long do you suppose we have to make nice with these people before we can kick them out and get to the consummation part?"

I laugh. "We could probably sneak upstairs after the cake. They should be well into their inebriation by then, and they'll have no clue we're off having all the dirty fun."

"I knew there was a reason I married you, you minx." My husband smiles when I whack him on the shoulder. "I love you, Pres. I'm going to do my damnedest to make you the happiest woman alive."

I trace the edges of his jaw with my finger. "You already have, Beck."

With one last kiss, we make our way back to the guests to celebrate the beginning of the rest of our lives.

"I swear to God, Beckett, if you smash that cake into my face, you're going to be sorry."

My new husband—damn, I love saying that—holds the piece of white cake up threateningly. "Really? Why does that make me want to do it more?"

I laugh. "Because you're a jerk?"

Beck wraps his arm around my lower back and nuzzles into my ear. "Don't worry, honey, I'll show you how nice I can be when we get upstairs. But for now..."

Oh, no.

I try squirming out of his arms, but his grip is too tight. He goes in fast but pulls back at the last second, right before the frosting touches my face. Beck's chocolate eyes are filled with humor as he allows me to take a small bite before setting it back on the plate. Just when I think I've escaped, he swipes his finger through the frosting, wipes it down my cheek, and follows the trail with his tongue.

I don't know what comes over me as I pick up the same piece and smash it into his face. I'm laughing so hard, I snort as a giant glob of frosting falls off the tip of Beck's nose. I'm not laughing for long when Beck seeks retribution in the form of a lengthy kiss. When our mouths part, my face is just as messy as his. I don't think I've ever been so amused, grossed out, and turned on at once. Of course, our guests are thoroughly entertained, hooting, hollering, and catcalling the entire time. After our faces are frosting free once again, Beck and I decide to make our rounds, meeting with each person briefly before we disappear for the night.

Beck tugs on my hand. "Well, I'll be damned, they made it."

"Who made it?"

I follow his line of sight and find a couple I've never seen before.

Beckett and the man do some guy hug thing before my husband pulls back and faces me. "Presley, I'd like you to meet Chase and Holly Bradshaw. Chase was in my unit."

I could totally see this guy being a SEAL. He's big and muscular with a dangerous air about him, but his dark eyes are haunted and soulful, a lot like Beck's are. The tall, beautiful blonde at his side smiles warmly as she turns her emerald gaze my way.

"Oh, my God, it's so nice to meet y'all." I smile as understanding dawns on me. "Is it okay if I hug you? I feel like a handshake is too formal."

"Sure," they both say in unison, chuckling.

"It's nice to meet you, Presley," Chase says, pulling out of my overzealous hug. "I've heard *a lot* about you over the years. I guess the girl who got away didn't get very far, after all."

"Beck's talked about me over the years, huh?" I glance at my groom out of the corner of my eye. "You don't say."

"Yeah, yeah." Beck wraps his arm around my back. "What can I say? I'm a lucky bastard."

Chase looks down at his wife. "I know the feeling."

The four of us talk for a while, and we even wind up taking the couple on a tour of the facilities for the healing center before they have to head out. Beckett and I wind up staying at our reception a bit longer than initially planned, but neither one of us have any regrets. The entire day turned out perfectly. When my husband carries me over the threshold, waving goodbye to our guests, I think about how lucky I am. Today, I got to marry my best friend. My soul mate. The future father of my children. And after what I suspect will be a long, fantastic night tangled in the sheets, I'll get to wake up in his arms, ready to spend the rest of my life proudly by his side. How could it get any better than that?

Epilogue
Presley – Eight Years Later

"She looks so happy."

I press a hand to my heart, watching our oldest daughter, Addie, talking to the instructor. She's been around horses her whole life, but this will be her first time riding one independently. Today is the orientation for the ranch's youngest group of kids. When they're this little, we start 'em out with Daisy, our sweet pony, and keep the lesson groupings as small as possible. Besides Addie, there's only one other child, a seven-year-old little boy named Cash.

As Beckett and I watch, Addie takes a few steps closer to her new friend and whispers something in his ear. At first, he gives her a funny look, but then in the next moment, he smiles when Addie grabs his hand.

I lean into my husband. "This seems familiar."

He smiles. "Lord help that little boy. She is definitely her mama's girl."

"What's that supposed to mean?"

"Darlin', I never had a chance of resisting you. You were a pushy little thing. Wouldn't take no for an answer."

I laugh, playfully jabbing him. "Really? Is that how it went?"

"That's how I remember it." Beck shrugs.

I give him a wry look. "I think your memory is failing you in your old age."

"Honey, I just turned thirty-nine. My memory—among other things—works just fine." He gives me his *I'm undressing you with my eyes* look, which, predictably, makes me shiver.

"I'm perfectly aware of how well those 'other things' work. You've knocked me up every other year since we got married, Beckett." I rub my small baby bump. "And she's takin' up the last bedroom in the house, so I think you've made your point."

"You're back to thinkin' it's a girl again?" He smirks. "I thought we've discussed this. Fourth time's a charm for a boy."

"First of all, I believe the saying is third time's a charm. Secondly, it's definitely a girl. I can't stop craving Cream of Wheat and fried okra."

For a solid month, that's all I wanted to eat when I was pregnant with Addie, and the same craving lasted two months with her sisters, Bailey and Savannah.

Beck wraps his free arm around my shoulder. "We'll find out one way or the other soon enough. And if you're right, we'll just have to build a bigger house."

My eyes widen as I take a few steps away and point

an accusatory finger at him. "Oh, no. You keep your super sperm away from me. I'm done after this."

"Mama, what's pooper sperm?" Bailey asks from her perch on her daddy's hip.

My husband laughs. "Yeah, *Mama*. What is that?"

I glare at him as I adjust Savannah on my hip. "You're lucky I like you so much."

He laughs, pulling me into him again. "Oh, honey, you more than like me. When we get these little angels to bed later, I'll be happy to remind you."

"I'm sure you will." I laugh, rolling my eyes.

He nods to the kids. "Pay attention, woman. This is history in the making. Mark my words: that little boy will be smitten by the time this lesson is over."

"Smitten?" I raise my eyebrows. "Is that what you were on the day we met?"

"Damn straight, Pres." He kisses my temple. "And I wouldn't have it any other way."

I smile. "Me neither, Cowboy. Me neither."

———

Would you like to read a bonus epilogue? Scan the QR code below to sign up for Laura's newsletter and you'll have instant access. You can unsubscribe at any time.

Acknowledgments

To my husband, Tad: Thank you for being you. I couldn't do this without your constant support.

To my beautiful children: You two are my world, even when you're driving me nuts.

To my agent, Bethany: Thank you for helping bring my stories to new markets. I can't wait to see more translated versions of my book babies!

To my lovely betas Crystal Eacker, Jen Durfey, & Heather Bryant: Thank you for being the first people to read Redemption. As always, your feedback on Beck and Presley's story was invaluable.

To Reanna: Thank you for being my horse expert and answering all of my strange questions.

To all the seriously awesome book influencers: I value you so much, as a reader and a writer. The time you take to help others find new books is much appreciated.

To my incredible ARC team and Loungers: Thank you for always bringing a smile to my face and for encouraging my Chris Hemsworth obsession.

To my editor, Ellie McLove of My Brother's Editor: Thank you once again, for squeezing me in because I'm always pushing deadlines. Your feedback on this story was especially helpful. The final product is so much better because of you.

To my proofreader, Christine Estevez: I miss working with you at Wildfire every day, but I'm so glad I still get to keep you as my proofreader! You'll never escape me now! Muhahahaha! *insert evil Elmo GIF

Last but never least, to my readers: Thank you, thank you, thank you for reading my words. I know you have a lot of options out there, and I'm forever grateful you took a chance on me. Whether you've been with me for a while, or you found me through this book, I appreciate your support more than words can say. I couldn't do what I love for a living without you. XOXO

Also Available By Laura Lee

Standalone Novels

Beautifully Broken

Happy New You

Dealing With Love Series

Deal Breakers

Deal Takers

Deal Makers

Bedding the Billionaire Series

Billionaire Bossman

Billionaire Bad Boy

Billionaire Bosshole

Windsor Academy Series

Wicked Liars

Ruthless Kings

Fallen Heirs

Broken Playboy

About the Author

Laura Lee is the *USA Today* bestselling author of steamy and sometimes ridiculously funny romance. She won her first writing contest at the ripe old age of nine, earning a trip to the state capital to showcase her manuscript. Thankfully for her, those early works will never see the light of day again! She is also one half of the romantasy author duo, Poppy Ireland.

Laura spends most of her time in the Pacific Northwest, typing away on a laptop with a furry friend curled up in her lap and an iced matcha by her side. When she's not hanging out with her family or talking to the fictional people inside her head, she's probably nose-deep in a book that features anti-heroes or an enemies to lovers trope.

Laura is represented by Bethany Weaver at Weaver Literary Agency. For subrights inquiries, please email: weaverliteraryagency@gmail.com

For more information about the author, check out her website at: www.LauraLeeBooks.com

You can also find her "working" on social media quite frequently.

Facebook: @LauraLeeBooks1
Instagram: @LauraLeeBooks
TikTok: @AuthorLauraLee
Reader's Group: Laura Lee's Lounge